THE LAUNDRYMEN

Mark Stretch

THE LAUNDRYMEN

Mark Stretch

Copyright © 2016 by Mark Stretch

www.MarkStretch.co.uk

Mark Stretch asserts the moral right to
be identified as the author of this work.

All rights reserved. This publication or any portion thereof may not be reproduced or used in any manner whatsoever without the express written permission of the publisher except for the use of brief quotations in a book review.

This is a work of fiction. Names, characters, businesses, places, events and incidents are either the products of the author's imagination or used in a fictitious manner. Any resemblance to actual persons, living or dead, actual events or localities is entirely coincidental.

Contains language, from the outset, which some readers may find offensive. Contains scenes of a sexual nature. Recommended to 16+ readers.

All rights reserved. No part of this publication may be reproduced, stored in a retrieval system, or transmitted, in any form or by any means, electronic, mechanical, photocopying, recording or otherwise, without the prior permission of the publishers.

THE LAUNDRYMEN

Mark Stretch

This book is dedicated to my family:
Sara, Daniel, Jack, Daisy & Ruth.

* * *

Special thanks to the following who read
the drafts and contributed valuable feedback:

Tim Newman, Johanne Spittle,
Andrew Trigg, Mike Bullen, Jack Barratt,
David Rann & Fahmi Mursaleen

Extra special thanks to my wife, Sara,
(who is the real writer in our house)
for her help and support with this book
and for letting me borrow her dream
for a while.

Part 1

It is often said that corrupt or bad people have a sense of honour or integrity, or justice, even if it is a bit skewed.

Chapter 1

'Shit, shit, SHIT!' he said through his teeth, as he tugged at the edge of his overcoat to free it from the car door. He staggered backwards as it came loose and he noted the corner of the caramel-coloured garment was now smudged with black grease.

'Fuck!' He looked imploringly to the sky. Pressing the remote to lock the car, he turned and dashed straight across the road. A motorcycle courier swerved to avoid the running man then twisting round in the saddle, yelled a muffled 'Wanker!' through his helmet and shook his gloved fist before roaring off.

He reached the office building just in time. There was a faint sheen of perspiration on his forehead as he strode briskly across the paved plaza outside the fifteen-storey office complex. He aimed to arrive as close to nine o'clock as he could. Not before, if possible. Definitely not after. Today it had been perilously close. But he'd made it. It was another petty little challenge to liven up his daily routine. Tiny risks in a protected environment, like overtaking just one more car before diving into the inside lane at the motorway exit slip road during the morning journey or parking in a side street spot barely big enough to fit the car. Sometimes, on the journey into Birmingham, he would re-tune the radio as he drove and try listening to a different station just for some variety. Inevitably, though, the songs obstinately remained the same. He often wondered whatever happened to originality on the airwaves.

Sighing with the sheer inevitability of his day, he took a last look at the outside world and then mounted the steps for another eight hours of office incarceration. The glass entrance door slid open and he stepped into the large air-conditioned foyer. His name badge on its lanyard tugged at his neck as he held it out it at the anonymous bored-looking security guard on the reception desk and he was the only occupant of the narrow brushed-steel lift up to the eleventh floor. Not for the first time, he wished there was a mirror so he could check that his hair was in place and there were no remnants of breakfast clinging to his mouth. The lift pinged to announce its arrival. Along the carpeted corridor, he juggled his briefcase from one hand to the other as he removed his coat. At the coffee machine he pressed the third button down for his usual white Americano with sugar and then made his way to his office opening the door with his elbow balancing the coffee in one hand, briefcase in another and coat draped over his arm. He placed the coffee on the drinks mat, hung his coat on a hanger and placed his case under the desk. Almost as soon as he was seated, and before he had even turned his computer on, one of his team appeared in the doorway.

'Morning Kevin, have you got a minute?'

'Yes, of course, Sian. Come in. What's up?'

'It's about Mandy,' she said furtively, as she quickly slid onto the large black faux leather chair nearest his desk. 'She's crying, in the toilets. I think maybe you should have a quiet word with her.'

He sighed. Another domestic, no doubt. He asked Sian to go and persuade Mandy to come and see him. Two minutes later Mandy entered and occupied the same chair that Sian had vacated. Her face was red and her eyes looked puffy.

'Mike has left me', she announced flatly.

Kevin had met Mandy's husband Mike briefly twice before. Once about eighteen months ago at a bowling alley during a staff night out and then again a few weeks later at their wedding reception held in a dingy room above a pub in Kings Heath. At the initial meeting, they found themselves on the same bowling team and, to make polite conversation, Kevin had enquired about Mike's employment and had discovered that he re-upholstered car interiors. Mandy tearfully continued, and for a brief selfish moment, Kevin thought that it was a shame if it was a permanent break-up as, if he ever got the classic car he often dreamt of, he might have had need of Mike's skills – and as his wife's boss he might have got a useful discount. Now that was looking highly unlikely.

'He's gone back to his ex-girlfriend.'

Kevin noted her blotchy tear-stained face, running mascara and greasy hair. He could understand why Mike might have decided to look elsewhere.

'How awful for you.' he said. 'When did this happen?'

Between sobs (he handed her the box of tissues he kept for these occasions) she explained about the strange absences several times a week at odd times, the new aftershave, the increased frequency of showers, the silences, then finally how she read the texts on his phone and eventually confronted him.

'He packed his bag. The one I bought him for Christmas, and left.' The sobs became louder.

Kevin chose his words carefully. Sometimes these things were final but over the years he'd observed that more often the couple would sort it out, so it was best to at least appear to be sympathetic for the time being.

'Mandy. I'm so sorry. If you need to take some time off..'

'No thank you. I'm amongst friends here and the work will take my mind off it.'

Kevin was relieved. 'Okay – well if there's anything I can do ...'

'Thanks, Kevin. Thanks for listening. It's been a great help. It'll probably be alright in the end.'

Then she was gone. Back to her section, where the other girls crowded around her. The sisters taking time off from bitching. He glanced at his watch and hoped that they'd soon get back to work.

The rest of the day passed uneventfully and after waiting until the last of the staff had departed for the day, Kevin grabbed his coat, picked up his case and walked back to the car. On the drive home, he reflected on Mandy's situation. Perhaps it was another example of young people getting married too young. Or maybe it was just a bump in the road. They hadn't had any children yet, so it was easy for them to split up and re-group. It was a shame for the parents who had probably paid for the wedding, though. He concluded that it was more likely however that Mike would soon get fed up with the old girlfriend and come back with his tail between his legs, promising it would never happen again. After making him grovel for a while, she'd take him back and then throw a dirty scowl at anyone at work who ever dared mention the incident again.

Pulling onto his sloping drive and firmly applying the handbrake, Kevin admired his house. This was his second house, a big step up from the small terraced house he started with. Now he had something more impressive. But it still needed work. He walked inside and hung up his coat on the coat-rack which had originally come from a junk shop and had since been stripped, sanded and waxed. He strode down the hallway into the kitchen and put the kettle on. As the kettle noisily heated itself up, he heard the front door open and click shut, then footsteps on the tiled floor of the hall.

'Hiya.'

'Hiya.' he replied and automatically got out another mug.

'Had an extraordinarily crap day at work. How was yours?'

'Same as usual. Want some coffee? Or tea?'

'No thanks. I'll have a glass of vino I think.'

He put the mug away again and poured her a glass of Chardonnay from the half-full bottle in the fridge.

'Thanks.' she said as she took a seat at the small table against the wall in the kitchen. 'Shall we get a takeaway tonight? I really don't fancy cooking.'

'Okay. I'll pick it up. Chinese, Indian or chippy?'

'Indian I think. Yes. Chicken Balti & mushroom rice for me. Oh, and some naan bread too. Peshwari.'

He shuffled through their collection of takeaway menus, called the Balti Raj and recited the order. She went upstairs to get changed. He gulped down half his coffee, poured the rest down the sink and went out to collect their meal.

'So why was your day so awful?' he said later, as they ate.

'Oh, AFD just pinched the Marshall Developments account from us. It was one of our biggest accounts. So a few people are going to have to go. There was a real atmosphere in the office all day.'

'Not you, though?'

'No. I don't think so. Not this time anyway.'

Later that night as they lay reading in bed, she asked him about his day. Marginally surprised to be asked, he told her about getting collared by Sian as soon as he walked in.

'Hadn't even had chance to sit down before Mandy was in the office blubbing all over me.'

'Hope you made sympathetic noises.'

'Of course I did. Just wish they would sort themselves out without involving everyone else. Imagine if it was me and I walked into Simon's office to pour it all out!'

'She probably hoped you'd tell her exactly what to do to make it better.'

'As if! Trouble is, what I really wanted to say was *"You stupid cow. What the fuck do you expect? You were probably quite sexy eighteen months ago. Nice hair, nice clothes. Now, since you've been married. You've cut your hair short and wear hideously frumpy clothes. You look like an old crone and I don't blame Mike for dumping you. You want to get him back? Well, make some bloody effort. And remember what attracted him to you in the first place."* Maybe I should have said it. It might have made her think.'

'It's probably a good job you kept quiet.'

'You may be right but isn't crazy to be thinking one thing and saying something else. Seem to have to be doing it more and more.'

'Welcome to my world. It's like that all the time at the agency. Lydia bollocks me to get more money out of the client. Then the client is bollocking me because their artwork is wrong. I just want to say '"Shut the fuck up" to all of them. Instead, I have to smile sweetly and soak it up. Makes you want to scream.'

Chapter 2

Kevin had first met Anne at a crowded student house party in Selly Oak near Birmingham. Crushed together briefly in the long entrance hall of the run-down terrace, they had made small talk until they could escape from the crowd and rejoin their friends. Later on at the same party they chanced upon each other again in the tiny back garden as they had both escaped the smoky haze to get some fresh air. Surrounded by traffic cones, plastic patio chairs, a rusty barbecue and a faded pub sign, they resumed their conversation and discovered that they came from the same area but while he had attended the local public school as a day boy, she had been a pupil at the nearby sixth form college and whilst they discovered that they had a few mutual acquaintances, including the hosts of the party, their paths hadn't knowingly crossed previously.

Kevin's friends stumbled out into the garden interrupting them to say they were leaving to go to another party and asked if he was coming too. Kevin chose to leave with them. Emboldened by the drink, he leant forwards, gave her a quick kiss on the cheek and whispered his phone number into her ear as he left.

She didn't phone him. But they did run into each other several times over the next few months. However, the relationship failed to develop any further as they were both involved with other people on each occasion.

Two and a half years later they met up again by chance at the opening night of a new wine bar in Shirley, on the outskirts of Birmingham. On this occasion, the timing was better as they were both single. They got on well and after several more dates they settled into a comfortable relationship, eventually moving into a rented flat together.

'How do you feel about marriage?' Anne had said once a few months later.

'Ah, I wondered when this question would arise. I don't think it's really necessary. Can't see the point. Why go to all the fuss of getting married? Unless kids come along, of course,' said Kevin whose parents had split up when he was fifteen.

Kevin had dropped out of Aston University after two years. A lack of money, one poor mark for an assignment which knocked his confidence, and a burning desire to get a real life led to the abrupt resignation from the degree course. On the day he quit, he went directly to a job agency in the city centre and took the first job he was offered. After a few months of factory work he eventually secured a clerical job at an insurance company. A few promotions later and Kevin was approximately where he had expected to be had he completed his degree.

Kevin had always been interested in music and photography. He'd played guitar in a band at school and then worked on the student radio station at the university and put a few bands on at some of the surrounding pubs to earn a bit of extra cash. On leaving the course and joining the real world, he felt his involvement in the music scene was also at an end. He had also had to abandon the photography when his camera and lenses were stolen from his student accommodation. There was no insurance and he couldn't afford to replace them.

After her A-levels, Anne took a gap year and travelled around Europe. On her return, she took up her place at Birmingham University. She achieved a second-class degree in marketing. Anne enjoyed travelling so after graduating her parents had given her a thousand pounds which had paid for her to spend three months travelling around Thailand and Indonesia before settling into a job as an account executive at a large advertising agency based in Redditch.

Thirteen months after moving into the rented flat together, they bought their first property, a small terraced house in the city's suburbs. Two weeks after moving in and overruling Kevin's doubts, they were married. The wedding was in a registry office with a few friends and family. The honeymoon was a few days in Paris. Twelve months later the terraced house was sold and they bought a larger house in the same area. This house needed a bit more work and Kevin threw himself into it, acquiring new skills in plastering and decorating along the way. He spent most of his spare time working on the house and doing up old pieces of furniture while Anne found herself working longer and longer hours to keep the agency and clients happy. Although the idea of children was never discussed, when Anne unilaterally stopped taking the pill it became a possibility.

One week before the Mandy and Mike discussion, Anne had finally brought up the subject over breakfast.

'How do you feel about having kids?'

'Kids? Blimey, what prompted that? I'm sure they'll come along eventually. I suppose it would be fun to try and conceive one every now and then'.

It had long been Kevin's opinion that they weren't having sex as often as they used to. Certainly not as often as he would like. He presumed it was the same for all married couples after the first flush of lust had worn off.

'I'm not sure that they will. Maybe we need some help.'

Kevin studied the paper.

'What do you mean, help?'

'Well, I'm pretty sure everything is working okay but nothing has happened has it? Maybe we need to get checked out.'

'Your taking the pill is probably having something to do with it'. He re-folded the paper so that he could read the sports pages.

'I'm not taking the pill and haven't been for a while now.'

Kevin lowered the paper and stared at Anne.

'Sorry. Did I hear that correctly? You're not taking the pill?

She nodded.

'Does that mean yes you're not taking the pill or yes you are?

'I'm not.'

Kevin put the paper down and leant forwards over it.

'You're not taking the pill? Since when?'

'Since a few months ago..'

'Well, thanks for checking with me. Surely there should have been a discussion about this. Don't you think it should be a joint decision to have kids?'

'No, not really. I wasn't ready before but I am now. And something is obviously wrong with one of us.'

'Hang on. Let me get this straight. First you stop taking the pill without asking me and then you suggest that there's something wrong with me.'

'I didn't say that. It's not necessarily you. It could be me.'

Kevin didn't want to hear any more. He got up and left for work, slamming the door behind him but not so hard that it damaged the stained glass panes he had restored and fitted himself. At lunchtime, Anne called him on his mobile.

'Sorry.'

'I'm still cross with you.'

'I know. It's just that I can't stop thinking about having a baby now. Everywhere I look I see pregnant women. Or mothers with babies in prams. I'm really sorry I didn't tell you about the pill thing. I had anticipated telling you at the same time as I announced I was pregnant.'

'I thought we always discussed things first. It's a huge step having a kid.'

'You're right. I'm sorry. But you do want one, don't you? I've seen you looking at Scalectrix sets. By the way, I've bought you something.'

'What?'

'It's a surprise. For later. Got to go now. Bye.'

He pressed the red button on the phone and pocketed it. Sometimes she really annoyed him. She acted like he was an actor in a play that was all about her. But she was probably right. He wasn't sure but maybe he did want kids. After all, wasn't the normal order of things is to get married, buy a house, then have children? So this was the natural next step. Although it still seemed a bit soon to him. But the fact that she hadn't got pregnant despite being off the pill was a tiny bit worrying.

The present was a baby-doll nightie. While he was watching television that evening, she came walked seductively into the lounge wearing it and nothing else. Seconds later he was chasing her upstairs and then removing it as quickly as he could. Now that he knew she wanted to get pregnant he was going to apply himself with relish. They had sex every night and every morning that week. The night of the Indian takeaway they had sex on the sofa and again in the shower. By the time they went to bed the desire was still there but they both fell asleep.

Several months went by and so did several periods. With each passing month, Anne became increasingly depressed and volatile. Kevin was confident that things would happen in time and although he was enjoying all the sex he wasn't so keen on her bad moods and subsequent tears when the periods arrived. The pregnancy test kit box remained steadfastly unopened on the top shelf of the bathroom cabinet.

Anne eventually made an appointment for them to see the doctor. Despite her telling him the time, four o'clock one weekday afternoon, Kevin failed to appear at the surgery and Anne had to see the doctor on her own. That evening she stormed into the house and marched up to him as he sat at the kitchen table trying to prise the back off an old clock with a screwdriver.

'What happened? Where were you? Tell me. I felt a complete idiot on my own there. Why didn't you turn up? I told you when it was.'

Kevin spluttered his excuses. He had found it difficult to get away from work. There was a meeting. That he had tried to call but there was no signal. He tried to explain but Anne turned her back to him and, sinking down onto the floor, she began to cry. He desperately wanted to tell her the truth. That he really wasn't sure whether he wanted kids yet. That he didn't want their life to change. That he didn't want her to turn into a 'mum' and get fat legs. That he wanted his wife to stay a 'babe'. And the truth was that he really didn't think there was anything wrong with him and he definitely didn't want a doctor messing with his tackle. So he just blanked the appointment from his mind. He knew she'd be upset but assumed that she would get over it. There was plenty of time to have kids when they were both ready.

That marked the end of their quest for children. Anne busied herself at work. She only sulked for a week or two. Then, to his surprise, she seemed to be more cheerful. Kevin thought Anne had taken it rather well really as he continued to sand down, then wax, the pine farmhouse chest of drawers he had recently salvaged from a garage sale.

Chapter 3

Three months later when Kevin's boss Simon called him in for a meeting, he wasn't expecting to hear that the department was being merged with the company's Southern division. Everyone in the department was going to have to re-apply for their own jobs and the successful candidates would be re-located to the new offices in Milton Keynes. A formal announcement was due to be made the next day but as Kevin was a senior employee he had received advance notice. Simon had every confidence that Kevin would be successful in his application. He smiled, shook Kevin's hand and showed him to the door. In shock, Kevin mumbled his way through the rest of the morning. At lunchtime he felt a bit queasy and so, uncharacteristically, decided to take the afternoon off.

As he arrived home he saw Anne's car on the drive and next to it was parked another car he didn't recognise, so he had to park on the road which irritated him. Kevin turned to glance at the car as he turned the key in the lock and let himself in. It was a silver Lexus. As he closed the door behind him he heard voices upstairs. He called up 'Everything alright? Whose is that car on the drive?'

Even as the words were tumbling out of his mouth he suddenly knew it wasn't alright. He heard thumping and muffled exclamations from the floor above. He resisted the temptation to run upstairs and burst in. Instead, he just sat down in the kitchen. His head dropped into his hands. The front door slammed. A car engine fired up. When he looked up Anne had appeared in the kitchen doorway. Her blouse was done up but the buttons weren't lined up with the buttonholes so it sat lopsided. Her neck and cheeks were flushed. She was staring at him.

For several seconds that stretched to fill the void, there was silence. Kevin was wryly thinking that in the movies the cuckold always croaks 'Why?' He decided against it. He could think of a few reasons why. But he still didn't like how it felt now it was happening to him. He looked up at Anne briefly. She was nervously biting her bottom lip waiting for his reaction. Not sure what to say, or do, Kevin stood up, brushed past her, slammed the front door shut, walked down the drive to his car and gunned it down the road. The radio was on and a cheery presenter introduced the latest single from yet another bland boy band. Kevin allowed about five seconds of the song before yelling 'Fuck off!' at the radio and stabbing the off button with his finger. As he roared along the road he didn't notice the Police van parked tucked away with the hidden camera registering his speed that was seventeen miles an hour over the limit. He continued driving in silence, alternately speeding and then crawling. As he drove out of town the suburbs gave way to villages, then eventually to the trees, hedges and fields of the countryside.

After several miles of aimless meandering, he realised that he didn't recognise the area and needed to stop to collect his thoughts, so he pulled off the road and parked up in front of a gateway to a field. He sat in the car for a few minutes listening to the engine ticking as it contracted. He suddenly felt nauseous so he got out of the car and locked it and held onto the gate as he bent over to be sick. But nothing came out. After waiting for the feeling to recede, instead of getting back into the car, he climbed over the gate, dropped to the other side and walked across the field. His brown leather brogues slipped and slid over the lumpy muddy ground. He clambered over stiles and walked through woodland criss-crossed with soggy paths. He brushed aside branches, stepped over logs and skirted dirty pools of water. He kept walking until eventually his passage was barred by a river. After walking up and down in each direction for a few hundred yards, he couldn't see a bridge.

Kevin sat down on the trunk of a fallen tree near the riverbank and stared into the dark water as it slid by. More and more of it, a continually replenished supply. It occurred to him that nothing would ever be the same again. His smooth and reasonably successful, but mostly uneventful, life had altered dramatically in one day. His happy past was flowing away with the water. In his darker moments, Kevin had occasionally wondered how it would feel to lose everything and had tried to imagine it, but it was always so painful to even contemplate that he had never thought about it long enough to establish how he would react if it actually happened. So he had no plan.

He continued to stare at the water. Some ramblers appeared and smiled at him cheerily as they passed by. He smiled back mildly, even though he hated ramblers with their sensible brightly-coloured waterproof clothes, walking boots and stupid sticks and he didn't really feel like being polite.

Kevin knew he couldn't just sit on the log forever. Sooner or later he would have to rejoin his life and face up to the mess. So much was swarming around in his head he didn't know where to start. He decided to try and deal with each problem separately, even though they were inter-connected, starting with the least difficult one.

The job. Christ. He knew he didn't want to live in Milton Keynes. Who would want to live there? And applying for his own job. How ridiculous was that? He mulled over the fact that might not even get his own job. He wondered what would happen if he didn't get it, or if he did, but then decided not to relocate, what the alternative was. Perhaps he'd be offered redundancy. He'd started at the insurance company for eight years ago. Eight years, crikey was it that long? That's got to be worth something. But did he want to wait around until it all happened just to pick up a payoff? He could leave now. But what about having to give notice? He vaguely remembered something about his contract requiring him to give three months. Or was it one month? He couldn't remember for sure. Fuck them. After putting him in this situation, they couldn't force him to go to work. Maybe he'd just not go back. He briefly tried to imagine the Work Police breaking down his door with one of those big red battering rams, smashing the beautiful stained glass panels, just so they could drag him into the office. He didn't think it was very likely somehow. Or maybe they just wouldn't pay him if he did that. That led him neatly to the next problem if he didn't have a job.

Money. His heart sank still further. He wished he had saved some now. In a separate account, in his own name, perhaps. He had friends who had secreted money away in case their marriages broke down. However, he had always felt that it wasn't really in the spirit of marriage. But then nor was your wife fucking someone else in your bed, in your house, while you were being told you had to reapply for your own sodding job.

That thought made him jerk his head up hard. Anne. The pain was really beginning to hurt now.

The pain of regret, of loss, of disloyalty, of ignorance, of being taken for an idiot. His fingers stretched out and gripped the gnarled bark of the log. His knuckles went white. How could she? How dare she? Who was that fucker who invaded his house and his wife? He picked up a large stone and hurled it into the water. Disappointingly, it hardly made a splash and just disappeared into the dark flowing mass.

He thought about those glib sayings that some of his fellow managers had pinned to their office walls, 'Problems are just opportunities in disguise', or 'In the middle of difficulty lies opportunity'. Which is all very well until you have a real problem and then it's just a fucking problem.

He looked around him. It was beginning to get dark. Kevin realised he didn't have anywhere else to go. He and Anne had been so consumed with each other and their jobs and the routine of their lives that he had neglected his friends. Most of them had moved away from the area, some to London. Reluctantly he decided to return home and start facing the music. Maybe there was a way that they could work something out.

The house was in darkness and Anne's car wasn't on the drive. Depressingly, there on the kitchen table leaning against the novelty penis-shaped ceramic salt and pepper shakers was an envelope with the word 'Kevin' written on it in small clipped letters.

He opened the fridge. There were no bottles of beer. Just a lonely can of Boddingtons. He pulled the tab, waited for the widget to do its thing and then took three long swigs before sitting down to open the envelope and read the note.

Kevin,

I don't quite know where to start. I suppose a good place is with an apology. I love you and I'm really sorry. But I think you know why this has happened.

He hated 'sorry buts'. It was one of his pet hates and she knew it. There should never be a 'but' after 'sorry'. Either you are sorry or you're not. The fact that she'd used one, despite him telling her many times how much he loathed it, annoyed him even more. And actually no, he didn't know why this had happened. Perhaps she would enlighten him.

When we got together I thought we'd have a lot more fun in our lives. That we'd go travelling together and explore the world. That we'd laugh and be carefree. After the wedding I thought our trip to Paris would just be the first of many romantic getaways. Instead, we seem to have ended up tied to our jobs in the Midlands and occasionally having a takeaway as a treat.

His instant reaction was to defend their life together. Surely, the way they lived was a joint decision. Wasn't it? Obviously not, from this note.

And when, a few months ago I started to think about getting pregnant I felt that it might somehow make up for the lack of excitement in our lives. Being a mother would give me the fulfilment that is missing from our marriage. I know you probably weren't as keen on the idea as me but when you didn't come to the doctors, and I didn't get pregnant, I couldn't bear the thought of us just carrying on the way we were. Then Tom joined the agency.

Ah, Tom. So that was the fucker's name. Tom. He tried to imagine what Tom looked like. The kind of smooth operator that drives a Lexus, clearly. All shiny suits and expensive after-shave. He was already planning the confrontation in the agency office. He would march in past the protesting receptionist who would make a pathetic effort at stopping him entering the main office. He would march over to Tom's desk (he felt sure he'd recognise him) and point at him while shouting *'Hey you! So, you're the bastard who's been shagging my wife in my bed while I've been at work? Go on deny it. No need to. She's told me all about it. It's all in ...this ...fucking... note.'* He would brandish the note in Tom's face then get into a light scuffle before feeling arms pulling him back and then being firmly ejected from the building by Colin, the elderly office security guard, who, once outside, would sympathise with him as ten years earlier his wife had run off with a jumped-up office twat too. Good riddance to her.

Tom is kind and thoughtful

Oh God. She actually likes him.

And although I didn't encourage him,

Yeah right. I bet you didn't.

.. we struck up a friendship. Well more than a friendship really.

More like a fuckship really dear.

And one thing led to another. And you know the rest. I don't know if Tom and I have any kind of a future but I want to give it a try. So I'm moving in with him. He's got an apartment in Solihull.

Solihull. Fuck! It just took a turn for the worse. Soli-fucking-hull. Reportedly, the wife-swapping capital of Great Britain. Except that it didn't appear that Tom had kept his end of the deal. And just to be sure, Kevin looked around just to make absolutely sure that Tom hadn't deposited his wife as part of the swap.

We'll have to get divorced I suppose. I do hope this hasn't come as too much of a shock to you. But at least you've got your job, which I know you love, and the house too. Until it's sold, of course. I'll only ask for half,

even though my parents put up most of the deposit, or you could buy me out but I don't think you've got that sort of money saved up. And then we'll both be free to start again. We're both young enough.
Goodbye and good luck.
Love.
Anne x

Kevin sat back and dropped the note onto the kitchen table. He sighed a sigh so deep that, if it was any deeper, his lungs would collapse. This was it then. The end. The end of his marriage and of the life he knew. Clearly, there was no point in having the confrontation in the agency office, as it was already a done deal.

Shock was slowly replaced with anger. He would reply. He felt he needed to put forward his side of the argument and make sure she knew how he felt. He found a pen and some paper and started to write feverishly. Then stopped abruptly. He screwed the paper up into a ball, tossed it into the corner of the room and started again. He had five attempts, some bitter, some sympathetic, some begging and then gave up and sat back. What was the point? She'd made her mind up. She'd had an affair. They couldn't undo that. He would never be able to forgive her. Or forget it. Writing to her would be futile. There would be plenty of letters going backwards and forwards during the forthcoming divorce proceedings. He'd heard all about the sheer misery of divorce from some of his fellow managers at work who had experienced it. It seems that the husband gets stitched up nearly every time especially when there were kids involved. He didn't relish the prospect.

He got his mobile out of his pocket and thumbed through to Anne's number. His finger hovered over the green icon. He tried to imagine how the conversation would go. Only one way to find out. He pressed the button. It rang. She answered.

Kevin said 'Hi, it's me'

'Hi,' then he heard a whispered '*Shush, it's Kevin*'

'Got your note'

'Oh right. Okay.' Then a delay. 'I'm really sorry. I probably should have told you how I felt earlier. But I don't think you would have taken it seriously.'

There it was again. The 'sorry but'. Annoying and utterly pointless.

'Are you okay? I mean you aren't going to do anything stupid are you? Tom plays rugby and he is quite good at karate. I think he has a black belt in it so you probably shouldn't try and fight him or anything silly like that. Anyway, we're going away for a while, to Cyprus, just for a few days.'

Kevin held the phone in front of him and stared at it. He could hear Anne repeating his name. Then with as much vigour as he could muster, he threw the phone at the wall and watched with some satisfaction mixed with regret as it shattered into several pieces and fell to the floor.

The following day Kevin took more time off work and went to see a solicitor.

When he got home there was a letter from the Camera Enforcement Agency. It was a speeding ticket and meant a fine plus a further three points on his licence. He already had nine points from two previous speeding offences and (rather unfairly, he thought) a failed brake light. So this would probably mean disqualification.

For the next few weeks, Kevin just carried on as normally as possible under the circumstances. The solicitor's correspondence started flowing backwards and forwards almost immediately. The letters had been just as acerbic as he imagined but the law did seem to be reasonably fair when it came to the house and contents. The house was placed on the market.

Just four days after it was advertised online, an offer was accepted for the house. It was sold to a young couple from Newcastle-upon-Tyne, who were relocating to the Midlands because of their jobs. Being first time buyers, with help from their parents, meant there was no chain and the deal went through in just a few weeks. During this time, Kevin hired a box van to take his remaining possessions to his father's house in Swindon where there was an empty garage, which could be used for storage. Luckily, there were only a few things that Kevin really wanted to keep, which were mainly the pieces of furniture that he had restored and Anne didn't contest those. While he was away in Swindon, Anne returned to the house and removed her remaining possessions.

House prices were rising fast. The house had appreciated in value over the time that they had owned it. Kevin's work to restore it had also added value so there was sufficient equity in the house, even after the estate agents and solicitors costs had been paid, to allow them to walk away with a lump sum of several thousand pounds each.

A month before the house completion date, and with some satisfaction, Kevin handed in his notice at the insurance company. He didn't want to wait for redundancy. Simon had readily agreed to relocate and so expressed some surprise that Kevin was turning down the opportunity to move to Milton Keynes as well. It was, as he saw it, a big step up the social scale from Birmingham.

On his final day at work, Kevin handed back the keys to his company BMW. As is customary, he packed his few personal items from his desk into a cardboard box. The staff had organised a collection for him and presented him with a card and a wooden box containing an engraved clock. The back was engraved 'To Kevin – the Best Boss Ever. Good Luck.' He thanked them and returned to his office. He placed the clock in the cardboard box, gathered his coat and his briefcase, said his goodbyes and left. Once outside the building he placed the cardboard box in the nearest rubbish bin. Then he looked down at his briefcase and quickly stuffed that in too.

Kevin went back to the house one last time and looked around, partly to make sure he hadn't left anything that he might want in the future, and partly to put off the final departure. He went through the post. The letter from the courts was amongst the junk mail. He had now accumulated twelve penalty points so he was disqualified from driving for twelve months. He screwed the letter up, went outside and dropped it in the dustbin. Back inside, he leant against the lounge window for a moment, remembering the cosy evenings in front of the television with Anne. He thought of the summer days pottering in the garden while Anne sunbathed topless out of sight of the neighbours. He recalled their early days decorating together with electro music blaring out of the stereo. He thought of their honeymoon in Paris. The romance and the sex. Then he frowned as he thought of his wife and Tom writhing around in his bed and shook his head rapidly trying to erase the image. He flicked off the lights, gave the stained glass in the front door one last look before pulling it shut and listening for the click of the latch as it locked. He slid the key carefully under the flowerpot and stepped off the front step and into his new life.

Chapter 4

Two hundred and twenty-four miles away Robert Grigson was walking briskly down the road towards the Pig and Drum pub with an i-pad and a laptop hidden snugly under his jacket. He reckoned that altogether these should fetch a hundred and fifty pounds or so which would enable him to fill the rusting old Peugeot estate with diesel allowing him to get away from this freezing Northern outpost.

As it turned out the most he could get was ninety-five. He took the cash and gave the finger to the buyer as he left the pub. He slid fifty pounds of it under his landlady's front door. He put thirty pounds of fuel in the tank and headed towards the south, determined that he was never coming back.

Feeling hungry he pulled into the services south-east of Birmingham and after squirting his last of the ninety-five into the tank he used the small-change he had in his pocket to buy a meal deal consisting of a coffee and a muffin. While the machine gurgled and spluttered into the paper cup he pondered where exactly he should aim for. In his desire to leave Scotland, he hadn't really thought about destination options. He poured two sachets of sugar into the cup and stirred it with the wooden stick provided, then slipped on the plastic lid, picked up the muffin and headed to the checkout. After sipping the coffee and wolfing down the cake, he headed the car towards the exit of the services. He spotted a hitchhiker by the end of the slip road with a small hand-penned sign saying 'London'. Of course. That's where he decided to go. He looked again at the man behind the sign. The company might be useful, and the guy didn't look like a tramp, so he pulled in, just past him.

The hitcher tucked the sign into his jacket, picked up his bag, ran over and opened the passenger door.

'Going south?'

'Uh-huh.'

'Thanks.'

Kevin got in. He was carrying a smart leather holdall containing a few clothes, a cheap digital camera, laptop and toiletries. He placed this carefully between his feet and then rubbed his hands together. The car was pleasantly warm after standing outside in the chilly night air. He could smell the coffee that was sitting in the cup holder. He was hitching in preference to having to use public transport. His first lift had taken him fifteen miles and dropped him at the motorway services. He'd been waiting two hours for the next ride.

Robert accelerated out of the services and onto the motorway. He looked over his shoulder and indicated as he made his way into the middle lane where he remained. After a few minutes of silence, Kevin tried to strike up a conversation.

'Whereabouts are you going?'

'London, hopefully,' with a glance at the petrol gauge which was now less than a quarter full.

'Me too.'

Another few minutes of silence passed. Robert reached over and pushed the radio 'on' button. He adjusted the volume. It was an interview with Paul McCartney.

'Jesus! When will he give it up?' said Robert in exasperation.

Kevin smiled. That was exactly what he was thinking.

Robert quickly tried some other channels but obviously didn't like what he heard as he turned the radio off again.

'Have you come far?' asked Kevin.

'Yeah. Scotland. Too damned cold up there so I'm moving to London.'

Kevin glanced around. The back seat and the luggage area at the back of the estate were empty. Obviously the guy travelled light. He tried to place the accent. It definitely wasn't Scottish. Maybe North Midlands, Derby perhaps.

'And you? What's in London for you?'

'Well, a new life hopefully. Just split up from my wife, sold my house, left my job and lost my licence, hence the hitching.'

'Jeez. That's a bit grim. Got anywhere to stay down there?' Said Robert, thinking this guy sounds a bit posh. Maybe he's got relatives in London.

'Not yet. I think I'll try and find a cheap hotel for a bit then rent a room or something. Don't really know. Have to see how it pans out.'

Robert thought the guy's plans sounded just as vague as his.

'What about you? What do you do?'

Robert thought for a second about how he should answer that. Strictly speaking he was a joiner but he hadn't been doing much joinery for a while now. He had been working in a pub but supplementing his income by fencing stolen goods.

'I'm between jobs at the moment. Hoping to make my fortune in London. I heard that the streets are paved with gold.'

'I'm not so sure about that, but I gather that there are plenty of jobs down there. I'm hoping something interesting will turn up. My last job was with an insurance company. Eight years. Now I look back on it, it was a bit dull really.'

'Is that why you left?'

'No, not really. They wanted me to relocate to Milton Keynes'.

'Figures.'

More miles passed in silence. Robert tried the radio again. He switched it the AM waveband and they listened to a lively phone-in about urban foxes. Kevin settled back and contemplated the move to London. He was conscious that he could have chosen to move anywhere in the country, or the world for that matter. But he had to select somewhere so he picked the capital as a starting point. He imagined that London might prove to be a fizzy antidote to his steady suburban life with Anne. He knew a few old college friends had moved there but he hadn't seen any of them for years, so he could hardly turn up and ask for a bed for a while until he got established, but he did contemplate that once he got there, he might try and look some of them up again.

Robert leaned forwards and switched the radio back to FM. An old Ultravox track, prior to Midge Ure, was playing and both of them were murmuring the words.

'Shit!' said Robert suddenly. Kevin looked over to the dashboard and noticed that the orange petrol light had now lit up.

'If it's getting low on petrol maybe I could pay for some more?' offered Kevin.

'I think you'll need to if we're going to get there, as I'm nearly out of cash.'

'It's fine. If you pull in at the next services, I'll pay. It's still cheaper than the train.'

Later, as they reached the outskirts of London the traffic began to build up. Robert slowed the car as they joined the end of a long queue. Both men were lost in their thoughts. There was a sudden screech of tyres from behind, followed by a loud grinding crunching sound, then a huge bang as the car was shunted forwards hard into the car in front. Both men's heads first hit the headrests and then lurched forward straining violently hard against the restraining seatbelts, accompanied by the sound of tinkling broken glass. The car was old so there were no airbags. Then the forward movement stopped as instantly as it had started and they fell back into their seats. Kevin was dazed and trying to piece together what had happened. Robert was quicker on the uptake and yelled 'What the fuck?' He fumbled with the seatbelt until it came off and wincing at the bruising on his shoulder he attempted to get out. His door was wedged shut so he pushed Kevin, who was able to open his door and throw his bag out onto the verge and then staggered out allowing Robert to scramble over the seats and then rush round the car to confront the driver of the van behind them. Kevin picked up his bag and followed.

'Jesus! What were you doing? You bloody nearly killed us, you idiot!'

The other driver was nursing a cut forehead. He was pale and obviously shaken. He just sat in silence while Robert yelled at him. Other drivers were getting out of their cars to see if they could help. As the people approached and asked if they were alright, Robert abruptly stopped shouting and took Kevin's arm. He pulled him to one side, away from the crash while the other drivers circled the van checking on the condition of the driver.

'Actually, we really need to get out of here. Now.'
'Why?'
'Don't ask questions. Just do as I say. We can't get involved. Let's go.'

As they walked briskly away towards a side road, Robert looked back over his shoulder and stated loudly that he was going to call his insurance company. He waved his phone at the onlookers. They reached the corner of the road and moved quickly out of sight. Robert started walking more hurriedly. Kevin lengthened his stride to keep up.

'Is there a problem? No tax? Insurance, maybe?' said Kevin

'Yes. Partly that,' said Robert, 'Plus, it wasn't my car.'

'What? I'm not sure I understand. Whose was it then?' said Kevin.

'Don't know,' said Robert. 'Are we being followed?'

Kevin glanced back as they crossed the road. 'No. I don't think so.'

Then it dawned on Kevin that the car must be stolen. No wonder Robert wanted to get away. It occurred to him that he was now an accomplice and he felt sick.

All his life Kevin had tried to be honest and truthful. His parents had drummed it into him. They told him to always tell the truth as lying just made things worse. He had avoided any possibility of getting into real trouble. When he was at school one of the boys in his class had smashed open the school payphone, scattering coins all over the courtyard. His classmates all grabbed as many as they could before slipping away leaving the perpetrator to collect the rest. Kevin had watched in amazement, tempted to help himself but fearful of the consequences. So he had quickly made himself scarce in case he was associated with the crime. The identity of the boy became known a few days later and he was immediately expelled. The others were suspended. Kevin was relieved that he had been able to resist the temptation to join in.

Now he found himself in a situation where he didn't know what to do. He could return to the scene of the crash and own up. He knew this was the right thing to do. If he explained about being a hitchhiker people might believe him. He slowed his walk while he weighed up the possibilities of getting caught against getting away with it. Nobody knew their names. It occurred to him that even Robert didn't know his name. There were several roads between the scene of the accident and them by now and, looking back again to check, he was sure that they weren't being followed. He didn't have any kind of criminal record (other than the minor traffic offences) so even if the police found his fingerprints in the car, they wouldn't match anything they had on record plus he doubted that they'd bother anyway just for a traffic accident. The guy driving the van probably wouldn't pursue it, as the collision was his fault. Kevin mentally tallied up the probability of getting caught. He reckoned he might be okay. But he was still very pissed off with Robert as he ran to catch him up.

'Listen. You should have told me the car was nicked. What if we'd been stopped by the police? Or worse still, what if we'd been injured? It's a lot harder to get an insurance payout if you're in a stolen car even if it's not your fault.'

'Oh yes. Of course I'm really going to announce that it's a stolen car, aren't I? Want a lift mate? By the way, I've just stolen this car. Get real. Anyway we weren't injured, were we? Apart from my shoulder, of course. So it doesn't matter. Does it?'

'Doesn't matter?' Kevin was incredulous. 'Are you fucking insane? You've made me an accomplice to a crime. And now we've both left the scene of an accident. Which makes it ten times worse.'

'Look mate. It's up to you. Go back if you want to. Just keep me out of it, though. I've got enough problems without having the police down here on my back too.'

Kevin kept walking and thinking, rapidly evaluating the situation. Every step took them even further from the scene. He was torn. Then, although he wasn't entirely comfortable with it, he made a decision. He wasn't going back. He felt that the risks were probably acceptable. Feeling distinctly uncomfortable with himself, he sighed and after a while he calmed down.

The adrenalin ebbed away as they kept walking. The bag was heavy. He could smell food. His stomach nagged at him. He realised he hadn't eaten for hours.

They approached the gaudy shopfront of a McDonalds. 'You hungry?' asked Kevin.

Robert nodded. With one last look around them they turned and went in. Kevin stood in the queue while Robert found a table. For a moment, Robert considered making a quick exit but he was starving too and decided to wait until he'd eaten something before parting company with Kevin.

Kevin placed the plastic tray of food on the table and slid into the seat opposite. Robert divided up the burgers and fries.

'I'm still trying to get my head around this. What kind of trouble are you in? I think you owe me some sort of explanation about what went on back there.' said Kevin as he dipped fries in the barbecue sauce and took the first bite of his burger.

'I don't owe you anything. And, it's a long story.'

'I've got all day. And you also owe me for this meal - and the petrol.'

'Well, you did get the benefit of the petrol until that bloody idiot hit us. Alright, if it will make you happy, here's a very quick summary. Up until a few months ago I had a family, a house and a decent job. I was living and working in Tamworth, Staffordshire. My wife and I split up. Then the company I worked for went bust. They made windows. The boss was good at running a business but hopeless with the horses. He lost a lot of money at the bookies and then couldn't afford to pay the VATman. In the end, he went bankrupt and had to close the company down. Around the same time my wife and I got divorced. She got custody of our kid. So I had to get out. I didn't fancy dedicating any more years of my life to another company only to have the same thing happen, and I didn't really have any ties to Tamworth, apart from my ex-wife and kid that she won't let me see, as she's now shacked up with someone else, so I moved away and ended up in Scotland. I found a pub job for a while, just behind the bar, you know, and then met some guys who were pub regulars. They seemed friendly enough but a bit shady, as it turned out. I got involved with them and made a bit of money on the side. And I enjoyed it for a while.'

He paused and then continued, 'But it was all getting a bit heavy up there so I left. That's all there is to tell really.'

'So, was it drug dealing?'

Robert smiled. 'No, not drugs. They're not my thing. But I have been known to handle things occasionally that came to me without the owner's permission. Kind of matching up supply and demand. It was just a means to an end, though. It's not who I am.'

I bet they all say that, thought Kevin. He was intrigued. He'd never met someone so openly dishonest. Most of the dodgy people he'd come across before were ordinary people trying to defraud the insurance company by inflating their claim. He didn't regard them as thieves, although technically they were stealing. But this guy, he obviously just takes what he needs whoever it belongs to. Kevin made a mental note to keep an eye on his travel bag, which, he double-checked, was now underneath the table.

'And just how much trouble are you in?'

'That depends on how you look at it. The police were becoming interested in our activities and there are some people in Scotland who are probably feeling a bit aggrieved that I've left.'

'Do you think they are likely to follow you down here?'

'I very much doubt it. Although, I wouldn't put it past them. Anyway, there's no need to worry about me, I'll be off in a minute and you won't see me again. So none of this is your problem.'

A mobile phone started ringing. Kevin glanced around at the other diners to see who answered. When he looked back Robert was holding his phone to his ear.

'What? No. Not interested. No. Thanks mate, but I'm not into all that any more. I've moved away. Listen pal, I've told you. NOT INTERESTED.'

Robert shrugged, clicked his phone off and put it back in his pocket. He gathered the remnants of the Big Mac meal packaging onto the tray and started to get up to leave. Kevin abruptly said 'Wait. Listen. Why don't I come with you?'

Kevin had no idea why he just said that. Maybe it was the thought of being alone again. Maybe he wanted to find out a bit more about Robert and get to the bottom of his story. Maybe he just wanted some excitement in his life. Even as he uttered the words, Kevin felt that he was almost certainly making a huge mistake. He'd been incredibly lucky earlier after the crash, but he probably wouldn't be so fortunate next time. And maybe for the last few hours of his life he had felt an exhilaration that had been missing from his previous existence.

Robert held his hand out and smiled, 'Listen pal, thanks for the meal and that but it's probably best for you if you don't hang around with someone like me. That was the Scottish lot on the phone. So, as you've already seen, trouble has a way of finding me and I guess you don't really need that.' Robert made to leave the restaurant.

'Wait. Listen. I've got money. Well, I've got enough money for a few months, anyway. I really have no idea what I'm going to do and maybe it's fate that you stopped at the services and picked me up. Maybe I can help you. I don't know. Anyway what's the harm? Let's at least finish the journey and get into London. Then we can decide.' Kevin was beginning to backtrack, but his mouth had other ideas. Maybe this wasn't such a good idea.

'My name is Kevin, by the way. Kevin Walker.'

'Robert Grigson.'

They shook hands.

'Okay, let's get into London and take it from there.'

They caught the Tube and stepped off at Kings Cross. They looked right and left along the platform. People were scurrying backwards and forwards in front of them.

'Where to now?'

'I don't know about you but I'm knackered and it's getting late so let's find somewhere to stay. Things might look a bit clearer in the cold light of day.'

A short walk away, and after rejecting a few other hotels because they had no availability or looked too run-down or too pretentious, they arrived at The Bellbrook Hotel in Argyle Street. It looked reasonably smart but not too pricey. The receptionist didn't even look up as they tried to book two single rooms for one night.

'Sorry, only got one twin room left.'

Kevin and Robert looked at each other. Then Kevin said, 'okay, that'll have to do. It's just for one night.' and handed over his debit card.

'Would you like a paper in the morning?'

Kevin declined. He didn't want to chance, however unlikely, reading something about two guys leaving the scene of an accident involving a stolen car. The girl handed Kevin the form to complete.

'Name, address and signature please.'

Kevin hesitated for a moment. Robert just shrugged. So Kevin wrote down the address of his former marital home. He handed the form back and they went upstairs to locate the room.

Robert immediately disappeared into the small en-suite bathroom.

Kevin slumped on the bed nearest the window and looked around. The room was small and was in need of a bit of brightening up but this was London and so it was a relief just to know they had a roof over their heads for the night. He was thirsty so he decided to go and get something to drink. He called out to Robert in the bathroom, 'I'm just going out to get something to drink. Want anything?'

'Yeah, some beer would be good. Thanks. Oh and maybe some nuts. Just salted, not dry roasted.'

Kevin took the key and went out but as the door was shutting behind, he remembered his bag. He didn't want to leave it. So he went back in quietly and retrieved it. As he passed the bathroom door again he could hear Robert on his mobile shouting 'Look, you'll get your money when I'm ready. Just leave me alone will you.' and then slamming the phone down.

'Forgot my wallet. Back in a bit,' Kevin said to the bathroom door as went out again. Out in the street, he looked around for an off-licence. There wasn't one but in the next street there was a small late night shop that seemed to sell everything. The shopkeeper was just replenishing the beer shelves and handed Kevin a six-pack before leading him to the counter where he bagged the beer and nuts while Kevin counted out the cash.

As he mounted the steps of the hotel, he hesitated. It wasn't too late. He had his bag. He could take off now. Robert probably wouldn't care either way. It was Kevin who had everything to lose. He grimaced. Actually, what exactly did he have to lose? He didn't really have anything any more. And what he had thought he had, turned out to be false, empty and meaningless. He stood motionless for a moment and then continued up the steps. He decided to stay the night and leave in the morning.

The girl on reception continued to read her book. He climbed the stairs and entered the room. Robert was sitting on the bed nearest the door, his thinning hair slicked back and wearing just a towel and fiddling with the remote control.

'Ah, you got the beer, and the nuts too. Good man.'

They drank the beer, ate the nuts and silently watched the second half of a film on the TV. When the credits appeared at the end, Robert turned out the light.

Chapter 5

Sylvia McAvoy poured herself her second cup of coffee, stirred in half a spoonful of sugar and then picked up the paper again. The economy seemed to be in free-fall. More corrupt politicians were named and shamed. Another paedophile TV presenter had been uncovered. There had been a massive earthquake in Thailand causing destruction and hundreds of deaths. Migrants were still streaming across Europe. The England football team was involved in another brawl on the pitch. Same old news.

She neatly folded up the paper and pushed it to the other side of the table and began scrolling through the texts and emails on her Blackberry. The second day of the week-long management course was due to start in forty minutes. The business centre where the course was taking place was just two tube stops away. She had plenty of time. Once she had deleted the spam and replied to one urgent email from the bank, she scanned the hotel restaurant. It was the usual mix of hotel guests. There was a group of bustling Asian tourists taking their breakfast very seriously and a few single business types with their laptop bags parked discreetly under their chairs. A group of women were seated together, laughing and ribbing each other loudly, probably down for a hen do or maybe a works outing.

She eyed the two men that walked in and sat at the table next to her. One was well-dressed in chinos and a pullover with a neat haircut and smart leather shoes. The other was slightly shorter and a little rougher looking, with a slightly receding hairline, wearing jeans, rugby shirt and ugly trainers. When people-watching she liked to make up stories about people but these two didn't quite gel in her mind. The best she could come up with was that maybe they played squash together or something like that. She glanced at the time on her phone. Time to go. As she got up, one the two men, the one in the trainers, asked if it was okay to read her paper. She told him it was fine, passed it to him and left the restaurant.

Robert opened the paper and started reading it. The waiter came over and took their order for coffee. Kevin helped himself to the buffet.

'Why do these Koreans or Chinese always look so serious?' He asked as he sat back down with the small plate of sausages, bacon, egg and beans.

'No idea. Maybe it's really miserable where they live and they forgot how to smile,' offered Robert before looking back down at the paper.

Kevin ate his breakfast and looked around. He thought it was a pity the good-looking woman had left. After a few minutes, Robert went over to the buffet and came back with some croissants and honey. The coffee and toast arrived. Robert read the paper while he ate.

'It's alright here, and not too expensive. I thought it might be good to use as a base while job-hunting,' said Kevin

Robert looked up 'For you, maybe. Not for me. I can't afford to stay here. I'll have to find somewhere else. I've got friends in London. I'll look them up and stay with them.'

'It's up to you. But you don't have to.' said Kevin. 'It'll only be for a few days. Once I've got a job I'll rent a place. Hopefully, you can get fixed up too. So if you don't mind sharing I don't mind footing the bill, for a bit anyway.'

'Okay. Thanks. Just a few days, though.' He looked at Kevin and then glanced around and grinned, 'Don't want people thinking we're queer or something.'

'Quite. Anything interesting in the paper?'

'Just the usual stuff. Politics, NHS delays and so on. I was just reading this article about a bunch of city types scamming ten million with some insider dealing, but they got caught and it looks like they are going to get pretty hefty prison sentences.'

'I suppose that sort of thing would appeal to you.'

Robert lowered his voice. 'Hang on Kevin. Don't get me wrong okay? I've done some pretty stupid things in my time and some slightly dodgy deals but I'm not a professional thief so don't keep suggesting I am. Anyway, I've left all that behind. I was never that comfortable with it anyway. Particularly with the kind of people I was having to deal with. My plan is to get a regular job and go straight now.'

'Glad to hear it. What sort of job are you going to look for?' said Kevin changing the subject. Obviously Robert was a bit touchy about his past.

'I thought I'd look for bar work again. Don't really want to go back to factory work and I don't know if there is any around here anyway. What about you?'

'Don't know. Thought I'd try a few agencies and see what's available. Actually though, I thought that, for today, I'd just have a wander round and see a few sights. There's plenty of time for working.'

'Good idea. I think I'll go and try and find those friends I mentioned and leave the job hunting until tomorrow too.'

'Need any cash?' offered Kevin

Robert looked a bit embarrassed so Kevin peeled off some twenty-pound notes and Robert slipped them in his top pocket. 'Thanks'.

They finished breakfast and went their separate ways. Kevin headed for the Kings Road. When he was younger, he had come down to London with his friends and been amazed at the weird niche shops and bizarre fashions. After nosing around the shopping areas, he made his way to Abbey Road and walked across the famous crossing. Then he went back and did it again. He considered putting his camera on self-timer and trying to get a picture of him on it, but decided there was a strong likelihood that someone might nick the camera while he was posing.

When Kevin returned to the hotel that evening he really didn't expect to see Robert. He imagined that Robert would locate his low-life mates and they would persuade him to stay with them. And actually, Kevin half-hoped that Robert had gone. He felt that Robert was probably what his mother would have called a 'bad influence'. It was worth the money he'd given him to be rid of him and removing the possibility of being led into more trouble.

He hadn't spotted it earlier, but just inside and to the right of the entrance to the hotel, there was a small bar area and as he passed through reception Robert called out, 'Hey Kevin. Over here.'

Kevin spotted him and entered the bar area. He sat on the stool next to Robert who was sipping a pint of lager. He ordered a beer.

'How did it go? Did you find your friends?'

'No,' said Robert 'I hunted around Streatham looking for their flat. When I found it, the people living there told me that the previous tenants had moved to Brighton. So I went back into the centre of London and did the tourist thing for a bit then came back here.'

A stylish female, probably in her late twenties, came into the bar, ordered a gin and tonic and sat down in one of the comfy chairs and took out her phone. Kevin and Robert both studied her casually wondering where they had seen her before and then they realised that it was the woman from breakfast. They resumed their conversation.

'Excuse me,' said Sylvia, interrupting them. 'You wouldn't happen to know anything about Blackberry phones, would you? I'm trying to send a message with a picture attached. Not done it before.' Robert shrugged his shoulders and shook his head. His mobile was just a cheap pay-as-you-go phone. He had acquired smart phones in the past, but they usually weren't in his possession for long.

'I used to have a Blackberry,' said Kevin, thinking of his phone as it smashed against the wall while he was talking to Anne. He went and sat down in one of the soft chairs opposite her and she handed him her phone.

'It's a picture of the London Eye. It was lit up last night and looked quite spectacular. Even though I'm useless with a camera, this photo looked quite arty so I wanted to send it to my friend. She's doing an MA in art at Bristol.'

Kevin fiddled with the phone for a few seconds and then said 'There. You just need to press send now.'

'Excellent. Thank you.' She quickly tapped the phone and sent the message. 'It's gone. Can I get you two a beer to say thanks? It's on expenses. Same again please, Mister Barman.'

Kevin beckoned Robert to join them. Robert came over with the drinks and sat down.

'All sorted?' He said to Sylvia.

'Yes. It's sent now, thanks to your friend here.'

'The name is Kevin'

'Hello, Kevin. I'm Sylvia' She looked over at Robert.

'I'm Robert. Thanks for the drink. What brings you here?'

'I'm on an extremely dull management course for the week. My boss should have been on it, but he wormed his way out of it as it clashed with an interbank golf match and the course was paid for, so I've ended up doing it. I could do without it really. What about you guys?'

Kevin told her that he was thinking of moving to London and was using the hotel as a base for job hunting. Robert provided a rather sketchy reason for being in London involving old friends and job opportunities.

'So you are both looking for new jobs?'

'I'm not in a great rush,' said Kevin 'But if I can find something I like, I'll take it and see how it goes.'

'What are you interested in?'

Kevin thought for a moment. He tried to remember if his soon-to-be ex-wife had ever asked him that question. In all the years that they were together, he couldn't remember if she had ever asked him about what he really wanted to do in life.

'I quite enjoy restoring furniture and stuff. And I used to be really into music, promoting gigs and so on but that all stopped when I left college. I am quite keen on photography too. I had an expensive Nikon camera for a while and took a lot of photos but our flat was broken into and it was stolen. Now I just have a small digital one. For the last few years, I've worked in insurance but I'd quite like to get into something a bit more creative.'

'What about you Robert, what are you into?'

Kevin turned to look at Robert, intrigued to hear what he'd say.

'I'm quite into music too, as it happens. I used to be in a band, playing guitar, but, like Kevin, I had to give up the music scene. I got married young and we had a little girl a few months later. So my nights out with the band just ended. Apart from music, I'm quite good with my hands. I trained as a joiner but can also do a bit of welding, plumbing, even decorating and building. Had to, when I got married. Couldn't afford to pay anyone else to do it. So I can turn my hands to most things to earn money.'

Kevin waited to see if Robert would add anything else, like burglary, fencing stolen goods or driving stolen cars, to the list of things he could do. But unsurprisingly, he didn't.

'What about you Sylvia? What's your line of work?'

'Oh, my job is pretty boring really. I work for a bank.'

'A banker! Are you one of these city traders or do you work behind the counter?' asked Robert.

'Actually, I'm in the fraud prevention department.'

'Presumably that's where you are looking at credit card usage to see if the spending is outside that person's normal pattern?' asked Kevin.

'Well that is a big part of fraud prevention obviously and that's the bit that most people are aware of. But I'm involved in the higher end stuff. We keep an eye on people within the bank to make sure that they aren't stealing from the bank or its customers.'

'And who keeps an eye on you?' said Kevin. Then added, 'Only joking.'

'Is it a big problem in the bank? Staff helping themselves?' said Robert.

'No, it isn't, thankfully. But probably only because there are complex systems and procedures specifically designed to prevent it. The possible damage to the banks reputation it is something we have to take very seriously.' replied Sylvia. She sipped her wine and then continued, 'The banks all have the same potential problem and play it down as much as they can. You don't want customers thinking that they are handing over their hard-earned money into an institution that will steal it off them. Banking is all about trust. The customers trust us to look after their money. And we need to be able to trust our staff. But occasionally we can't. So we need to prevent them from being tempted. Or, we have to catch them before they do too much damage if they decide to cross the line.'

'Sounds fascinating,' said Kevin enthusiastically.

'It's not really. It's just a job. And like all jobs it has its moments, but usually it's just routine. Checking bank records, checking employee records, checking customer records, checking computer printouts, then re-checking everything looking for clues, patterns or anomalies, anything that leads us to an internal breakdown of trust. Sometimes we are alerted to the fact that money is being siphoned off and we have to work out how and where it is going. Other times we suspect someone and we're looking for evidence and proof so we can deal with them.'

Kevin and Robert sipped their drinks while they took it all in. Sylvia looked as if she'd be more at home managing a local branch of Top Shop than involved in high-level financial investigation.

'What are you guys doing about eating tonight? Maybe we could join forces? I found a nice little French restaurant last night or I gather there's a good pizza place about two hundred yards up the road.'

'Sounds good to me' said Kevin. Robert looked more doubtful. 'It's my turn to pay,' said Kevin diplomatically. Robert looked up and said 'Okay that's fine then'.

They chose the pizza place and sat near the window. The waitress took the order and brought their drinks.

'Did you two meet up at the hotel then?' asked Sylvia.

'Actually we met on the journey down here.' said Robert, deliberately not mentioning the car.

'And you both found you were staying at the same hotel? That's quite a coincidence.'

'Not exactly. We met on the journey down and then chose this hotel.'

'I see,' said Sylvia.

There was an awkward silence for a few seconds. It was broken up by the arrival of the pizzas and pasta.

Changing the subject, Robert asked if Sylvia lived very far away.

'Not too far, actually. I've recently moved to Chiswick. I could have stayed at home for this course, but the hotel had been booked for my boss so I thought I'd take advantage of it. It's just easier than getting across town.'

'Plus you've met us,' suggested Kevin with a grin.

'True. The people on the course are all typical middle management types. You know the kind, all suits and laptops. So it's nice to meet new people who aren't just more employees of the bank.'

Robert was looking around at the restaurant while he was eating.

'This is smart for a pizza place. Where I used to live pizza places were just greasy spoons with extra garlic, a picture of a Vespa on the wall and, if you were lucky, there was a table cloth too.'

'I've been here before actually' said Sylvia. 'I came here before with my ex-boyfriend once. He's a photographer and did some promotional shots of this place during the day and we came here for a free meal afterwards. It was a while ago, though. The boyfriend is history. Hence moving to Chiswick. Got my own flat now.'

The rest of the evening passed with pleasant camaraderie and finished with a final drink at the hotel bar before they all retired to their rooms. As they got ready for bed Kevin said 'She's alright isn't she? Attractive too.'

'Nice enough. Not my type, though.' said Robert. 'Bet she's high maintenance.'

With that, Robert rolled over and went to sleep. Kevin sat up in his bed for a while in the dark musing over the developments of the last few days. Eventually, he laid his head on the pillow and listened to the rhythmic breathing coming from Robert's side of the room until he drifted off to sleep too.

Chapter 6

Kevin was successful in securing a job the next day. He completed a number of application forms in three agencies and was politely requested to apply online in two more. On the way back to the hotel, he passed a large antique showroom, which also had its own auction house. At first he was attracted by the pieces of furniture stacked up on the pavement outside and so went inside to have a better look. As he passed the counter a 'vacancies' board caught his eye. The vacancy advertised was for an 'Assistant Sales Manager'.

After a swift interview with the owner of the business who was relieved to finally see someone who could speak English fluently, Kevin was offered a part-time position requiring him to work four days a week during a three month probationary contract period which would then be reviewed.

Kevin was pleased. He wasn't ready to return to a job with office politics. He hoped that he could indulge his love of old furniture and antiques for a while before, perhaps, having to return to the sort of work he was used to. He had agreed to start the following Monday.

His next task would be to find somewhere to live but for today he felt he had achieved enough. He was looking forward to telling Robert about the job and hoped Sylvia would join them again. He realised he had enjoyed some female company the previous evening.

Initially, Robert was not so lucky. He tried several bars asking for work. All of them asked for his c.v. He didn't have one with him or the means to produce one easily and he really needed to earn some money.

He couldn't rely on Kevin to bankroll him for much longer. He located the local job centre. It was depressing in there surrounded by badly dressed no-hopers and foreigners. There were plenty of jobs on offer, but they all were very low-paid and appeared to be spread all over London.

Ideally he wanted a job that was within walking distance of the Bellbrook. Then it occurred to him that it might be worth trying the hotels and bars in the immediate vicinity. He tried several but had no luck in any of them. Tired and fed up, Robert eventually returned to the hotel. As he was passing the reception area, he spotted the duty manager coming out of his office and decided to try one more time.

'Excuse me.'

'Yes sir, how can I help?' asked the manager

'I was wondering if you had any job vacancies here?'

The manager looked momentarily surprised to be asked for a job by one of the hotel's guests, but he recovered quickly and said, 'Please step into my office sir and let's discuss this.'

After a short interval, Robert came out the office complete with a new job. It turned out that the hotel barman had booked a month's holiday so he could return to Poland to visit his family. Robert was offered his job on a temporary basis starting at the weekend. Equally importantly he was also offered staff accommodation on the very top floor. Robert had a big smile on his face as he met Kevin returning to the hotel. They congratulated each other and celebrated with a drink in the bar.

Later they rang Sylvia's room and asked her if she wanted to join them for dinner again that evening. She agreed and they met up on the steps of the hotel before making their way to the French restaurant this time. As the sulky waitress went off to the kitchen with their order, Kevin told Sylvia about their success that day. She was pleased for them.

'So that means you are both going to be staying in London for a while?'

'Looks that way' Said Robert. 'How was the course today?'

'I'll be glad when it's over.'

'What do you do on this course?'

'After the usual introductory bollocks to break the ice, we've had to listen to a series of dull speakers telling us about various management techniques and then we look at case studies in groups. Finally, we have to present our conclusions. It's tedious. Really tedious.'

'Surely it's better than being at the office?' said Robert.

'Not really. It's okay for a change, but I'd rather be doing my regular job. It can be dull at times there are times when we're onto someone and there's a thrill about the chase that I enjoy. A bit like being a detective I guess. So I'll be glad to get back to it next week. There are only two more days to go here. Anyway, let's drink to you two getting jobs.'

They raised their glasses and toasted each other. Later that evening Sylvia found she was really enjoying herself. Kevin and Robert were so different to the other men she knew. Kevin was intelligent, gentle and had a nice smile. Robert was funny with a wry sense of humour. Neither of them was trying to impress her or attempting to be sophisticated. They just seemed to be naturally confident. For a fleeting moment, she thought about the fact that she'd probably never see either of them again after the next two days were over. She made an impulsive decision.

'So you aren't starting your new jobs for the next couple of days are you?'

'That's right' said Kevin. 'I thought I'd try and find somewhere around here to rent.'

'Do you think that it would be useful to have a second opinion and maybe a third opinion too?' She said, looking at Robert.

'What about your course?' said Kevin.

'Sod the course. I shouldn't even be on it really. I haven't learnt anything.'

'But won't they miss you? Surely they'll notice you aren't there?'

'I'll phone in sick,' she said.

Robert smiled. He had phoned in sick many times in his life and usually his day was a lot more interesting, and profitable as a result. 'Do it,' he said. 'We'll all come with you Kevin and help you choose a decent place.'

So it was agreed.

After breakfast together in the hotel the next morning, Sylvia made her call citing a migraine headache, and then the three of them ventured out together.

The first stop was the newsagents where they bought the local paper. The next stop a coffee bar where they pored over the classifieds, circling in pen any potential targets. As they walked the streets between each guided tour of bedsits and small flats they chatted about jobs, ex-wives and boyfriends. Robert even began to allude to some of his shadier dealings obviously believing that he knew Sylvia well enough now to let his guard down a tiny amount.

After seeing several unsuitable places, too small, too smelly, too dark, too far away, they stopped for lunch. They reviewed the paper and selected a second batch of potentials. Sylvia insisted on paying for the meal as she felt that they had rescued her from the dreadful course. Robert put up no resistance. The afternoon was more fruitful and Kevin eventually paid the large deposit on a small two bedroomed sparsely furnished flat near Islington. Kevin thought the rent was extortionate. He told Sylvia that for the amount he would be paying he could be buying a nice four-bedroom house with a garage and garden in the Midlands, but she assured him it was good value for the area. Even though it was slightly unusual, he persuaded the landlord, who it turned out lived next door, that he would move in at the weekend. The landlord's token resistance was brushed aside when he saw Kevin's deposit and first three month's rent being paid in cash.

'Perhaps tomorrow we could help you get some odds and ends for the flat to brighten it up?' suggested Sylvia

Kevin agreed readily. Robert did too as Kevin might need some muscle if he was going to move things around.

As they walked back to the hotel, they fell silent.

Eventually, Sylvia piped up with 'So this is probably our last evening together.'

'Not necessarily' said Robert. I'll be working at the hotel. So you'll know how to find me. And we all know where Kevin's going to be. And we know you live somewhere in Chiswick.'

Sylvia laughed and delved into her handbag. She extracted her purse and took out two business cards. She leant against a shop window and wrote her home address on the back of the cards. 'Here's my address,' she said as she handed the cards out. 'And my work and mobile numbers are on the front.'

That evening they were back in the pizza restaurant discussing their lives. Sylvia related details of some of the unsuccessful relationships she'd had. One was with her married ex-boss at the bank who had resigned and moved to another bank after their affair ended. Another was with a flamboyant hairdresser, but he spent more time preening his locks than he did on hers. He was dropped fairly quickly. She also went out with a county rugby player for a few months but, despite his rugged appearance complete with battle scars he turned out to be gay and was just testing out his sexuality. The most recent relationship had been with Neil the photographer. She had met him when he approached her in the street, told her she was beautiful and asked if she had ever done any modelling.

'Every woman dreams about being asked to model, so even though it was the corniest of chat-up lines I said yes immediately.'

She described the first modeling session where she was pampered by hair and make-up staff before being photographed in glamorous, designer outfits. 'It was fantastic' she said 'And the photos looked amazing. Nothing like me, of course. Neil edited them using Photoshop to make me look attractive.' There were several more sessions after that including a few where he asked her to wear just a bikini or her underwear followed by some sessions in which she posed topless and then nude. It was after one of those sessions that she fell into a relationship with him and eventually moved into his combined flat and studio.

'And then he started photographing other girls and was less interested in me so it was only a question of time before we had ended the relationship and I moved out.'

Robert told them more about his marriage. His eyes glistened when he talked about his daughter Chloe. He really wanted to be a part of her life but his ex-wife Janice felt it was confusing for Chloe to have her real father around and the new man in Janice's life who Chloe sometimes called 'Daddy'. So it had been better, as Janice saw it, for Robert to back away and leave them to try and get on as a family. Initially Robert had fought with Janice about it but he could see that the arguments were having a negative effect on Chloe so in the end he capitulated, making his trips to see Chloe more and more infrequent. But it hurt and the longer it went on, the harder it got. To think of your daughter calling another man Daddy was painful and Robert confessed that even though he had gone along with Janice's request, he really wasn't sure if he had done the right thing. And now it may be too late. Robert had always hoped that one day he would be able to sit Chloe down and explain to her why this came about but he wondered if she would ever understand or forgive him. Moving to Scotland had put some distance between them and he had now come to terms with the fact that he was never going to have the kind of relationship with his daughter that he would have liked.

When Robert stopped talking abruptly, Kevin filled the void by describing how that by comparison his life had been totally uneventful until the one day where everything changed in a couple of hours. He related the routine of his life and his job. He explained how he thought Anne was happy with their life together only to discover, too late, that she wasn't, and that he hadn't spotted any of the warning signs first. His mood changed to one of bitterness as he described finding the note on the table and then smashing the phone against the wall.

Robert and Sylvia listened in silence.

'So now I'm going to live my life my way, the way I want to live it. I'm going to do what I want when I want and it's all going to be on my terms.'

It was obvious to Sylvia and Robert that Kevin was still smarting from his wife's unfaithfulness. It occurred them all that they had all suffered rejection by their other halves.

Sylvia turned to Robert and said 'So, what did you do up in Scotland?'

Robert cleared his throat and then said, 'I got involved with the wrong kind of people and did some things that weren't entirely legal.'

'Ooh, tell me more.' Said Sylvia.

Chapter 7

Robert explained how he'd ended up to Stranraer. After his wife had taken up with their neighbour and then when Janice had told him that it was confusing for Chloe to have him keep coming round, he decided that he should get as far away as possible for a while. The thought of bumping into Janice with her new bloke holding hands with his daughter was too much to bear. He had heard of a job possibility over in Ireland. He'd got as far as Stranraer to catch the ferry but before he could make the crossing he heard that the job had fallen through.

He needed money quickly so he had found a bar job locally. Then he found some cheap digs. After a few weeks, the pub regulars had started to include him in their conversation. He thought they did it so they wouldn't have to keep their voices low all the time to prevent him overhearing. He described how they would talk about the various 'jobs' they had carried out and then where they were trying to 'fence' the stolen goods. Occasionally they would ask him if he wanted a phone or a lawnmower or a whole variety of items they had acquired. At first he had refused. But sometimes he realised he knew someone else he'd met in the pub who was interested in precisely those items. So he began to match the supply with the demand and taking a commission from both buyer and seller. At first this was just small relatively low-value items but as time went on the value of the items started to go up and Kevin was having items acquired to order. He became known as someone who could obtain things at a discounted price as long as no questions were asked and people would come into the pub just to see him. The pub regulars became his sourcing team and everyone did nicely out of it. For a while.

Then the plain-clothes police started arriving in the pub. They may have been out of uniform, but they stood out a mile with their black shoes and their awkwardness. They had heard rumours that the pub was the centre of the ring and they started dropping in at all sorts of times. The communication with the team became difficult and awkward. Sometimes the instructions were misunderstood and the wrong items were sourced. Robert refused to pay when the goods were wrong and had stopped placing the orders while he waited for the police to give up. The team became disgruntled and blamed Robert. He was running out of money and knew that it was only a question of time before he would be tied into the thefts. So he decided it was time to leave. The last item stolen to order was the car that had been shunted by the van driver.

Sylvia's mouth was gaping open the whole time Robert was talking.

'No doubt your opinion of me has just nose-dived. Sorry,' he said. 'In my defence, I didn't intend to get involved. I just sort of fell into it and then couldn't get out easily. I'm glad I left when I did though as it was all getting a bit heavy.'

'I don't quite know what to say. I'm just surprised,' said Sylvia.

'Well, that has put some flesh on the bones,' said Kevin sitting back in his chair and stroking his chin, 'And now you've got an opportunity for a fresh start.'

'I think I know a way to defraud the bank and not get caught,' said Sylvia quietly.

Kevin and Robert stared at her.

'What?' said Kevin.

'Forget it, I was just thinking out loud. Don't even know why I said that!'

Sylvia leant forward and started busily lining up the beer mats on the table. Robert touched her wrist briefly and asked her to repeat what she said.

'No. Honestly. It was nothing. Let's change the subject.'

'Go on. I'm interested in what you were saying.' said Robert. Kevin gave him a long withering look before turning his gaze back to Sylvia.

'Alright then. Here goes.' said Sylvia before taking a deep breath. 'I'm not sure I should have said anything and I know it sounds crazy but while I have been investigating all those different ways of stealing from the bank I think I have found a kind of loophole.'

'What kind of loophole?'

'It's not a loophole as such. It's more of an area that isn't really being looked at, plus a way of moving funds that is almost impossible to detect.'

'Surely the bank, and your department in particular, knows every conceivable trick and got it covered?' said Robert.

'Yes, you'd think so wouldn't you but I've never come across this one before and as far as I know no-one has tried it. I've been researching it for months now.'

'I'm assuming you aren't really tempted?' asked Kevin

'Again, I'm aware that I may come across is being a bit weird about this but oddly enough, I am tempted, actually. Obviously no plan is completely foolproof but I just think this one would work and I can't believe no-one has come across it before.'

So why haven't you done anything about it? Or maybe you have?' enquired Robert.

'No. I am absolutely certain it will work, and be undetectable, but I suppose I've just been waiting for the right time, or ..' she hesitated 'found the right people to help me.'

Robert and Kevin looked at each other. Now it was their turn to be open-mouthed. They could hardly believe what they were hearing from this well-dressed seemingly loyal and trustworthy employee of the bank.

'Look. I'm not dishonest. I've never stolen anything from anyone.' She glanced at Robert when she said this, 'And, if the idea ever entered my head even for a second, I always said to myself that if I was going to commit a crime it should be one where the rewards were worthy of the risk. I think this is risk-free. My problem would be what to do with all the money that it would generate.'

'Ha, now I know you are just pulling our legs' laughed Robert and called the waitress over for some more drinks, hoping that no-one was expecting him to pay.

Kevin just smiled when he realised that Sylvia had just been joking and reached for his drink.

Sylvia leaned forwards and they leaned in towards her. 'No, listen, I'm completely serious. I honestly think we could take the bank for a million pounds each and get clean away with it. Aren't you the slightest bit tempted?'

'It's just ridiculous,' said Kevin. 'And I can't believe you are being serious. You're not wired are you?'

'Don't be ridiculous. This isn't the movies. I'm not wired and I really think we could do this. I can't do it on my own, though. I need people I can trust.'

'I assume you mean us?' said Robert. Sylvia nodded.

'But why? You've only known us for a couple of days.' said Robert

'True, but I think I'm a good judge of people – past boyfriends notwithstanding.' Sylvia laughed which lightened the mood. 'Never mind. Just forget I mentioned it. It was just a mad idea. Let's talk about something else.'

'How?' said Robert

'How what?' said Sylvia

'How would you do it?'

'I can't really explain it to you in a few minutes. It's too complicated. It's to do with dormant accounts, interest and timing. But it doesn't matter. I can see you're not interested. Can we forget I even mentioned it?'

'Maybe I am interested,' said Robert after a few seconds.

'Ha! So much for you going straight' said Kevin 'I thought it was too good to last.'

Robert twisted round to face him directly. 'Listen Kevin. I've had a pretty crap life so far and, unlike you, I tend not to land on my feet. Getting the job here at the hotel was the single best thing that's happened to me in a long time and now I'm hearing of an opportunity to make some serious money that may never come round again I'm not just going to dismiss it out of hand without at least giving it some consideration. So I'd like to hear a bit more about it first.' And then added 'If that's okay with you.'

Kevin was silenced. He was shocked to hear Sylvia's idea and disappointed that Robert seemed to be taking it all in. He got up and paid the bill. On his return, he said sternly 'I think it's time we left' and led the way out onto the street. Robert and Sylvia followed behind, talking quietly amongst themselves. At the hotel, Sylvia suggested a nightcap. Kevin was going to refuse, but she insisted, as this was likely to be their last night together at the hotel.

Kevin and Sylvia sank into the comfy chairs. Robert went to the bar and organised the drinks. While the drinks were being poured, he chatted to the barman about how he felt to be going home and promised that he would do his best to make sure that the manager stuck to his promise of the keeping job open for when he returned.

'I'm sorry,' said Sylvia.

Kevin waited for the 'But'. There wasn't one.

'To be honest, I'm really surprised at you' he said. 'Don't you have any loyalty to the bank?'

'I do' she said 'And I'd probably feel the way you do now if someone had suggested something like this to me. It's just that there are lots of people working at the bank making crazy amounts of money. I mean, millions of pounds and huge bonuses, for seemingly doing very little. I'm surrounded by them, all walking around in their new suits and suntans, bragging about their new houses, cars, holidays and so on. I work really very hard. The hours are long, the work is tiring and I don't make a huge amount by comparison. Certainly nothing like as much as those posh-boy traders. You can see why this is so tempting for me. It would be a sort of re-balancing. But let's not talk about it any more. I know you aren't interested and unless I can find some people to help it will never happen. Please just erase the conversation from your mind.' Then switching the subject, Are we still on for bric-a-brac shopping tomorrow?'

Kevin was still shocked by what she had said and wanted to decline, but something in him felt that he didn't want tonight to be the last he saw of Robert and Sylvia. 'Sure' he said as Robert arrived with the drinks.

The following morning, as Kevin and Robert walked through the reception area to reach the breakfast area, Sylvia was at the desk checking out. She had requested that the hotel store her luggage until later that day.

She joined them for breakfast and then the three of then went shopping. When Robert had offered his muscle, he was thinking more of moving furniture around inside the flat. He hadn't anticipated having to carry large shopping bags containing lamps, framed photos, kitchen utensils, cushions, and a large hat-stand bought for twelve pounds from a junk shop. They stopped at the flat and persuaded the landlord next door to let them in and deposit their purchases.

Back at the hotel Sylvia retrieved her bag. Kevin thanked her for all her help with the shopping. She hugged them both before leaving in a taxi. Robert and Kevin rejoined to the bar.

'So. That's that,' said Robert. 'She's gone and it's back to just the two of us.'

'And tomorrow it'll be just you.' said Kevin.

'What did you think?' asked Robert

'About what? Her?'

'I know you like her. It's pretty obvious. No, I meant her plan. The money.'

'Oh no, not you as well. I was trying to forget she'd even mentioned it.'

'But don't you think we should find out more and see if it's feasible?'

'Listen to yourself! Feasible! It's mad. It's illegal. It's a completely crazy notion and anyone thinking otherwise has got to be completely insane.'

'Well. I want to know more. I think it's possible it might work. She seems pretty certain about it. She must know more about the internal procedures, and how the security works. Plus she's taking most of the risk.'

'If, for one tiny incredulous moment, I even considered it, you seem to forget that we hardly know her. For God's sake, I hardly know you. And every time you open your mouth more crazy stuff comes out, so I'm not sure I want to know more about either of you.'

'You're intrigued though aren't you? You've got to admit it. No-one could be offered a million pounds and not give it a moment's thought.'

'No. Seriously, I'm not. I made a decision early in my life to be honest.'

'And look where that got you.'

Kevin was about to retort when it occurred to him the Robert had got a point. Where had it got him?

'Look, all I'm saying is that we should find out more. I don't think there's any such thing as the perfect crime. I think she must have overlooked something. And if so it's definitely a non-starter. But if, by some miracle, she's right and it could work, without any risk, we should at least think about it.'

Whilst Kevin was definitely not interested in her plan, he was interested in her. He hoped that he would see her again and maybe pretending to want to know more about the crazy idea, as long as it never went any further, was one way to do that.

'Okay, let's look into it a bit more in a while. Happy now?'

Robert smiled. 'Yes, another pint?'

The following morning Kevin settled up for the room and said goodbye to Robert who was already dressed in his smart barman outfit. Apparently being the barman in the evening also required him to serve coffees in the morning. As he left for the flat Kevin slipped some folded notes into Robert's hand.

'Thanks very much for your help yesterday. Hope this will see you through till you get paid.'

Robert nodded his thanks and then followed Kevin out of the hotel. He stood at the top of the hotel steps watching Kevin cross the street and head off towards the flat. When Kevin was out of sight he turned around, clicked his heels and commenced his hotel duties.

Kevin reached the flat and after unpacking his bag he spent some time arranging and rearranging the furniture and other items bought the previous day. Then he went out to get a paper and did some grocery shopping. He returned to the flat and made a cup of coffee and sat in the old armchair, which he was pleased to find was agreeably comfortable.

As he relaxed and read the paper he found his mind wouldn't stay on the newsprint in front of him. It kept wondering to thoughts of Sylvia. He imagined her trying to share the mirror with the hairdresser boyfriend and then tried to imagine her posing nude for Neil the photographer. He thought about her smile, her dark brown eyes, her hair and her perfume. He wanted to see her again. He retrieved her card from his jacket pocket and studied it. Sylvia McEvoy, Senior Inspector, Financial Security Division of the National Standard Bank, Butlers Wharf, London. He flicked the card in and out of his fingers.

He resolved to buy a new phone.

Chapter 8

Sylvia was in the shower when she heard her mobile ringing. She debated with herself whether to answer it or not. She grabbed the towel and wrapped it around her as she ran into the bedroom to pick up the mobile phone from her bedside table.

'Hello.'

'Oh, hi Sylvia, it's me, Kevin.'

She was glad she'd made the dash, even though she was now dripping all over the polished wooden floor of her apartment.

'Hi Kevin, how's it going? How's the new job?'

'Well I've only been there a few days but it seems to be working out fine. I've sold quite a few pieces and Peter the manager says he is pleased. So, all in all, it's all going okay right now. How are things with you?'

'I'm fine. Straight back into the swing of things at work. Busy, busy, busy.'

'You didn't get into any trouble for missing the last couple of days of the course then?

'No, of course not. I doubt if anyone even noticed. These courses are just box ticking, so the bank can say it offers regular training for all staff.'

'Good. Erm, I was wondering if you wanted to meet up for a drink or something?'

'You know, I was thinking of ringing you and asking you the same thing, but I realised I didn't have a number for you. But now that you've rung me, I should be able to save your number on my phone. Yes. A drink. That would be lovely. How about Saturday? Is that good for you? Where shall we meet?'

'Maybe we could meet up the hotel. The Bellbrook. We can check on how Robert's getting on too.'

'Excellent idea. Eight o'clock?'

Kevin reached the bar first. He'd bought a new jacket and splashed out on some designer jeans. Robert was behind the bar and was pleased to see him.

'Back already? Nice to see you.'

'And you. Job okay?'

'Yes. Long hours though, but I do get a big chunk of the daytime to myself. I go out exploring. I'm getting to know the local area quite well. How is it in the antique business?'

'So far, so good. The boss seems to like me, and the sales results have been pretty good.'

'So are you making decent money?' Typical Robert. Straight to the point.

'Not bad. And I get a bit of a bonus if I exceed the monthly target.'

Robert's looked over Kevin's shoulder and adjusted his focus. 'Look out, here comes Madame.' And then looking back at Kevin, he raised one eyebrow.

Kevin turned around and looked at Sylvia. He took in the vision. She was dressed in a long lavender-coloured dress which clung to every inch of her shapely body. She smiled and Kevin felt his heartbeat quicken.

'Hope I'm not late' she said as she leant over the bar and kissed Robert on the cheek and then did the same with Kevin who eagerly breathed in her perfume.

'No, I had only just arrived and was just saying hello to Robert. Would you like a drink?"

'Good. Yes, a gin and tonic please.'

They had a drink and offered Robert one as well, but he refused.

'No drinking on duty,' he said, 'Are you two off out somewhere nice?'

'What time do you finish?' said Sylvia 'Maybe you can come too.' She looked at Kevin to see if he'd mind. Actually he was hoping to get her on her own but Robert helped by telling him that he was working until midnight as it was Saturday.

'My early finish nights are Monday and Tuesday. Then I'm free from eight o'clock. The manager runs the bar on those nights.'

Some more residents came into the bar and Robert attended to them. Kevin and Sylvia finished their drinks, waved at Kevin and left the hotel. They walked the streets for a while before pausing outside a small restaurant. 'Will this do?' said Kevin. 'Perfect,' said Sylvia so they went in.

The waiter asked if they had a reservation. He looked doubtful when they said they didn't. They looked around the half full restaurant. The waiter suddenly jerked as if he'd just remembered something and then said 'Yes we do have a table. It's by the kitchen, though. Is that okay?' They said it was.

Kevin looked at Sylvia. She was a very beautiful woman. He hadn't really noticed before, but now he was definitely aware of it. The thought made him nervous. His conversation was a bit garbled and random. She reached over and put her hand on his. He stopped talking and looked down at her hand. She withdrew it gently and said 'So tell me about the job and how you are getting on in the flat.'

Before he could answer, the waiter arrived and took their order. He came back a minute later with their drinks. Kevin then told her about the targets and bonuses, and the customers. He told her about the people who bought antiques and those who just looked saying 'Oh we used to have one just like that at home. Imagine it being an antique now. We must have been sitting on a fortune.' Sylvia laughed as he told her about people buying antique beds and wanting to try them out in the showroom first. 'One couple even had the woman bending over the headboard to make sure it was the right height.' Sylvia giggled.

The food arrived, and realising that he was probably talking too much, Kevin switched the conversation to Sylvia and her life. She told him about getting back into the job and how sympathetic her boss had been when she told her she had to miss two days of the course because of the migraine. She told him about a member of staff they were tracking, and she lowered her voice as she told him, reminding him that this was between them and should go no further, as the member of staff was working in the same building as her but on the floor below. She told him how this person had opened a series of fake accounts and was moving money between them. They were closing in on this person waiting for a slip-up. Then they would pounce.

Then they talked about Robert for a while. Sylvia asked if Kevin knew what had happened between Robert and his ex-wife. 'No' he said 'I don't know much more about Robert than you do. He certainly seems upset when he talks about his daughter, though.'

'It must be hard.' said Sylvia. 'I'm lucky. My parents are still together. They live in Australia now, though. Most of my friends' parents split up along the way. Sometimes I was envious that they seemed to get two of everything, two birthdays, two Christmases, two holidays and so on but on balance I think it's best if parents try and stay together.'

'My parents split up when I was fifteen, then my mum died three years later.' said Kevin. Most people think that by that age it doesn't affect you much. But it did. It rocked my faith in marriage. And, of course, my marriage failed too.'

'You didn't have any kids then?'

'No. Anne wanted children, but I wasn't so keen. If it had just happened I would have been okay with it. But actually deciding to bring new people into the world was a step too far. Something wasn't right. At the time I thought it was just the timing and I wasn't ready to be a father. As it turned out our relationship was about to fall apart so perhaps it was for the best.'

Sylvia was aware that Kevin was still raw from the whole experience so she changed the subject.

'Had any more thoughts about the project I mentioned?'

For a moment, Kevin had no idea what she was referring to. Then it dawned on him.

He lowered his voice and actually lowered his head too. He hissed, 'No. I thought we weren't going to discuss it any more?'

'It's just that the timing is a critical part of it and if we are going ahead we need to start soon.'

'Shhh, keep your voice down. Someone might hear.'

Sylvia smiled, 'Hear what? No-one knows what we're talking about.'

'I can't believe you are so blasé about it. We're talking about a lot of money... and a crime.'

'I know' said Sylvia 'And I don't want the opportunity to pass. Have you actually thought about it? You know, seriously I mean?'

Kevin felt strongly that he was being put on the spot. 'Robert is quite keen as far as I know,' she said.

'Why? Have you been discussing it with him?'

She looked distinctly sheepish as she told him that Robert had phoned her the same day Kevin had and had indicated that, if Kevin was game, then he was too.

Kevin thought about it for a while and then said 'Look I don't like the idea one bit and every fibre of my body is telling me to walk away but if you want to arrange a meeting with Robert let's talk it through. There's almost certainly a flaw in your plan somewhere and once we've found it, hopefully, we can drop it.'

'That sounds perfectly sensible' she said and raised her glass of wine to him.

Kevin's heart sank. What had he let himself in for?

Chapter 9

They met up the following Tuesday at Kevin's flat. It was Robert's turn to have bought some new clothes. He was wearing black trousers, a white shirt and a beige jacket. Sylvia thought he looked decidedly cleaner and tidier than before. After the initial small talk and drinks, Sylvia opened the proceedings by explaining the workings of the bank. She described the role of her department, its functions and how the bank security worked. She told them about some of the fraud cases they had uncovered and how they detected them.

Kevin was feeling decidedly uncomfortable, particularly when Sylvia explained how the fraud had come to light and how the perpetrators had subsequently been caught and sentenced. He kept hoping that they could get to the end of the discussion and change the subject. Sylvia then began to outline her proposal. It involved taking money from dormant bank accounts that hadn't had any activity for a number of years.

She explained that accounts became dormant for a number of reasons. The death of the account holder was the most obvious one. Serious illness was another. Sometimes people just forgot that they existed or forgot how to access them. Most of the accounts had less than fifty pounds in them although there were a sizeable number where the amount was much larger than this. Most people couldn't be bothered to write letters and so on to regain access. She estimated that there were several million dormant accounts within the global banking industry.

The reason the Sylvia felt it was undetectable is because nobody in the bank was constantly monitoring these accounts. Dormant accounts came under her department's domain and it was her responsibility to look at them every now and then. By definition, there was never anything to report on them as they were accounts that had no activity going on. As soon as some activity went on, they ceased to be dormant. The addition or removal of interest was not seen as activity.

The amount of interest payable on these accounts was tiny but when added together would result in a sizeable amount. She explained that initially the interest only would be diverted. As long as that didn't cause any alerts she would then arrange for some of the capital in accounts dormant for a number of years to be removed electronically. She estimated that over the course of twelve months they could accumulate approximately three million pounds. She felt that a year was the right period. Any longer and the loss might be spotted by the external auditors.

Sylvia went on to say that the biggest problem was going to be moving the money around so that it didn't accumulate in one account and arouse suspicion. So it would have to be laundered. This is where she needed help.

Kevin was shaking his head. This was crazy. It went against everything he had ever believed in. He almost felt like pinching himself to see if he was dreaming all this up. For the whole time that Sylvia was talking he felt sure that there must be something that she had overlooked. Nothing was ever that simple.

Robert said, 'So, once the money has been diverted to us, we would need to move it around by spending it on something that provides us with a legitimate paper trail.' This had never been an issue for Robert in his previous dealings as the amounts of money were never so large that he needed to worry about it. In fact most of the money was spent before he even received it, so he never really got ahead of the game.

'Exactly' said Sylvia.

Robert and Sylvia spent a few minutes tossing ideas around and then dismissing them as the drawbacks of each option became obvious. Kevin listened in silence. He still could not believe that a blatant flaw in the plan had not yet come to light. Without being aware of it, he had been analysing the problem of laundering the money. Then he had an idea and blurted it out.

'How about antiques?'

Kevin immediately regretted his contribution and restrained himself from putting his hand over his own mouth.

Robert looked at him with surprise and then at Sylvia and grinned. 'Yes. That might work.'

They pondered this for a moment. Then Robert added, 'But what about storage?'

'Clearly there's no way we're going to do this but, purely hypothetically, I was thinking that it should be possible to buy antiques, and then re-sell them through an auction house like the one where I work. Then we don't really need to store them.'

Robert and Sylvia glanced at each other. Their eyes acknowledged that it was very early days, but it looked like Kevin was at least allowing himself to give the idea a cursory airing, even if he was still some considerable distance from getting fully on board.

They continued to discuss the various permutations and there were certain aspects they agreed on in principle. As they were airing them, Kevin said, 'For the avoidance of any doubt I just want to reiterate that I have no intention of getting involved in this. Apart from the obvious moral issues, I'm still convinced that it would never work in practice. But if by some miracle we did decide to go ahead with this, it would need to be organised properly. It would need meticulous planning. There would need to be total agreement about a range of things. Like a set of rules about how we operated. For example, one of the main rules would be that we mustn't suddenly start splashing out on fancy stuff, like new Ferrari's. And we'd need another one about what happens if one of us wants to stop, and so on.'

Sylvia and Robert knew that Kevin was the natural leader amongst them and so if he wanted rules, he would have a set of rules. They spent the next hour talking through the parameters and Robert suggested that they draw up a list. 'Just as an exercise to see if we can agree on things,' he said, reassuringly, while looking over at Kevin. Sylvia found a pad of paper and a pen. She also acted as scribe. After much discussion and argument, they finally came up with a set of ten. When she had finished writing them down she read them out.

The Rules

1) *The aim of the venture is to collect £3 million. It will be divided equally amongst the three of us. We will stop when all three of us have received £1 million each from the venture.*
2) *We will stop in exactly 12 months from the date we commenced or see note 1 – whichever comes first.*

3) But if any one of us wishes to stop at any stage, we will all stop.

4) If there is any indication that any one of us is under suspicion, or that anyone is going to get hurt, we will stop.

5) We will not start to spend outside of our normal pattern on ourselves (other than the laundering exercise) until after we have stopped and we are sure that we are not under suspicion. And even then we need to be very careful not to attract attention to ourselves.

6) We will not reveal anything to do with this venture to ANYONE outside of the 3 of us.

7) No other people will be introduced into the venture without the agreement of the three of us.

8) If any one of us is caught we will do everything we can to prevent the names of the other two being passed on, (although recognising that fraud investigators would quite easily be able to link us together).

9) We will all use every means we can to hide our involvement in the venture. (e.g. Nothing written down. No computer records. No emails. Pay as you go phones and regularly replaced sim cards).

10) Once the project is underway we will try to avoid all being seen all together at the same.

Kevin was a bit unsure about the last one as it might be a barrier to the fledgling relationship between him and Sylvia developing much further if they couldn't be seen in public together. They agreed to commit the rules to memory so that the piece of paper with them written on could be destroyed. They agreed to meet up in one week's time for a final decision meeting. The week would allow all of them to have a 'cooling-off' period allowing them to back out if they wanted to.

For the next few days, Kevin's head was in a whirl. He felt a new chapter of his life was just starting and all of a sudden it was thrown into turmoil by the remote, but still being discussed, prospect of this very definitely criminal venture. But somehow he didn't want to be the one who would call it off. He hoped that an obvious spanner in the works would appear and he could justifiably excuse himself. He thought about Robert and whether he could be trusted. He seemed to have little to lose so he didn't think he would back out although he couldn't be certain as Robert was evidently a bit unpredictable and maybe his desire to straighten his life out would overrule his tendency towards criminality. But of the three of them, Kevin felt that Robert was the most likely to press on with the plan.

Even though she came up with the original suggestion, he thought that Sylvia was the most likely to change her mind. On the surface, she seemed to have a good job. She was young and beautiful. She appeared to have everything going for her and the least to complain about. He really couldn't understand why she was even considering risking everything to do this. He decided to find out.

Chapter 10

In the small snug bar of the Ferryboat Inn in Stranraer, Big Mitch was striding up and down the flagstone floor in front of the bar berating his team.

'So where the fuck is he then?'

The other four men just shook their heads.

'What have you idiots done to find him?'

'I've tried his flat. And I've been round to see that tart in Glen Street. She hasn't seen him for over a week,' said Charlie

'Well, I've tried his mobile. He cut me off. Twice. Bastard.' Said Monkey

'I think he's legged it.'

'That's pretty bleedin' obvious fuck-face' said Mitch thrusting his large shaven head against Jimmy's small tattooed forehead. 'The question is where has the little shit legged it to?' Then turning to the others, 'Who saw him last? What about you Ralph? When did you last see him?'

'Last Friday, when we delivered that Peugeot. He was pretty pissed off 'cause it was an estate and said he wasn't 'aving it' said Ralph 'I told him it was the best we could do at short notice. He told me 'is client wanted a saloon. I thought a saloon meant one with four doors.'

'Okay Ralph, being totally brain-dead really hasn't held you back much, has it?'

Ralph look confused.

'Jesus! You are all fucking useless. Has anyone seen him after Friday?'

They all mumbled that they hadn't. Mitch walked over to the window, pulled the net curtain aside and looked out across the street.

'Right, so it looks like he cleared off around then. And, as the car's gone, we'll have to assume that he took it. He owes us five grand at least. So that's a grand each as I see it. Where was it he came from originally? Tamworth wasn't it? Didn't he have a wife and kid there? I think we need to pay them a visit.'

Chapter 11

Kevin spoke briefly into the entrance intercom. Sylvia buzzed him in.

'I'm glad you rang' she said as she took his coat and hung it over the back of a chair. He followed her into the open plan sitting room and took in the real polished wooden floor and tasteful furnishings. The room was warmly lit with floor lamps in the corners.

'I must just see to the food. Pour us both a glass of wine will you please Kevin?'

Kevin poured two glasses of wine while Sylvia moved round to the kitchen area.

'Gorgeous flat,' said Kevin as he looked around taking in the muted colours and decorative artworks on the walls. He examined one of the paintings. 'Makes mine look a bit like a shoebox.'

'I'm lucky. I managed to persuade the agent to let me have it when there were lots of other people after it. I flirted outrageously with him until he said it was mine. The food's about ready now. Take a seat.'

Kevin sat down and Sylvia brought in the lasagna. She served it onto the square white plates.

'There's Parmesan too.' Kevin added some and then ate a mouthful. He sat back in his chair 'Ah, this is just delicious.' Between mouthfuls, he said 'This is the first proper home-cooked food I've had in ages.'

She was pleased he liked her cooking. 'I guessed you might be getting fed up with takeaways and I thought it might make a nice change from going out. When you rang you said you had something to ask me?'

'Yes. I did. Can we finish this first?'

They emptied their plates. Then Kevin finished what was left in the dish. Finally, he leant back. 'I'm completely stuffed. That was amazing. You're an excellent cook.'

After a couple of minutes while they sipped their wine Kevin leant forward and explained that he had been thinking about the meeting in his flat and how he couldn't stop thinking about whether to declare that he was in or out. Then he said 'It's just that I know why I might possibly consider getting involved. And I've got a fair idea why Robert might. But with you, I just don't know. What I'm trying to say is ..'

Sylvia interrupted his awkward speech 'You don't know why I'd want to do this when it looks as if I'm doing just fine.'

'Exactly.'

She said that she could understand perfectly why he or anyone else for that matter would think that but that appearances could be deceptive. She then explained that she had always anticipated having a certain kind of life and had realised she was never going to get from the salary she received from the bank.

'It's a very good salary' she admitted quickly, 'In fact, it's very generous and many people would really feel that they had arrived if they were earning my salary but in order to keep receiving it I have to keep going into work every day and will continue to have to so for the next thirty or forty years. I've always felt that there must be more to life than this. I want to be able to pick and choose what I do. I want some control over my life. Being young, fit and healthy won't last forever. The truth is that eventually my looks will fade and my body will get old. I want to be able to really enjoy this bit right now, and not to be continually working just to get the next paycheck like a rat on a wheel. I suppose what I'm really looking for, is freedom. Freedom from the job, freedom from relying on anyone else for money and freedom to travel and explore. And, if I'm brutally honest, I think it will be exciting to pit our wits against this institution and succeed.'

Some of what she said made sense to Kevin. He wondered what the possibility was that they could conceivably get away with it without alerting suspicion. On the face of it, and he found he was trying to convince himself, it appeared to be as close as possible to a victimless crime so nobody would actually lose out or get hurt.

'Would you like dessert?' Kevin nodded. Sylvia collected up the plates and went back round to the kitchen area. He was surprised how quickly she could flit from talking about something as momentous as bank fraud, to whether he wanted a pudding.

'Have you thought about the consequences if we were caught? Have you any idea how you would cope with the police, the courts and all that?'

'You worry too much. The whole point of this is that what I'll be doing in the bank is undetectable. I'll make sure of that. The only problem will be if we are stupid with the money and people start asking awkward questions.'

'How can you be so sure? Surely the account you'll be using is monitored and so your actions will be traceable by somebody who was looking.'

'There are a number of spare accounts not allocated to specific people and everyone in the team has access to them and we can use them to access the accounts of any member of staff. In fact, they can be accessed from anywhere. There are also lots of accounts of members of staff who have left, which aren't always removed from the system by the IT department until several weeks or months later. I can get in and out of the system electronically and no one will ever know it was me. I don't even have to be in the bank. I've tested it. It works.'

She returned with a coffee and chocolate mousse. She sat back down opposite Kevin.

'Okay, but where do we move the money to?' He said.

'I can set up a group of accounts that then automatically transfer money between them and eventually to our payout accounts. The way I look at it, it's going to be down to you to administer the money after that.'

Kevin was surprised to hear that Sylvia was already allocating tasks.

'It makes sense you see. You can monitor the payout accounts and move the money so that we can create a legitimate trail. Your idea of antiques was perfect. Presumably you can buy them and move them on getting receipts for the purchase and the sale. It will look like a legitimate business. Then the money can be fed into our own accounts in equal shares.'

'Until we've reached a million each'

'Yes. Then we stop as agreed. Then, after a period of time, I will leave the bank.'

'Then what? Assuming we pulled this off, what would you do then?'

'I haven't thought that far ahead and have no fixed plans obviously but I'd like to travel for a while and then settle down somewhere warm, away from the grey drizzle of this country.'

Kevin considered that. He had always lived in England. His foreign holidays had always been in Europe. It had never occurred to him to live anywhere else other than his home country.'

'And what would Robert's role be in all this? You seem to have it all figured out.'

'I'm only suggesting things. I know what my job is going to be and so I've been thinking about where you and Robert fit in, if you both agreed. I pictured me in the bank, you in the central monitoring position and Robert as our man on the street. So for example, when the money starts flowing, you would withdraw it and decide where it was spent, then Robert can do the actual purchasing, delivery, collection and so on. It was just how I saw it panning out and playing to our strengths.'

Kevin had to admit that it sounded feasible and that each of them would be doing what they were best at. Yes. It sounded like a plan. Then he checked himself. Only a few days ago he'd never even met these people and now they are talking about robbing a bank of three million pounds. How could he possibly trust them? It all seemed a long way from his safe and steady job at the insurance company.

Chapter 12

Robert carried the drinks into the restaurant and could feel the vibration of his phone in his trouser pocket as he walked. He deposited the tray of glasses on the side workstation so the waitress could take them to the table. He returned to the bar and checked his phone. There was a missed call from Big Mitch. His heart sank. This was trouble.

When Robert had first met Mitch's gang when they came into the pub in Stranraer, they had seemed friendly enough despite the tattoos and aggressive haircuts. He then began to realise that they weren't the brightest people in the world. Of the five of them Mitch was the only one who wasn't completely stupid. They were also disorganised, inefficient and lazy.

Robert had given them regular 'work', requesting specific items and had advised them on times and places. Everything went smoothly for a while and everyone had profited, apart from the people and firms they stole from, of course, but Robert assumed most of them would be insured.

Towards the end of his time up in Scotland, there had been a couple of deals that had gone badly wrong. The clients had refused to pay up which meant that Robert didn't have the money to pay Big Mitch and his crew. Then there was the car that he and Kevin had abandoned after the crash.

He had hoped that he had left his troubles behind. The call from Mitch indicated that he was mistaken. He felt like ditching the phone and getting a new one but the number was the only one his ex-wife Janice and more importantly Chloe, had for him. They hadn't been in touch recently but he hoped that

Chloe might ask after him and perhaps Janice would call him and let her speak to him.

He wished the bank job had already started. Then at least he'd have the money to pay Mitch back if he had to.

Chapter 13

As Sylvia said goodbye to Kevin that evening she wondered whether she should have let him stay the night. They had kissed briefly at her front door then he had smiled and waved as he walked off down the corridor. The kiss was the sort that good friends might give each other. She hoped that she had reassured him. They needed to get started soon as she wasn't sure how much longer her job would last. Cutbacks were always being made and she didn't think that her department would be immune, plus there were constant rumours of a takeover bid.

Kevin waited on the platform of the Tube station running the conversation through his mind. He looked around him. There was a young couple necking behind him. A business type was checking his phone. In fact, most of the people around him were staring at their phones as if they were conduits to another, better, world outside the tube station. He was almost decided. He just needed to talk to Robert now.

He knew it was late but he called him anyway. Robert answered.

'Hey, Kevin. I'm glad it's you' he said.

'Really? Why?'

'Oh nothing, it's just good to hear a friendly voice.'

'Have you finished work yet?'

'Yes. Just. About five minutes ago.'

'Just wondered if you had got time for a chat. I know it's late but I'm not too far from you.'

Robert was curious to know what Kevin wanted to talk about so he said 'It's fine. Come over. I'm on the top floor. Room ten.'

Twenty minutes later Kevin was gently tapping on Roberts door. Robert opened the door and handed Kevin a bottle of beer.

'Thanks' said Kevin and sat down in the chair next to the bed. 'Don't splash out on the staff here do they?' he said as he looked around and took in the tiny sparsely furnished room.'

'No. But it's a lot better than sleeping under a bridge. And I've done that more than once.'

'I've just come from Sylvia's place.'

'Thought you might have done. Getting the jitters are you?'

'As it happens, she has reassured me on a few points. She seems to have it planned out rather well. I don't fully understand exactly what she's going to be doing within the bank but once the money starts flowing it would be up to us to handle it and for you, in particular, to be out and about moving it around by buying and selling antiques. How would you feel about that?'

'Sounds good to me. I get several hours off during the day so it should be fine. And if it gets too busy I can always give up the job and find somewhere else to live.'

'Do you trust her?'

Robert looked at Kevin. 'I don't know. Can you trust anyone? She seems pretty straight and she's left herself wide open. We could get her fired tomorrow on what she has already told us. So she must trust us. To a point anyway.'

Kevin thought about that for a moment. 'I think I'm falling for her.' Then he qualified it. 'A bit anyway. But it's probably just a rebound thing.'

'That was fairly obvious' said Robert. 'But you mustn't let that cloud your judgement. You should try to look at it as a business arrangement.'

'So I take it that you are fully behind it?'

'Listen' said Robert 'I don't know if it will work. She seems very sure. But if we don't try, we'll never know. The way I look at it, we've got one shot here at creating a better life and I'm going to take it. If something goes wrong, we can move on, maybe abroad.'

Kevin noted that both of them had now mentioned the possibility of leaving the country.

'It's all about trust, isn't it?' said Kevin. 'You need to trust me. I need to trust you. We both need to trust Sylvia. And trust is gossamer thin.' As he said this he was thinking of Anne, sneaking back to his house with that fucker Tom.

'Are you just thinking aloud? Or are you asking if you can trust me?' said Robert.

Before Kevin could reply Robert said 'Look, and I speak from bitter experience here, I don't fully trust anyone. Even people with the highest integrity seem have a point where I think they'll crack. Usually, it's money or sex. My attitude is to look for people who have a higher than average trustworthiness quota and trust them up to a degree. After that, I have to look after number one. For what it's worth though, you can trust me and I'm going to trust you. I think we both agree Sylvia remains a bit of an unknown quantity.'

Kevin nodded in agreement and sipped his beer.

Chapter 14

The rest of the gang stayed in the car and watched Monkey as he reached down and opened the little white painted gate and then closed it behind him before walking up the path and ringing the doorbell of the terraced house in Tamworth.

A woman came to the door and they spoke for a while. The woman shook her head. Then the door shut. Monkey walked back to the car opening and closing the gate carefully behind him. He got in, closed the car door and said, 'He's not there. Hasn't been there for months. She hasn't seen him since he went up to Scotland.'

'I fucking bet she hasn't,' said Mitch as he leapt out of the car and slammed the door.

He kicked the gate open and thumped his fist three times on the front door. The door opened a crack. This time, there was a chain across the gap. A frightened looking female face appeared briefly to the watchers in the car. They heard raised voices then the door slammed shut. Mitch kicked the door hard then strode back to the car. 'Let's go' he said.

'Where?' said Ralph.

'I don't fucking know. Just drive. Idiot.'

Once out of the estate Mitch said, 'Okay. Stop and park here. You two ..' gesturing to Jimmy and Charlie, 'Go and watch the house. Keep out of sight. Anyone goes in or out I want to know about it. Call me as soon as you see anything. We won't be far away.' They got out of the car and walked off in the direction of the house.

'Right, Ralph. Take us to a pub. I need a pint.'

They drove to the nearest pub and ordered drinks.

'I think she might be telling the truth. I suggested we might hurt the kid if she was lying but she was adamant that he hadn't been there. Monkey, try him on his mobile again.'

Monkey got his phone out and prodded it before holding it up to his ear. 'Bob, it's Monkey. Where are you? We've looked all over for you ..'

Before Robert could respond Mitch leant over and grabbed the phone 'Hey shit-face, you owe us a lot of money you bastard. We're going to collect it. You can give it to us easy or we can cut it out of you. Where are you? You'd better tell us or your missus and the kid will wish you had.'

At that moment, Mitch's own phone started ringing. 'Find out where he is,' he said as he handed the phone back to Monkey.

'What?' Mitch yelled into his phone. 'Right, we're on our way.'

'Jimmy and Charlie have just seen him going into the house,' said Mitch 'Let's go. Come on Monkey, let's talk to him face to face.'

Monkey ended the call and pocketed his phone. They downed the rest of their pints, slammed the glasses down in unison and ran outside to the car. Ralph raced the car back round to where Jimmy and Charlie were loitering on the pavement outside the house. They all marched up to the front door. Monkey went to press the doorbell but Mitch brushed his arm aside. 'We know you're in there. Open up or we're coming in.'

The door opened and a man dressed in a tracksuit looked at the assembled group on his doorstep.

'It's not 'im' said Ralph.

'I can see that Shit-For-Brains.' Then to the man in the doorway 'Who are you?'

'Who the fuck are you more like?' said the man. 'What do you want? If you're looking for Bob Grigson he's not here and hasn't been here for ages. He doesn't live here. I do. So if that's all, you can piss off,' and he slammed the door shut.

Mitch grabbed Jimmy and Charlie by their collars and dragged them down the path and into the road before releasing them roughly.

'You fucking dickheads! Next time make sure it's the right bloke before getting on the phone. Monkey, come here and give me your phone.'

He found Robert's number and rang it. 'Me again, Dipshit. We're outside your missus's house. Did you know she's shacked up with someone else? Can't blame her really. Where are you? Look mate, we just want our money. Tell us where we can meet you. You can hand over the money and we'll leave you in peace. Okay?'

Then Mitch held the phone away and looked at it. Then back to his ear. Nothing.

'Fuck! He's hung up. The little shit. I'm going to fucking kill him.'

Chapter 15

The second meeting at Kevin's house was even more business-like than the first one. At the outset, Sylvia wanted to know whether they were in or out. She asked Robert first. He said yes without any hesitation. Then she turned to Kevin. He crossed his legs. Then uncrossed them and sat forwards.

'I'm still not sure.'

'Kevin, we agreed that at this meeting we would be sure. If we're going to do this, we all need to be a hundred per cent committed to it. Are you in or out?'

'I don't know. We would have to stick to the rules. If we don't, it'll never work,' said Kevin.

'I'm happy with that,' said Robert.

'And so am I,' said Sylvia.

'And if there's even a suspicion of getting caught we must all agree to pull out.'

Robert and Sylvia nodded.

'And we stop at three million.'

Sylvia repeated her question 'In or out? We can't wait much longer Kevin. We need a decision.'

Kevin opened his mouth. For a moment, there was no sound as if the words had stuck in his throat. Finally, after what seemed like several seconds he whispered 'Okay. I'm in.'

As he uttered those three words Kevin knew he had crossed the line. His life had changed with immediate effect. There would be no turning back. Now they just had to make a success of it.

'Good.' said Sylvia with relief, 'Thank God we got there eventually. Now, let's get down to the nitty-gritty. I'm going to start work on this first thing tomorrow. I'll identify the initial set of accounts and make the changes. I'll be diverting the interest to the fake accounts. I have already started setting up these accounts with small amounts of money in each. The first of the money should be flowing to the payout account by the end of the week. Then I'm going to revert everything back to how it was before so we can test to see whether there is any reaction to the changes. If there are no adverse issues, and I'm certain there won't be any, I'll start it up again. I have worked out a sequence that will apply the process to random accounts and then revert before moving to the next set. I'll arrange for a card to be delivered to you Kevin so you can withdraw most of the money. Just leave a hundred pounds or so in there. Then you can start spending it on antiques. Have you thought how you are going to do that?'

Kevin continued, 'I'll identify a couple of more expensive pieces to start things off. I'll give you the cash Robert. And you can buy them. And you'll receive a receipt. Then you can immediately enter them into the next auction. We'll store them for you at the saleroom. Then, at the auction, you can be selling those pieces and buying the next lot either in the auction itself, or from the shop. There will be invoices and receipts for all of the payments. Those items can then be sold at another auction house while you buy more and bring the items you've bought back to our auction house and so on. We have a number of regular buyers and sellers. I've already met a few of them. Robert, you'll just become one of the regulars. The shop might be able to buy some of the items off you. If we end up moving a lot of stock, we'll just have to move further afield. For smaller items, we can probably use Ebay with a Paypal account.'

Robert and Sylvia looked at each other and smiled. Kevin had obviously been thinking seriously about how it could work.

'Sounds good to me,' said Robert. 'Lets go for expensive but small items, please. I don't want to be struggling up the road with a Victorian wardrobe thanks!'

'What about if the item makes less at auction than you just paid for it?' asked Sylvia.

'Nothing,' said Kevin, 'That happens all the time to regular dealers. We'll try and identify lots that will make money, though, and that will almost be legitimate profit!'

They went through all the details again just to be sure they fully understood them. Then they went through the rules again. They had all learnt them by heart and they recited them to prove it.

Kevin went over to the kitchen area and opened the fridge saying that he thought he might have a bottle of cheap fizz somewhere. He found it, opened it and, with some misgiving he poured some into three glasses.

'To success.' They toasted each other.

Chapter 16

Mitch and the gang were driving back towards the motorway. They had decided to head back up to Stranraer to see if anyone up there had heard from Robert. Maybe he hadn't left town after all. Maybe he was just lying low somewhere until the dust had settled. Ralph was driving again. Mitch was starting to doze off in the passenger seat. Ralph looked in rear-view mirror at Jimmy, Charlie and Monkey on the back seat and asked, 'Anyone got a fag?'

Charlie leant forward and passed Ralph a cigarette. As he did so he said

'Remember that car we nicked that Bob didn't want? You know, the Peugeot saloon estate? Well, I heard it had turned up in London, all smashed up. My mate was told that the guy who had owned it got a call from the police asking if he still wanted it, or if the insurance company were going to write it off.'

Mitch sat bolt upright with a jerk, 'What did you just say?'

Charlie repeated what he'd just said.

'London? For fuck's sake! Turn this fucking car round. That's where he is then. Jesus, I'm working with a bunch of complete fucking retards. Charlie. You get back on to your mate. Find out what else he knows about the driver and where he is now. Do it!'

Ralph took the next turning and within two minutes they were heading back the way they had just come.

Charlie was on the phone to his mate. After a few minutes chatting, he ended the call and said. 'The police told him that the driver and passenger left the scene of the accident on foot.'

Chapter 17

Anne contemplated her naked body in the mirror. At thirty her body wasn't quite as taut as it had been in her teens but she was quite pleased that everything seemed to be holding up quite well. Sadly the tan from Cyprus was beginning to fade now.

The first few days of the holiday had been great fun. The villa was luxurious. It was spacious with four bedrooms and even had its own pool. They had spent long lazy days around the pool or down on the beach. In the balmy evenings, they had dressed up and enjoyed some delicious meals in the surrounding array of restaurants. And when they got back to the villa there had been bouts of adventurous sex culminating in them collapsing exhausted into the huge bed while the ceiling fan whirled silently above them fanning their perspiring bodies.

After a few days, Anne started to think about the new life that awaited them back in Solihull. When she tried to discuss this with Tom he told her there was no need to think about any of that yet and then would keep changing the subject. She put it down to him wanting to avoid anything serious because they were on holiday. So Anne kept her concerns to herself.

When the holiday was over and they returned to the apartment in Solihull, Anne found it even more difficult to discuss anything with him. And she seemed to irritate him. He didn't like the way she ironed his shirts. He was picky with the food she cooked. He complained about some of the clothes she wore. They even disagreed about the television. She liked watching soaps like Coronation Street or films. He preferred programmes about customs officers in Australia, or Police chase programmes She began to realise that, apart from their jobs and the sex, they had little in common. Although she fancied him, even the sex was getting a bit stale now. All his early attention to her had soon diminished. Now it was quick shag then he'd roll over and start snoring.

She looked around the room. Like the rest of the apartment, it was light, airy and tastefully furnished, by the 'bloody expensive interior' designer Tom had explained. Everything in it was high quality and state of the art. There was an amazing music system with speakers positioned throughout all of the rooms. It had a remote unit that he controlled most of the time so he got to choose the music, which meant that she had to endure heavy metal one minute and eighties synth-pop the next.

She compared the apartment to the house in Birmingham that she had owned with Kevin, full of all the quirky stuff he rescued from junk shops and jumble sales. And all his old records and cd's everywhere. Their house had always looked untidy and unfinished, but it had character. This place was perfect. Not an item was out of place. She had to spend a lot of her time tidying to keep it immaculate. She missed the garden. The apartment had a large terraced balcony, but it wasn't the same.

As she looked at herself and running her fingers over her flat belly, she asked herself again if she had done the right thing by leaving Kevin. More than once the thought that it may not be too late had flitted briefly through her mind before being dismissed as the cogs of the divorce were grinding their way to its conclusion. She wondered where Kevin was now. She had tried to call him several times but just got the unobtainable tone. She assumed he didn't turn his phone on now. She hoped he was managing without her.

The sound of the front door being opened signalled Tom's return from his daily jog. She quickly started to put her clothes on. Tom was always having a go at her about her not getting dressed straight away in the morning, even at the weekends.

'Anne' he shouted 'Are you up yet? Come on. I've got a squash game with Tim at the club in an hour and I was hoping to have some breakfast before I go.'

She went downstairs and made him breakfast while he showered. Then he ate it and read the paper. As he went out he said, 'I won't be back till late. After the squash match, a few lads are going to watch the rugby at the club. There's usually a bit of a drink afterwards. Usual Old Sils stuff. You know?'

Yes, she did know. It had already become a regular Sunday routine. He would disappear off in the morning and arrive home drunk and sweaty around midnight reeking of curry. After he'd gone she tidied away the breakfast things and then it all got on top of her. She sat down at the table, leant her head on her arm and stared out of the window.

Chapter 18

Kevin opened the letter and there was the bank debit card as Sylvia had promised. The next letter contained the pin. He walked down to the newsagents and bought a paper. On the way back he stopped at the cashpoint. For a moment, he wondered whether he should be wearing a hoodie to cover his face in case there were cameras on the machine. He decided that would look decidedly more suspicious. He inserted the card and typed in the pin. It recognised the pin. He then pressed the button for 'balance'. The system took a few seconds before presenting him with a figure of eight thousand seven hundred and sixty-one pounds and nineteen pence. Kevin sucked in air. Then he looked around him to see if anyone was watching. He withdrew five hundred pounds. It all seemed completely unreal but real money came out of the machine and he pocketed it quickly.

He phoned Sylvia and then Robert confirming that the money had arrived in the account and that he was withdrawing it at five hundred pounds a day. Sylvia explained that he should use the card to keep withdrawing cash every day 'Better use different cashpoints just to be on the safe side' and that he should pay for higher ticket items using the card. She went on to say that she had restored everything to the way it was before to see if it caused any alerts.

Robert advised him to be careful when withdrawing that amount of cash to make sure that he changed his routine regularly and to look out for people loitering around the machines. He then said he would drop into the showroom after he'd done the breakfast coffees on Monday.

The following Monday Kevin looked around the showroom for suitable purchases. He spotted a Lalique vase for twelve hundred pounds. He had fifteen hundred pounds in his pocket after visiting cashpoint machines on Sunday and on his way into work that morning. He even had a system of right-hand trouser pocket for his own money and left-hand pocket for the 'venture' money.

Robert arrived around eleven o'clock. He walked around the showroom humming and picking things up, examining them and putting them down again. Kevin approached him as if he was a customer. 'Good morning sir, can I help you at all'

Robert smiled and spoke loudly for anyone who might be listening 'Yes please I'm looking for a wedding gift.'

Kevin guided him to the vase. 'Something like this sir?' As he did so, he slipped the cash into Robert's hand.

Robert said, 'Yes this looks rather nice. Tell me about it.'

Kevin explained that René Jules Lalique was a French glass designer who became well known for his vases, perfume bottles and car mascots. This vase is of the opalescent Eucalyptus design, made around 1926. He went on to advise Robert that whoever received this would be delighted and he would expect them to cherish it and forever grateful to the buyer.

Robert gently nudged him and lowered his voice 'It's okay, it's only me. You don't need to go overboard impressing me with your knowledge'. Then raised his voice and said 'What's your best price then?'

Kevin and Robert pretended to negotiate the price and then moved over to the till. On the way, Kevin pointed out a Clarice Cliff conical bowl with a crocus design at three hundred pounds. Robert said out loud that it would make a nice present for the bride's parents. At the till, Kevin printed a receipt for fifteen hundred pounds for the two pieces. He then arranged for both items to be entered into the next Collectibles auction, which was taking place the following week.

Kevin showed Robert to the door and as he passed Peter the manager, said 'Thank you very much, sir. Nice doing business with you. We hope to see you here again in the near future.'

Out of the managers earshot, Robert said 'Well that was easy. Let me know when you want me to spend some more of our money on fancy crockery.'

'You'd better come back on Wednesday and see what else we've got. There's new stock coming in every day. I'll sort out some more pieces by then.' Robert left.

At lunchtime, Kevin visited several other antique shops and galleries in the area. He made notes of several items he needed to find out more about. In the end he bought two signed and framed photographs by Terry O'Neil for three thousand seven hundred pounds in total using the card and took them back to his flat before returning to work.

That evening he poured himself a glass of red wine and then turned on his laptop. He set up Ebay and Paypal accounts and added the photos on the online auction site. Until they sold he would enjoy looking at them on his mantelpiece. He particularly liked the one of Jean Shrimpton in a raincoat. He opened his notebook and did some online research into the other items he had looked at. He decided that two of the items were worth going back for. He still had about three and a half thousand pounds to spend.

Then he set up a spreadsheet detailing the date, items bought, price paid and which auction they were entered into. He added columns for the realised price, auction commission fees and the net price. Then inserted an extra column to show any profit or loss. It would be a useful record of where they were at any one time. For the sake of transparency, he uploaded the spreadsheet to a cloud storage account so the other two could access it when they wanted to see how things were going.

When he had finished he sat back and looked at the photos on the mantelpiece. There was a nagging voice in the back of his mind reminding that this was wrong. He hoped that as time went on the nagging voice would fade. He sipped his wine and wondered what Sylvia was up to right now.

Chapter 19

Sylvia was busy. She worked until ten thirty that night checking and double-checking all of the files, reports, alerts and messages to see if there was anything out of the ordinary. She pored over the reports. There were all the usual signals relating to cases she was involved in but nothing that would have aroused her suspicion had she not been involved.

Satisfied, she locked her desk drawer, turned off her laptop and left the office building. Once outside she rang Kevin. 'How did it go today?' she said.

'Not bad at all. We bought a couple of things. I've got another three and a half thousand to spend tomorrow. I know what I'm going to buy. Then Robert is coming back on Wednesday to see what we're going to buy next. It's important we don't overdo it in one place so we'll spread it around a bit.'

'And you are getting receipts for everything?'

'Yes, it all looks legitimate after the initial cash payment has been made'

'Good. I'll be turning everything back on tomorrow evening so there should be more money coming through on Wednesday morning. The average should be between eight and nine thousand pounds per day so you'll have to get on with moving the money around straight away'

'Should be no problem. The biggest headache is going to be keeping a record of everything. I've set up a spreadsheet on an online account. I'll let you know the details when we meet up.'

'When will that be?'

'How about the weekend, Saturday? Perhaps we could meet at the hotel again. Then Robert can join us when he has finished his shift.'

The next day Kevin went out at lunchtime again. He re-visited the shop and gallery where he had seen the pieces he was interested in the previous day. He engaged the sellers in lively discussion and managed to get slightly better prices. They shook hands on the deals and he paid for them in full, using the debit card. He advised the shop and gallery owners that the purchased items would be collected by his colleague the following day. Then Kevin found a key cutting kiosk and had spare keys cut for his flat.

On Wednesday, Robert came into the showroom at about eleven o'clock. Kevin spotted him and went through the motions of welcoming him back. He then indicated some pieces that he should purchase. Then, away from any listeners, he gave Robert the details of the where the pieces that needed collection could be located. Kevin told him to pick the items up and bring them into to the auction house and enter them into the next sale. Robert could then buy the items they had agreed on. Kevin would use the card at the till to make the purchase. Kevin also let Robert know that they were meeting up on Saturday at the hotel.

On his lunchbreak, Kevin checked the balance at the cashpoint. It was now reading eight thousand eight hundred and seventy-two pounds. He withdrew five hundred pounds in cash. He would withdraw five hundred every day on his way to work or at lunchtime.

When he got back to work he rang all of the major auction houses in London and ordered catalogues of their forthcoming sales to be sent to him. Peter, the owner, walked past while he was on the phone and he smiled. His new recruit was going about things the right way by checking out the competition and looking for sale items that he could purchase for the showroom. Strictly speaking it was outside his job remit but he was pleased to see him showing initiative. So far, Kevin had exceeded his expectations. He was knowledgeable, good with the customers and was easily meeting his sales targets. He was already feeling favourable about extending Kevin's contract.

Kevin knew that having the catalogues would help him in his day job, but it would also be a way of sourcing future items to launder the money.

Robert reappeared in the afternoon carrying a painting and large lamp-shaped item sheathed in bubble wrap. He went straight to the auction house desk, handed the pieces over and completed the paperwork to enter them into the next Art Nouveau and watercolour sales. When he had finished he found Kevin. Robert quietly reminded Kevin to buy smaller items in future that were easier to carry. Then he picked up the items they had looked at earlier and repeated the purchasing process. This time, Kevin slipped one of the keys to his flat into Robert's hand and told him to take the items there. These would be sold through Ebay.

When Kevin returned to his flat later that day he quickly scanned the flat looking for the two new purchases. They were on his table next to the laptop and the photos were still leaning against the wall on the mantelpiece. He was relieved. He would have been very disappointed in Robert if something had gone missing.

He cooked himself a simple meal and then set to work recording the day's purchases and then added the new items to the online auction. They had only managed to spend one thousand nine hundred and fifty pounds today. By tomorrow if another eight thousand or so went into the account they would have nearly fifteen thousand to spend. It was already becoming apparent that they were going to have to scale things up a lot.

Chapter 20

The gang arrived in London and drove the streets aimlessly. They didn't know where to even start looking. Eventually, Mitch told Ralph to drive to the nearest pub. They were used to pubs with car parks. They ended up driving several miles back out of London to find the sort of pub they recognised. The pub had rooms to let so they booked two rooms between the five of them. They would get the cost of this back from Robert when they eventually caught up with him. That night they all got very drunk and, as a result, spent most of the next day in their beds. They made a half-hearted attempt to search for Robert the following day then retired to the pub again. Then Mitch had an idea.

He told Monkey to find out where that smashed-up car was taken. It took Monkey a few calls and he had to offer more than one drink to his mate who eventually got back to him with a location. It was late, so it was the next morning before they drove to the car storage yard. Mitch spoke to the security man, found out they were fellow bikers and managed to find out where the car crash had happened. They drove to the spot on the outskirts of London and parked up in a side road. Naturally, there was no evidence that there had been a crash there but Mitch looked all around almost sniffing the air like a bloodhound.

'So you say he walked away from the scene,' he said to nobody in particular. He looked around him. Their car was parked in the most obvious route away from the where the car had crashed. 'He was in a stolen car so he would have wanted to disappear from view as quickly as possible. I reckon they must have walked up there.' He pointed to another road off the road they were on and started to stride off towards it. 'Yes. They will have walked up there and then turned left to get as far away and out of sight as possible. Let's get back to the car and we'll drive the route.'

They cruised the route that Robert and Kevin had walked so briskly down only weeks before. They passed the McDonalds where Kevin and Robert had eaten. Then they saw the Hampstead tube station. 'There,' said Mitch, pointing. 'That's where the bastard will have gone.'

They parked up and walked into the tube station and found the iconic tube map display. 'So we're here' said Jimmy and pointed to Hampstead. 'And they were heading towards London', said Mitch. He traced his finger along the Northern line. 'Euston or Kings Cross I wonder? Kings Cross I think. Monkey. Get five tickets to Kings Cross. We're going to find that little bugger even if it takes us the rest of the year.'

Chapter 21

As she arrived at work Sylvia noticed the silver police car parked in the 'reserved for visitors' spot just outside the entrance. She felt the cold clammy fingers of dread creeping through her body as she entered the building, even though she was certain that she had covered all her tracks.

As a nod to fitness now she was nearly thirty, she always used the stairs and, as she climbed purposefully to the eighth floor where she worked, she ran all of the details through her head again and mentally ticked off how she had ensured that she had left no trace.

She arrived at her department. It was a stylish open plan office with five large work-stations spread across the space. She half-expected to see her boss and a group of police officers surrounding her desk but instead she found one policewoman waiting patiently by the window.

'Ah, good morning,' she said, 'Are you Sylvia McEvoy?'

'Yes', replied Sylvia.

'I'm DC Parker with the Metropolitan Police. Your boss -,' she consulted her notebook, 'Erm, Brian, told me to ask for you, as apparently he's unavailable today.'

Playing golf again no doubt. Sylvia tried to remember if this was a scheduled day off or if he just wanted to get out of dealing with the police.

'Fine. What is this about?'

'Can we go somewhere more private?'

They made their way to one of the meeting rooms. After showing the officer in, Sylvia went to the kitchen to organise two coffees from the percolator.

Inside the kitchen, Sylvia leant back, placing her palms against the wall and tried to steady her breathing. Then, as she poured the milk, she spilt some and swore quietly as she quickly wiped it up with a cloth. She realised her hand was shaking slightly but kept reminding herself that she had done everything right. All the time, she was running all of the processes through her mind, checking, re-checking. She was surprised how sharp and clear each activity had become in her head. There was no confusion. No grey areas.

'It's about one of your colleagues within the bank who works in this building,' said the policewoman as Sylvia placed the coffee in front of her and then sat down opposite.

'Go on,' said Sylvia.

'We understand that you were involved with investigating this person internally and we've been asked to go over what you have uncovered so far to see if it looks like a crime has been committed and therefore whether there is a possibility of a conviction.'

'You'd better tell me the name of the person you are talking about to make sure we are discussing the same person.'

DC Parker consulted her notebook. 'David King.'

'I see,' said Sylvia. Although she had been involved in the early part of the investigation into Dave King's activities, she wasn't aware that it had reached the level of involving the police. 'I'll get the file.'

She spent the next hour with DC Parker going through the details of the investigation. At the end of it and after making copious notes, the police officer announced, 'I think there's more than enough information enough here to make a strong case. I'll need to discuss this with my senior officers and then we'll get back to Brian once we've made a decision. Thanks for your assistance. I'll see myself out.'

After she had left, Sylvia breathed an internal sigh of relief. While Dave King was under investigation it might mean that her activities were even less likely to be noticed. However, she didn't want to find herself in his position. She made a resolution to take even more care, if that was possible, when accessing the systems.

She looked forward to seeing Kevin and Robert on Saturday.

Chapter 22

In his room, before his shift started, Robert rang his ex-wife Janice and willed her to take the call. After three rings, she answered. Before he could explain why he had called, he had to listen to her account of being threatened by a 'gang of Scottish thugs' and how it was all his fault and how she wanted nothing more to do with him and how he was ruining her life. Eventually she stopped and allowed him speak to Chloe.

'Hi there, Chloe. Are you okay?'

'I'm fine Dad. Mum's cross with you, though. She thinks those horrible men came here because of you. They were shouting. Loud. They woke me up and I heard them. One of them swore. Shall I tell you what he said? He said ..'

'No thanks Chloe,' he said interrupting her. 'Listen. You mustn't worry about them, darling, they are just silly people who want me to pay them some money. I'll pay them as soon as I can then we'll never hear from them again. Anyway, tell me what you've been up to recently.'

Chloe started to tell him about school, and how her friend Kate was always getting into trouble for being cheeky, and how the teacher had hurt herself skiing and now walked with a stick, and how the cat had singed its tail on the hob, before the phone was taken off her by her mother.

He heard Janice say 'That's enough now Chloe. Your tea is ready.' Then to him, after Chloe had shouted, 'Bye.'

'Listen. Don't involve us in your problems. We don't need your trouble here. Understand? And if they come back looking for you, where shall I say you are?'

'They won't come back,' he replied, more hopefully than he really felt. 'But if they do, you can tell them I'm in London. I've got a good job now, working in a hotel. I should be able to send some money for Chloe soon, and maybe her own phone,' he added.

'Don't waste your breath. I've heard it all before. Bye.' The phone went dead in his hand.

Robert wasn't worried about Janice. She could take care of herself, or his replacement would. But he did care about Chloe. He was angry with Mitch and the others for going to Tamworth to find him. He had always intended to pay them back, eventually. Now he would still do it, but perhaps not quite so willingly.

His phone rang. It was Sylvia. His mood lifted.

'Hi Sylvia. How's it going in the hi-flying world of finance?'

'It's fine,' she said. 'Everything okay with you?'

'Great, apart from a bit of trouble with my ex-wife, but nothing I can't handle. We're meeting up on Saturday, right?'

'Yes, at the hotel. I'll come straight to the point. I need to ask for your help.'

'Okay. What is it?'

'We need to speed things up. I know we agreed that we'd do this gradually over twelve months. But I'd rather do it sooner if we can.'

'Suits me,' said Robert. 'The sooner I can lay my hands on some cash, the better. Any particular reason for moving things on a bit quicker?'

'Nothing specific but all the time these systems are being worked, there's a greater chance that some alert will get triggered. I just want to reduce the risk to an absolute minimum.'

'Right. I can understand that. So what do you need my help with?'

'Well, it's um, it's Kevin really. He's got his rules, and he's right to stick to them. We all should. But if we try and start bending them he's not going to like it, so I was hoping I could count on your support when I bring it up?'

'Sure. But it does mean we'll have to drastically scale up the movement of the money. We've only done a few thousand so far.'

'I know. Maybe you could have a think about how we can do that before Saturday.'

'Okay. Will do'.

Sylvia thanked him and ended the call.

Robert pushed the phone into his pocket and stared at the flowery patterns on the wall. Kevin had so far managed to keep the handling of the money mostly to himself. To move it quicker, it was going to need both of them on it, probably full time and Kevin was going to have to learn to trust him with the cash. He wondered whether he would prove to be worthy of Kevin's trust. Or whether the temptation would be too much for him.

Is there really honour amongst thieves?

Chapter 23

There were celebrations at the advertising agency. There had been a successful pitch and the agency had won a big new client, which specialised in female hygiene products. At the board meeting the four directors opened a bottle of champagne and the Andy Morris, the chief executive, announced that this brand new client had the biggest advertising budget of all their clients so he wanted the best team working on it.

'Malcolm, I want you to oversee the creative side personally,' he said to Malcolm Richmond, the creative director who nodded in agreement. 'And Lydia, with client services I'd like you to make sure we have a predominantly female account handling team, please. Any names in the frame?'

'Anne Walker springs to mind.'

'Good. She's about the right age and she's accumulated some experience here. Don't want to leave it all to a kid straight from college. I'm sure you've made the right choice.'

To James, the media director, he said 'The media budget is more than enough to allow for some radio and TV advertising so who do you think will handle the media buying?'

James thought for a moment and then said 'Guy has always handled the larger accounts in the past, but I think this one might be better handled by Tom, and myself of course. I know Tom's not been with the agency for very long. But he is good when it comes to hard negotiation. We'll probably get a better deal with Tom in charge.'

'And now Tom and Anne are an item, they'll be able to work on it at home too. More bang for our buck!

So to speak,' laughed Andy. The others joined in too. He gestured to all the directors 'Well done everybody. This is a big win so I've arranged a bonus payment for all of you to say thanks for all your hard work to help us win it. It will be in your next salary payment. This contract is going to secure this agency for at least the next three years so everything needs to be perfect. Okay? I think you understand what I'm saying. I don't want any cock-ups on this one.'

Anne was called into Lydia's office the next day and told that she was going to be heading up the account handling team for the new client. She was glowing with pride as she left the office that day.

When she got home she was about to give Tom the good news but he edged in first and announced that he had been appointed media buyer for the new client. She said she was pleased for him and then told him her news. He didn't seem quite as pleased as Anne had expected and when she suggested that they might work together on some aspects he actually looked quite glum at the prospect.

After a while, he cheered up a bit and said, 'Let's go out to celebrate'. Anne was pleased and bounded up the stairs to change. It had been a while since they had done anything nice together. In fact, the holiday in Cyprus had been the last time they had dined out together.

When she came down, he registered that she had changed into a long dress, put her long dark hair up, and added long dangly earrings.

'Oh, I thought we were just going to go up to the Old Sils for a drink or something but it looks like you've got dressed up for something a bit posher than that. Never mind. We'll go out for dinner somewhere.' Handing her the key, he said. 'Why don't you wait in the car, I'll just get my jacket'.

Tom drove them to Stratford upon Avon in the Lexus and succeeded in securing a table in the second restaurant they tried. The first had been fully booked. Tom seemed a bit irritated that they could only find a table at the 'second best restaurant in Stratford' so Anne felt she had better massage his ego a bit.

'It's great news about you getting the media buying role. Normally Guy gets to do it for new clients. I expect his nose has been put out of joint a touch.'

Tom considered that for a while. Then he smiled 'Yes I bet it has. I'll have to show them why they made the right choice.' Then he said, 'I wonder why you got the job. There are several account handlers with more experience than you. It's probably because you're a woman.' With that, he put a large forkful of rib-eye steak into his mouth, started chewing away on it and scanning the restaurant at the same time.

Anne ate the rest of her meal in silence. Sometimes Tom could be really bloody insensitive. Kevin would have been genuinely pleased for her. Admittedly, they wouldn't have been in a smart restaurant if she had still been with Kevin. They were far more likely to have had a Chinese takeaway on the sofa at home, but he would have said how proud he was of her and she would have felt like she had achieved something. Tom just made her feel small.

After they left the restaurant and were driving home, Tom said 'What's up? You were very quiet. Anyone would think that you weren't that bothered about getting asked to work with a new client.'

When they got home Anne lay on her side of the bed with her back to Tom and silently wished she was still with Kevin. Even without the prospect of having children, she felt that life with Kevin had been preferable to this.

Chapter 24

Sylvia arrived at the hotel ten minutes before Kevin. She ordered a cocktail at the bar. 'I should be finished about ten.' said Robert as he placed the glass in front of her with the gaily-coloured paper umbrella facing away from her. He went to the other end of the bar to serve the other customers.

Sylvia glanced down at the messages on her phone. When she looked up again Kevin was standing in front of her. She felt a sudden surge of affection for him and threw her arms around him. Kevin caught Robert's raised eyebrows from the other end of the bar.

'Hey. You again,' he said with a grin to Robert as he came over.

Robert patted him on the shoulder as he walked past with a tray of drinks destined for the restaurant. All the softer chairs were occupied so Kevin and Sylvia sat on the bar stools.

'So, how have you been?' said Kevin.

'Fine. Everything is going fine.' She could not be sure where friendship ended and business began so she just launched into it anyway.

'All the systems are working the way I had planned. The money should be coming through regularly now.'

'Yes. We had more yesterday and Robert and I had a long chat about how we can expand the operation.'

'And what did you decide?'

'We can go into the details later when Robert has finished work, but we're going to set up accounts at all the major auction houses, Sotheby's, Christies, Bonhams and the others. Then we can either bid by phone or in person. They sell higher value items, so we can move the money around more quickly. The ideal system would be to buy at one auction and put the items straight into another so we don't have to store anything, but we're also going to concentrate on smaller items like jewellery, small paintings and so on that we can store at the flat, if necessary, between the auctions.

'Good. How did you get on yesterday?'

'We bought some more items. We managed to spend about seven thousand pounds. The first of the items we bought earlier in the week will be in the next sale on Tuesday. The money they raise will be the first of the clean money. Have you set up an account for us to deposit that money into?'

'Yes. I'm setting up a business account. We just need a name for the business. Something fairly anonymous preferably.'

Kevin went on the describe some of the items they had bought and how Robert had struggled across London with a pair of candelabra, a large French clock and pewter coffee set which made them both laugh. At ten o'clock Robert came over and suggested that they move on to another bar. They stepped outside the hotel into the cooling night, crossed the road and walked into a bustling pub on the corner. Kevin ordered drinks while Robert and Sylvia quickly grabbed some newly vacated seats around a small table.

'I was just telling Sylvia about how you had to carry all that stuff halfway across London today,' said Kevin with a smile.

'Very funny. I'm glad it amused you. To be honest, I think we ought to get a van.'

'Why don't we get a van?' said Sylvia. 'It makes sense'. They all agreed. If they'd been taking notes it would have been in the minutes, and Robert would have been given the action point.

'So Robert, we were just saying the first of the clean money should be coming through next week. So we should be able to start putting some in our own accounts.'

'It can't come soon enough as far as I'm concerned. There are some things I need to get.'

'Don't go mad with it,' warned Kevin. 'Remember the rules.'

'Steady on, I just want to buy my daughter a mobile phone. That's hardly going to cause the Flying Squad to pay us a visit.'

'Okay. Just take it easy, though. Anything out of the ordinary and people will get suspicious.'

'And talking of rules,' said Robert, 'Sylvia's got something she wants to discuss with us.'

Sylvia looked at Robert as if to say she wasn't quite ready to talk about it yet, but Kevin asked what she had on her mind. With a reproachful look at Robert who just stared back impassively, she explained that there had been a visit from the police.

It was Robert's turn to look at Sylvia in a questioning way as she hadn't mentioned anything to him about this and Kevin immediately launched into her, 'What did you tell them? Do they know? I thought you said it was undetectable.'

'Don't panic Kevin. Calm down. It was nothing to do with what we are doing. It was about the colleague I told you about before. The police were brought in to investigate him too. They just wanted to examine our findings. If anything, this should make our job somewhat easier as everybody's attention is elsewhere. However, it made me think that we should try and get this over with in a shorter time than we originally discussed.'

Kevin sat back relieved. For a moment, he thought that they were on the verge of being discovered before they had really got things moving. While he was mulling it over, Robert said. 'I think Sylvia is right. The longer the systems are in place and diverting the money the greater the chance of being discovered, so if we can move it through quicker we stand a greater chance of not being caught.'

Kevin mentally scrolled through the rules and weighed up how important the actual timescale was compared to the prospects of losing everything. Robert and Sylvia were watching him, waiting for his reaction.

'It would mean scaling things up on the laundering front by some margin, but we had discussed doing that anyway. So it's okay in principle. How much quicker?'

'I was thinking of four months,' said Sylvia.

'Four months!' exclaimed Kevin

'Steady on Kevin, no need to broadcast it,' said Robert 'I'll get another round in.'

While Robert was at the bar Kevin examined Sylvia's face looking for signs of panic or unease. There weren't any. She just looked matter-of-fact about it. Kevin ran some of the figures through his head. Three million pounds in four months. One hundred and twenty days or so, that's twenty-five thousand pounds a day they had to spend. They would have to work three times faster.

She reached out and put her hand on his knee. 'It'll be okay Kevin. Nothing's really changed. We're just doing it a bit quicker. That's all.'

Robert returned from the bar. 'Well? What do you think? Are we agreed?'

Kevin felt strongly that they should stick to the original plan, but recognised that he was in a minority here so he reluctantly agreed as long as they agreed that none of the other rules would be broken. Robert and Sylvia nodded in agreement.

'Right. We need to move the money a lot quicker,' said Robert. 'We've been thinking how we can do it.'

Robert outlined how he felt that they should set up a legitimate antiques business. Kevin would oversee which items were bought and sold and would concentrate on higher ticket items. Sylvia could get involved at weekends and he, Robert, would be responsible to bidding at auction and would be the public face of the business. He felt they should specialise in certain types of items or a period like Art Nouveau. Most other dealers had a specialist area that they were known for collecting. They would buy at auction and then either find a private buyer through eBay or customers who had expressed interest in certain types of items or sell back into the trade at another auction.

'We could call the business Bellbrook Antiques, after the hotel where we all met. It's fairly anonymous,' said Sylvia with a conspiratorial look to Kevin.

Robert had really just repeated what Kevin had discussed with Sylvia earlier so he added 'I'm with you on that Robert. If we're going to set up a legitimate business, we'll need the van we spoke about earlier, maybe a secure unit too. I don't think we need a showroom just yet. And Robert, you may need to decide if you are going to have enough time to do this and do your job at the hotel too.'

Robert remembered his promise to the Polish barman and thought to himself that he would try and hang onto the job as long as he could.

'You can always move into the spare room at the flat if you are stuck for somewhere to live,' continued Kevin.

Over the next few days, Robert worked like a dog. He got up early and did the morning shift at the hotel. Then he got changed and went out to the auctions. He bid on items highlighted in the catalogues by Kevin. He entered items into auctions. He drove around London in the Sprinter van that they had recently bought for cash.

'Make sure it's taxed and insured,' said Kevin with a wink as Robert had gone off to collect it, his pocket bulging with the money that Kevin had given him.

In the evenings, Robert changed back into his work outfit and did his shift behind the bar. And the end of each night he would wearily climb the stairs and collapse exhausted onto his narrow bed.

Later that week, on his way back to the hotel, he was about four roads away, he drove past a group of men, one large, one small and three following, walking down the main road. Something about these men seemed familiar. As he passed them he was horrified to see that it was Mitch and the others. He quickly faced forwards and accelerated the van past them, hoping that they had not spotted him. As he turned off the road he stole a quick glance in the rear view mirror and saw them enter a small hotel. He parked up in a side street, briefly looking around to make sure there were no traffic wardens around. Then he made his way back on foot. He mingled with a group of busy shoppers in a cut-price store opposite. He watched and he waited. After five minutes or so they came out of the hotel. Mitch was shaking his head. They continued walking in the same direction they'd been travelling.

So they were hunting for him. And clearly they had tracked him as far as this part of London. They were getting close. So it was only a question of time until they found him. He felt sick with worry. He could deal with any one of them individually. Even Mitch. But as a group he knew he wouldn't stand a chance. His first instinct was to run. He could leave London and go somewhere else. But he would always be looking over his shoulder. They wouldn't rest until they had their money.

Robert returned to the van and made his way back to the hotel. During the evening, he kept his eye on the entrance, ready to make his exit at the first sign of trouble. The next day he slid a letter of resignation written on hotel stationery under the manager's door and packed his bag.

The manager called him into the office and asked him to stay on. The customers liked him and he could find something else for the Pole to do. Robert politely declined, asked the manager to hold the job open for the Pole and moved his pathetically small bag of possessions into Kevin's flat.

When Kevin questioned his sudden departure from the hotel Robert decided to explain.

'So they followed you down from Stranraer? And now they are sniffing around all the hotels in the area trying to find you? How on earth did they find out where you were?'

'That's about the measure of it. I have no idea how they knew I was in London,' sighed Robert.

'And how much do you owe them?'

'It's about ten grand, maybe a bit more.'

'Jesus.' Kevin lapsed into silence. Robert was in trouble. Robert was part of their team, so his problem was also theirs. If Robert had to go back on the run to escape them, their venture would be over, which might be a good thing and perhaps Kevin could return to a safer way of living. On the other hand, Kevin felt more alive now than he had done since he was a student. Although he had no experience of dealing with the kind of people who would travel from one end of the country to the other to hunt a man down for money, he felt that between the three of them they ought to be able to deal with the situation and get Robert off the hook.

After a minute or two while Robert sat looking miserable, Kevin said. 'We'll pay them. Get them off your back. Set up a meeting.'

Chapter 25

The buzzer went on her door intercom and Sylvia answered. 'Yes, who is it?'

'It's me. Kate! I've been in London to visit an exhibition so I thought I'd drop by and say hello.'

'Kate. Wow. What a fantastic surprise!' She buzzed her up and then went out into the corridor to meet her. They embraced and did some air-kissing. 'You look totally amazing', Sylvia said as they parted and looked each other up and down. 'So do you. Being single obviously suits you,' said Kate.

They entered the apartment and Sylvia uncorked a bottle of wine.

'Nice. Very nice! I just adore the colour,' exclaimed Kate as she strode around the apartment taking it all in.

'Thanks. It's lovely to see you. How long can you stop for?'

'No rush to get back. Next lecture is on Monday.'

'That's decided then. You must stay here for the weekend and we can catch up.'

They finished their wine and then went up the High Street to Nando's to eat.

'So tell me about the course,' said Sylvia as they sat down.

'I'm loving it. When I was an under-graduate, it was all about the parties, and the social life. The course itself became a bit of a distraction from having fun. Now on this post-grad course I'm really enjoying the actual content. It's hard work though, but it's really fulfilling. What about you? How's the job going? Remind me what you do at the bank.'

Sylvia told Kate about her work at National Standard and gave Kate non-specific overview of the current investigation that she was involved in.

'So you are like a detective within the bank?'

'Sort of. We are trained to look for movements of money that are out of the ordinary and to spot the signs of money leaking out of the system. We also get tip-offs from other members of staff who pass on their suspicions. Then we have to investigate.'

'And I thought you just counted other people's money all day! Bet the salary is good, with all that responsibility.'

'It's not bad, but you can never have enough money, can you?' replied Sylvia.

'Tell me about it. I'm trying to live on bugger-all while my student loan just increases week after week. And that's with working three nights a week in Tesco's. It's not even as if the course is going to get me a highly paid job or anything. It's just in History of Art.'

'And how's the love life?' enquired Sylvia.

'Ha! What love life?' retorted Kate, 'Since Jules and I split up there's been no-one of any significance. All the good men seem to have been taken. So I'm left with the screwed-up ones with tons of baggage or men who are still living with their mothers!'

They both laughed. Then Kate asked if Sylvia had met anyone else since she had moved out from Neil the photographer's.

'Well ... it's hard to say really.'

'Intriguing ..'

'I have met someone, well two people actually, but I'm not going out with either of them really. No, that's not right. I might be going out with one of them. I'm not really sure.'

'And what do they do, these mystery men?'

'They're both antique dealers.'

Kate sniggered. 'You are joking of course! I thought you'd be hitting the city's celebrity night-spots with a high-flying city trader in his Ferrari, not traipsing round old junk shops with someone dressed in brown corduroy and hush puppies!'

Sylvia laughed, 'You're right, but if you met these two, you'd see what I mean. There's something really nice about them.'

'If they were alright, they'd be taken already. There must be something wrong with them.'

'They've both been married before and ..' Sylvia's phone rang 'Excuse me' She said as she answered it. 'Hi. Yes, I'm fine, thanks. And you? Good. I'm out with an old friend at the moment. Can we make it tomorrow? Great. See you then. Bye.'

She ended the call. 'Sorry about that. It was...'

'One of your antique dealers?' asked Kate.

'Yes, actually it was. His name is Kevin.'

'Kevin. Kevin. That name just conjures up someone with white shoes and a dodgy haircut. But didn't you say he wore Hush Puppies?'

'No, that was you. And he wears nice shoes. Plus he's got a smart haircut too. Maybe you'll meet him if you are still around tomorrow. He's coming round tomorrow.'

'Wouldn't miss it for the world!' said Kate.

Chapter 26

Kevin slid his phone back into his pocket. The words 'old friend' were ringing ominously in his ears. Was it the photographer bloke she talked about? Or perhaps it was someone else from her past? Kevin felt annoyed with himself for the way he was feeling. Was it jealousy? He had no rights to any kind of exclusivity over her. They had had just one kiss and that could have been just a friend's kiss, or a lover's kiss. He wasn't sure.

He put those thoughts to the back of his mind. He had to concentrate on the task in hand. Should they pay the Scottish gang? Or could they get rid of them another way? In the short term paying them off seemed the obvious thing to do. After all, they had plenty of money at the moment. Kevin paced up and down the flat thinking of how this could be used to their advantage at some point to help mitigate the money.

Robert came back into the flat. He had gone outside to make his phone call.

'That wasn't a particularly enjoyable conversation,' he said. 'But I've set up a meeting with them for Sunday morning. They want us to bring the money and then they're off back to Scotland.'

'That gives us chance to explain to Sylvia what we're doing. I've told her we'll see her tomorrow night.'

'So we've got a bit of time to sort out the cash. Thanks for helping me with this Kevin. I really appreciate this.'

'I don't mind helping. And I'm sure Sylvia will be fine with it too. The money shouldn't be a problem. I've been getting five hundred in cash out every day so there should be more than enough. I just want to make sure it's the end of it and that they don't come back for more later on. Tell me everything you know about them.'

Robert described the gang to Kevin. He told him how Mitch had adopted the role of the leader of the group, and that he had been a biker for years and then worked as a security guard, then a debt collector before getting embroiled in petty and generally small-scale crime.

Ralph, Charlie, Monkey and Jimmy were just small-time crooks. They relied on Mitch to provide them with work and they repaid him with their loyalty. When Robert had started working at the pub, the gang had been pilfering from sheds and a doing bit of shoplifting. Once he had started to place orders with them for larger and more valuable items like motorbikes, cars and jewellery, they had to sharpen their skills and learn about alarms and more complicated security systems. Even though they might appear like a bunch of comic misfits, they had evolved into a reasonably efficient thieving team.

Mitch had been the conduit to the rest of the gang and Robert presumed that Mitch had been taking the lion's share of the profits. So Robert's disappearance and the subsequent reduction in their income would have hurt Mitch the most and probably dented his authority too.

'So I don't think he's going to let it go.' said Robert

'He's come this far, and I think you're right. He's not going to want to go back to Scotland empty-handed. He's either going to locate you and extract the money or we're going to have to pay him. But we need to find a way of working this to our advantage.'

'In what way?' said Robert

'Well. There may well be a time when we need some dirty work done. And maybe we'll need to get someone else to do it'

'Ah. I think I see where you are going with this.'

'Good. Leave the talking to me.'

Chapter 27

The first meeting with the new client went reasonably well. Andy made his gushing welcoming speech to the five client executives and then excused himself, leaving the agency team to introduce themselves. When it was Anne's turn she explained that she would be heading up the account handling team, so she would be the main point of contact for the day-to-day activities.

'I'm hoping that we can integrate seamlessly with your company and work together as a team,' she said before handing over to the art director who smiled at her and thanked her before outlining the agency's intentions with the client's image. Finally, it was Tom's turn to introduce himself.

He started by talking for several minutes about his past campaigns and various achievements in other agencies before he joined Hopkins, Bailey & Barnes. He then described in some detail how he would handle the media buying. He talked about each type of media and his proposals for the approach he would take.

That evening at home over dinner Tom asked Anne how she thought the meeting had gone. She said she thought it had progressed well and that the client's people seemed impressed at the agency's proposals. Then she said, 'Tom, I was just wondering if you needed to go into such detail at the first meeting?'

Tom looked at her for a few seconds and then said, 'Excuse me but just who the fuck do you think you are? I've been doing this since you were still a teenager. I know exactly what I'm doing and I'm fucking amazing at it. These people know virtually nothing so I'm letting them know just what an expert they are getting here. And I'd appreciate it if you'd keep your opinions to yourself.' With that, he slammed down his knife and fork and left the room. Moments later Anne heard the front door slam shut.

Anne sat at the table for a while asking herself what she had said to upset him. Then she cleared away the plates, filled the dishwasher and tidied the whole apartment. It would just make him even more annoyed if the place was untidy when he got back from the pub or wherever he had gone.

Later that night and after a glass of wine, she plucked up the courage to ring Kevin's father. When she and Kevin were together she had got on well with John, who had treated her like a daughter. Now she had hurt his only son she wasn't sure what reaction she would receive. She need not have worried. John was as affable with her as he had always been. Presumably the fact that they had behaved fairly and decently towards each other while they sorted out the remnants of their marriage had meant that there was no lasting hostility.

'Hi John, it's Anne how are you?'

'Anne! It's great to hear from you. I'm fine. How's life treating you?'

'Very well, thanks. I was wondering if you have any contact details for Kevin. I've been trying his mobile, but it doesn't seem to work.'

'Didn't you know? He's moved to London.'

'Oh. London.' Anne was surprised. She was assuming he had stayed in the area somewhere. 'Do you have a number for him? I need to contact him.'

'Yes, I do. Hang on a minute and I'll get it for you.'

While he was getting the number, Anne let the news sink in. London. She wondered why he had decided to move to the capital. She knew he had some distant friends there but even when they visited London as a couple Kevin had never suggested that they meet up with any of them. In fact, she was fairly sure that Kevin had not been in touch with any of them for the entire time they had been married.

'Right, got it. Have you got a pen handy?'

Anne wrote down the number and thanked John. He made her promise to call in and see him some time. As she confirmed that she would, she wondered if she would ever see him again.

Anne then updated Kevin's number on her phone. Just having it there made her feel slightly less lonely. She emptied the dishwasher and was polishing the wine glasses before putting them neatly in the glass-fronted wall cupboard when she decided to call him.

'Hi, it's me,' she said.

'Oh. Hi,' said Kevin. He was not expecting her to call and wondered briefly how she had got his number. He quickly concluded that she must have got it from his father. He made a mental note to ask his father not to give out his number to anyone else.

'Just thought I'd call you and see how things are going? I gather you are living in London now.'

'Yes. I just wanted a fresh start and ended up here.'

'And are you working?'

'Yes. Actually I managed to get work quite quickly. In an antiques shop and saleroom.'

'Really! I could always see you doing something like that. Following in your father's footsteps. A bit more interesting than the insurance company I guess?'

'A bit. And how is it going with old whatshisname?' said Kevin, wishing she would get to the point.

She could hear the bitterness in his voice and despite herself she said, 'Everything has been going well so far. In fact, Tom and I are working on a

project together right now.'

'I'm glad to hear it.' His tone betrayed the fact that he was not really glad at all.

'I was wondering whether, now that some water has passed under the bridge so to speak, we could perhaps meet up for a drink sometime. If you wanted to, that is? I know we are nearly divorced, but we were also friends for a long time too. What do you think?'

'I don't see why not,' said Kevin flatly. He was not sure if meeting her again was a good idea. He had tried hard to forget her.

'I could come to London. I haven't been for a while. How about Saturday the twenty-seventh?'

He realised that she must have planned this before phoning him. It was about three weeks away. 'That should be okay,' he said reluctantly.

'Great. I'll text you nearer the time and maybe you can recommend somewhere to meet up'

'Okay. Fine.'

'See you then.'

'Bye.'

Chapter 28

Kate noticed Sylvia's make-up straight away.

'Morning. Blimey, you've scrubbed up well!'

'I have no idea what you're talking about,' replied Sylvia 'This is just my normal weekend look.'

'Yeah, right. And what time are we expecting Mister Antique Dealer Kevin?'

'This evening. And it's nearly lunchtime now so you'd better get yourself dressed.'

'Will do, Sergeant Major'. Kate saluted as she disappeared into the bedroom.

Sylvia put the kettle on for a cup of coffee. Then she did a quick tidy up around the flat. Since Kate had arrived there seemed to be mess everywhere. She could hear the shower running and so she called Kevin.

'Hi, Kevin. Still on for this evening?'

'Yes. Still okay with you?'

'Yes. It's fine.'

'Robert's coming too. I assume that's okay?'

'Yes, that's fine. We'll see you in a bit. Bye.'

Kevin pondered who she meant by 'we'.

During the afternoon, Kevin went out and wandered around the junk shops. Robert stayed in the flat and watched the rugby on television. Later, as they drove towards Sylvia's, Kevin said to Robert 'By the way, Sylvia has got company, so don't barge in all guns blazing. Let's just wait until an appropriate moment to talk business. Alright?'

'I'm not a complete idiot you know. Who's with her?'

'I don't know. I suspect it's her old boyfriend.'

'Oh', said Robert. 'That explains the long face.'

'Shut up and drive.'

They continued the rest of the journey in silence.
Sylvia met them at the door. As they walked into the apartment Kevin could smell the aroma of Sylvia's perfume and another smell too. A different perfume. A door opened and Kate entered the living room.

Kevin was confused for a moment. He had expected to be meeting Sylvia's old flame and instead a stunning woman with strawberry blond hair had appeared.

'You must be the antique dealers I've heard so much about,' she said and then she kissed both of them.

Kevin looked questioningly at Sylvia. She explained, 'This is Kate, an old school-friend. She's just dropped in for the weekend. Kate this is Kevin.' They shook hands. 'And this is Robert.' Kate and Robert's eyes met briefly and they shook hands too.

'Now that's over, who would like some coffee?'

Kate wanted to know all about them and fired a barrage of questions at them. Robert fielded most of them and fired a few back at her. He asked her where she lived. What she did. Why she was still a student. Whether she had ever been married. What music she liked. Kevin and Sylvia sat on the sofa next to others listening to the interrogation. Occasionally Sylvia's hand strayed onto Kevin's knee and once he placed his hand on hers.

When the pace of questioning began to subside Kevin suggested that they go out for a drink. Sylvia and Kate withdrew to the bedrooms to get their jackets. Kevin nudged Robert. 'You two seemed to be hitting it off?'

Robert just raised his eyebrows.

In the pub, while Kate and Robert were at the bar, Kevin took Sylvia to one side and explained about the money that Robert owed. He said, 'I hope you don't mind, but I've taken an executive decision here. We need to sort this out and get these people off his back or he'll just disappear one day and that's no good to either of us.'

Sylvia agreed and told him that as far as she was concerned it was fine and that he should do whatever he thought was right but that he should be careful as these people after Robert sounded dangerous.

Then he told her about the scheduled meeting the next morning.

'Don't worry. I don't intend to do anything stupid. We're meeting them out in the open, in a busy place and the fact that there would be a lot of witnesses should help prevent any trouble breaking out. The main thing is that we make sure they don't think about coming back for more.'

Kate and Robert returned from the bar carrying a tray of drinks.

'What are you two looking so secretive about?' said Kate.

'We're just planning a trip away.' said Kevin suddenly.

Sylvia gave him a questioning look.

'There's an auction in Oxford coming up and I was just asking Sylvia if she wanted to go. So do you?' he asked. Sylvia looked a little confused for a moment and then said 'Of course. I'd love to'. There was a broad smile on Kevin's face as he raised his glass.

'Excellent. Cheers everybody.'

On the way back to Sylvia's apartment, Kevin explained about the auction.

'There are three lots that I'm particularly interested in and I'd like to see the items with my own eyes. There's a viewing day on the Saturday and the next day is the actual sale day. So I thought we could make weekend of it.'

'Sounds lovely,' said Sylvia.

She looked behind her. Robert and Kate were deep in conversation. 'They seem to be getting on well,' she said quietly.

'I wonder if she would be so keen if she knew anything about his past.'

'Oh, I wouldn't worry about that. She's had her fair share of rough diamonds in the past, take it from me. Robert is a shining beacon of good behaviour compared to some of them. She can take care of herself, so I wouldn't worry about her.'

'Are you saying I should be worried about him?'

'No. I'm just saying that Kate is an independent woman. She's experienced quite a lot in her life so I doubt that much could shock her.'

Kevin lowered his voice so Robert and Kate wouldn't hear. 'What about our venture. Would that shock her?'

'Yes. That would. Well, the fact that I'm involved would, anyway. In comparison with her, I've always been the goody-two-shoes. So it's essential that she doesn't find out. okay?'

'I certainly wasn't going to be the one who told her,' said Kevin remembering the rules. As he said it he took a look behind. Robert looked up and winked at him.

Chapter 29

Outside Buckingham Palace, the traditional Changing of the Guard ceremony was being watched by several hundred enthusiastic tourists. The vast majority of them appeared to be of Asian descent and nearly all of them were wielding phones and cameras. Amongst the crowd, spread along the pavement outside the palace, were five Scottish criminals. Monkey pushed through the throng to where Mitch was pressed up against the railings observing the precision of the soldiers. Mitch turned to him and said 'Well. Is he here yet?'

'No, I can't see him.'

'Get back out there and don't come back till you've seen him. Tell the others too.'

Mitch turned back towards the Palace. He wondered if the Queen was in. Didn't they signal it by putting the Union Jack up, or down or half-way up? He couldn't remember. Maybe she was looking out at him right now. He'd give her a wave if she was. He squinted his eyes but couldn't make out any faces at the windows.

Out of the corner of his eye, he caught a glimpse of Monkey making his way back towards him, gently asking if people could let him through. As he got close enough for Mitch to hear he shouted 'I've seen 'im. Or should I say, them. He's with another guy. They are walking towards us now.'

Mitch extricated himself from the crowd and signalled to the others to join him. They walked towards where Robert and Kevin had stopped. They halted about ten yards away.

'It's been a while. I see you've brought your boyfriend. You better have what I've come for,' said Mitch.

Robert said nothing and Kevin walked forwards to Mitch and stood directly in front of him. They were about the same height so their eyes were level as they weighed each other up. Kevin said, 'We need to have a few words.'

Mitch stared back at him. 'I don't know who you are mate. My problem is with him.' He gestured with a nod of his head towards Robert.

'As I understand it, he owed you some money?'

'Owes, not owed. And he'd better have it with him now. As my patience is wearing very thin.'

'Well, here's how it is. He has paid me the money he owes you. I have taken over his debt. So now you have to deal with me,' said Kevin.

'No mate, you listen to me. He's the little shit who did a runner and took our cash. So our beef is with him, not you.'

'I beg to differ. He has paid his debt. To me. And I have the money here. Before you get it though, we need to take a little walk. Let's go.'

Kevin walked past him. Mitch sneered at Robert who grinned back, then Mitch turned and followed Kevin. When they were out of earshot of the others Kevin said 'Look Mitch. I'm a reasonable chap. I imagine you are too, deep down, obviously. Now as I understand it, the amount of the debt is ten thousand pounds. Is that correct?' Mitch looked around quickly to make sure the rest of the gang couldn't hear, as he had told them it was only five, and then mumbled 'Yes, that's correct'. He wondered where this conversation was leading.

'Good. At least we agree on that. I happen to have the cash here.' Kevin extracted four envelopes from different pockets. 'Each one of these contains two thousand five hundred pounds.' He pulled out another envelope. 'And this one contains a further five hundred pounds.'

Mitch's wide eyes were glued to the envelopes.

'Now these can be yours, Mitch. All we want is a small favour in return.'

Mitch looked suspicious. 'I don't have to do any favours. That money is mine.'

'Not yet, Mitch. At the moment, it's mine. But of course, it can be yours. I just need you to agree that if I call you and ask to do a little job for me, that you will. Do you understand?'

'What sort of job?'

'I don't know yet. But it will be a job suited to your skills and you will be paid commensurate with the importance of that job. And in exchange for your agreement I will pay you this extra five hundred pounds. Do we have a deal?'

Mitch continued to stare at the envelopes. He had never really expected to receive the money. He had assumed he would have to resort to violence in order to exact some form of revenge for having been ripped off. To get this money, all he to do was agree to do something in the future. Something which may never even happen. Plus there was no way this guy could force him to do anything.

Mitch agreed. Kevin said 'Let's shake on it then. A man's handshake is a symbol of honour. Once a handshake has taken place a man places his whole integrity on the line. And without integrity and honour we are nothing. Right?'

Mitch hesitated for a moment and then said 'Right'. They shook hands. Kevin handed over the money.

'I'll be in touch when we need you. I'm a man of honour. You would do well to remember that.'

Mitch snorted and strutted off in the direction of the gang. Kevin took a moment before rejoining Robert. His realised that his hands were shaking so he clenched his fists, and he had to control his breathing. It must be the adrenalin, he thought. He didn't want Mitch, or Robert, to see how scared he had been. The gang left and Mitch gave Robert one last glare as he walked past. Robert gave him the finger.

On their way back to the flat Robert said, 'So, what did you say to him?'

'I told him we might need him one day. We shook on it. And I gave him the money.'

'And do you think he will keep his end of the deal?'

'I don't know. One day maybe we'll find out.'

Chapter 30

Over the next few days and weeks Kevin, Robert and Sylvia resumed their activities. Each one working diligently to make sure that everything went smoothly.

Kevin went to work as usual, stopping at one of the cashpoint machines along the route, withdrawing as much cash as could, and checking the balances each day. When he arrived at work he would deal with the salerooms day to day activities and paperwork. Then, when there were no customers requiring his attention he would study the auction catalogues and sales brochures identifying pieces to buy and noting the lot numbers.

Some of the items had guide prices and he made notes about the values and expected returns of each piece. He could then draw up daily lists of dates, auctions, lot numbers, guide prices and bid price limits. He had set up accounts with each auction house and would arrange payment by phone or on receipt of their invoices.

He also bought and sold some items on behalf of the saleroom where he worked remembering to list these items separately. As he arrived one morning, Peter, the manager of the saleroom, waved him over.

'Good weekend?'

'Great thanks, and you?'

'Yes, very good thanks. Kevin, I'd like to have a chat with you later.'

'Sure, I'll pop in when I've dealt with this paperwork.'

About forty minutes later Kevin hovered outside Peter's office and was ushered in.

'Take a seat, Kevin.' He sat down.

'I've been looking through our sales figures. And they are good. Very good indeed. In fact the best that they've been for a long time. I think it's reasonable to assume that some of this is down to you. So I'd like to extend your contract for a further three months. Assuming everything goes well, we may be able to offer you a full-time position after that.'

In any other situation, Kevin would have been delighted, and he was flattered, but he knew that it was very likely that he would be leaving before that period was up. Nonetheless, he smiled as he accepted Peter's offer and thanked him before returning to his desk in the saleroom.

As Sylvia arrived at her desk, a little flushed and slightly out of breath from climbing the eight flights of stairs she glanced around the office. Her work colleagues were getting on with their work. She made herself a coffee, sat at her desk and flicked her computer on. She had twenty-six emails. She scanned through them. They were all routine messages connected with the various jobs she was working on. She responded to as many as she could and then went downstairs to retrieve some print outs she had requested. On the way to the print room, she passed Dave King in the corridor. He smiled at her briefly and gave the faintest of nods. She smiled back.

When she returned to her desk another seven emails had arrived. One of them was from her boss who was working from home that day stating that Target Topaz, which was their code name for Dave King, was going to be arrested the following day and that she would need to get all the case files ready to hand over to the police. It was a chilling reminder of what would happen if they got caught.

The next day the police arrived. DC Parker was amongst the group who led Dave away. Sylvia watched from the window. She noted how they placed hands upon his head as they helped to ease him into the police car, just like in the movies.

That evening she worked late. She went through each of the systems to make sure everything was operating exactly as it should be, checking that there were no alerts being produced. Everything was in order. Not content with that, Sylvia began to lay yet another false trail by logging into a colleague's computer using one of the departed staff's password and diverting the money in several different directions before returning it to the payout account. If anyone discovered that the money was being drained, it might buy a little more time. Around eleven o'clock she left the office and wearily made her way home.

Robert went off in the van each day to collect items they had bid on previously and deliver them to the other salerooms to be auctioned off again. Each day Kevin would produce a list of auctions and sales with times, lot numbers and prices. Robert would arrive at the sales early and would take up a position near the rear of the room so he could look out for rival bidders.

As the lots were shown he would check his lists and prepare himself to bid. He had to admit that Kevin was not only adept at organising, but he also had a flair for pricing. He was never far off the final figure. When it came to the actual process of bidding Robert had developed his own style. He initially attracted the auctioneer's attention using his card, and then an exaggerated raise of his eyebrows accompanied with a slight nod of his head was enough to increase the bid.

He was surprised to discover that he enjoyed the process of bidding. It made him feel powerful and influential. When he won the bidding he had a sense of victory. If he had bid under Kevin's target figure and won the item he might have punched the air but he didn't, as he didn't want to draw unnecessary attention. However, as time had gone on the value of the items he was bidding on had increased often to several thousand pounds and people had begun to turn around to look at him while he was bidding. He would occasionally see the same people at other sales and they would acknowledge him with a smile or a nod.

Robert now felt part of the antique business in London. He noticed that Kevin was selecting items of a similar style or era and when lots came up that related to that period other dealers would actually look round at him as if they expected him to bid and it was almost as if they were indicating that they would step aside. Robert began to realise that within this business there were some unspoken rules and he was beginning to learn what they were.

Robert was also finding that he was becoming interested in the items he was bidding on. Some of them were exquisitely designed with beautifully crafted details. The Art Nouveau figures were ravishingly sexy and the furniture made him wish he had the skills to make something similar. He enjoyed the feel of the items and relished being the winning bidder and being able to actually own these pieces, even if it was only fleetingly. He decided that one day his house, when he could afford one, would be decorated with items like these.

At the close of each auction, Robert would shake hands with some of the other dealers and then go and sign the various sheets of paper that were drawn up by the auctioneers administration team. He would then call Kevin to let him know the outcome. Once the payment was made Robert would load up the pieces into the van and either drive them back to the flat or to another auction house to be sold on.

At the end of each day, Kevin and Robert would discuss the sales in detail back at the flat. Kevin wanted to know how the bidding had gone and which other people were bidding against him. If Robert had brought some items back, they would get them out and study them. If there was an item that Kevin particularly liked he would impart his knowledge of the artist or sculptor and Robert would listen with interest. He was surprised how much Kevin knew and also by how much he wanted to learn. Kevin explained that his father had been an antiques dealer for a while and he had learnt a lot from him, by going with him to auctions when he was a kid and also from manning his father's shop during the holidays.

Recently they had bought another laptop and they would sit opposite each other in the evenings with a beer each or a glass of wine. Kevin would update the spreadsheets while Robert would be dealing with the online auction sales and checking routes to the various sales he would be attending. Sometimes they would use the internet to carry out research and learn more about particular pieces. Most nights they would call Sylvia and check how things were going with her as well as updating her on their own activities.

One night, before phoning Sylvia, Kevin said to Robert 'Oh by the way. My ex, Anne, is coming over next weekend.'

'Right. Want me to make myself scarce?'

'No. No need for that. Hopefully, she won't be staying long. In fact, I don't really know why she's coming. Just thought I'd let you know. That's all.'

'Does Sylvia know?'

Kevin hesitated, 'No. Not yet. If I can get rid of her quickly I may not need to tell her.'

Robert did the eyebrow-raising thing again and said nothing.

Chapter 31

It had not been a good day. The client's marketing manager had been discussing with Tom the proposals for media buying and had made some alternative suggestions at which point Tom had told him bluntly not to interfere with his arrangements. The marketing manager had phoned and complained to Lydia who was heading up the client handling team. Lydia found herself in a difficult position. Tom seemed to consider himself to be of equal rank within the company although the truth was that Lydia was more senior and she had been with the agency for many more years. If relations with the client were going to run smoothly, she was going to have to deal with Tom. For a moment she considered asking Anne, as his girlfriend, to speak to him but she knew that it would put undue pressure on their relationship. She needed to discuss this with James, the Media director first but he was on holiday. Even though she found conflict difficult she knew she had to handle this herself.

Lydia asked Tom to drop into her office. At the same time as Tom was making his way over to her office to see what she wanted, Anne was going through some of the copy for a press advert with Sarah, her opposite number at the client, in the open plan area outside Lydia's office.

In her peripheral vision, Anne was aware of Tom going into Lydia's office and then, after a few seconds she saw him return to the office door to shut it behind him. Anne moved the conversation onto the newly designed packaging. She overheard Tom's voice getting louder found herself talking louder to try and drown it out.

Then the door opened sharply and Tom yelled 'Just fuck off, will you? Telling me how to do my fucking job. I'm the fucking media expert around here. That fucking idiot client should just get lost and leave me to it. And so should you. You're not even my boss. So just piss off,' and then added under his breath but so others in the area could hear it, 'Fucking bitch.'

He stormed out of the office and slammed the door. The office had been silenced.

A few seconds later Lydia came to the office doorway red-faced and looked out briefly before shutting the door again. Anne could just make out her picking the phone up. A few minutes later Lydia came out of the office and disappeared in the direction of the Chief Executive's office.

Anne apologised profusely to Sarah. They quickly wrapped up their meeting and Anne saw her to the exit. All the way there Anne was playing down the scene as much as she could, explaining that Tom was highly strung and that it was not to be taken seriously. But Anne was all too aware though that, barring kidnapping Sarah and hiding her in a cupboard for the next few days, there was no way that the reporting of this event was not going to find it's way back to client's most senior people.

When Lydia returned she called Anne into her office.

'I assume you heard Tom's outburst?'

'Yes, sadly it would have been impossible not to'.

'So you think that Sarah overheard too'.

She nodded. 'Yes, she did. I tried to smooth things over, but I didn't want to say anything to make it even worse.'

'I've been to see Andy. He's going to deal with Tom. Be clear Anne. Tom will not be allowed to continue to work with this client.'

'I understand.'

'I'm concerned that this may cause you a problem at home.'

'Right. Yes. It probably will. But that's my problem. Not the agency's.'

'Just so you know Anne, I am very pleased with you and your efforts with the client. This is absolutely no reflection on you or your performance.'

Tom was fired later that day. Word got round the office quickly. When the news reached Anne she was shocked and it took a while to sink in. When she looked around at the others in the office she couldn't help noticing how they wouldn't meet her eye. They looked away and pretended to be busy. She could hear the whispers, though. She felt that Tom's downfall could also cause hers by association and it made her fearful.

After work, Anne drove home and reflected on the day's events. All the way there, she was dreading what was waiting for her when she arrived.

She parked her car away in her usual space. She noticed that the space where Tom normally parked his car was empty. Maybe he wasn't home. She tentatively opened the front door and walked into the apartment. Tom was there, sitting on the edge of the sofa sipping a whisky and tapping his foot.

'They took the fucking car off me. Can you believe that? Had to get a taxi home. Bastards.'

'You should have said. I could have given you a lift,' she said lamely.

'And give everyone in your office the satisfaction of seeing me having to ask you for a ride home. No thanks love. I've still got some tiny shreds of dignity left. No thanks to that lot, though. They're going to pay for this one way or another.'

Anne crept out of the room. She felt that her presence could just inflame him further and she was not in the mood for a row.

At work the next day she was called into Andy's office. The other directors were already in the meeting. Andy looked worried. 'Anne. Thanks for coming in. I was just telling the others here that I've had a call from the client's CEO this morning. Tom's stunt yesterday has not gone down well and in effect they have given us the yellow card. One more mistake and we're history. I was just telling the others that if we lose this client I shall be extremely pissed off. So please all of you make sure that from now on everything is perfect. Thanks, everyone.'

They all turned to leave the office.

'Anne, I'd like a word please.' He waited until they were alone and the door had been shut. Anne's heart started banging in her chest. She felt sick. She started rubbing her hands together nervously.

'Tom really let himself down yesterday. I hope you understand that I had absolutely no choice. I had to let him go. It was gross misconduct and nearly cost this company a lot of money. Now I do realise that it's likely to be very awkward for you at home. I want to keep you on the team, but I need you to be clear that Tom must have no further input or involvement with this client. You must not even talk about the client to him or divulge any information to him about what we are doing. Is that understood?'

'Yes, of course' said Anne.

'Good. I knew you would understand. Let's get back to work then.'

With that, Andy reached over and picked up the telephone, and Anne realised she had been dismissed.

Later that day she called Tom at home but there was no answer. When she reached home he wasn't there. Anne prepared dinner. She ate hers reluctantly and put Tom's meal in the oven to keep warm. She watched television and sipped wine. Her phone was on the arm of the sofa and her eyes kept flitting to it in case Tom had made contact. She checked her watch. It was getting late and still no word. She tried his mobile. It rang out twice and then stopped. At eleven o'clock she turned the oven off, scraped his food into the bin and went to bed.

In the morning, she expected to find him passed out in the bed or on the sofa but he wasn't there. It was clear that he had not been home. She examined her emotions. She felt worried for him, but she also felt angry too. Why hadn't he phoned and let her know where he was, or that he wasn't coming home? Then she thought that maybe he might have collapsed somewhere or perhaps he had been involved in an accident. She wondered if she should call the hospitals or the police. What do people normally do in this situation? How long does it have to be before someone is classed as 'missing'?

Anne went to work the next day and kept checking her phone in case there was a text or a missed call from Tom. When her colleagues eventually asked after him she said he was fine and that he was already looking for a new job. She wondered why she didn't tell them the truth. Was it to protect her pride or his? She rang his mobile. It was off. She rang home. It rang out until the answering machine kicked in. She decided to wait until she had got home and if there was still no sign of him, she would call the police.

When she got home, he was there. He must have seen her car pull up as he was standing waiting for her in the entrance. Behind him were some suitcases.

'Are you going somewhere?' she said anxiously.

'No, I'm not. But you are. I don't want you here any more.'

'What? I don't understand. Are you throwing me out? What for?'

'It doesn't matter what for. It's my place. I just want you out. Ever since you moved in here my life has turned to shit. So, as far as I'm concerned it's all your fault and the sooner you are gone, the sooner my life can start to recover.'

'Look, Tom, can't we talk about this? And preferably inside.' Anne just knew that the other tenants would be listening in.

'No. There's no point. I've made up my mind. I'll carry these bags to the car. When you've sorted yourself out I'll bring the rest of your stuff. Let's go.' He started to pick up her bags. She reached out to stop him. He struck her arm out of the way and she tumbled backwards. 'Now. Get up.'

Tom strode off with the cases. Numb, with tears stinging in her eyes, she pulled herself up, grabbed the rest of the bags and followed him. He put the cases down by her car.

'Have a nice life,' he said as he walked past her and then was gone.

Anne dumped the bags in the back and then sat in her car staring ahead. Her mind was still reeling. Her vision was blurred with tears. She considered going back to the apartment to try to reason with him. But his whole attitude had been so fixed, so rigid that she knew it would be useless to try and discuss it with him. It was at that moment that she knew for sure that it was over.

Like an automaton, she started the car, reversed out of the parking space and then drove to her parents' house. Her parents welcomed her, listened to her, hugged her, sympathised with her, fed her and then quietly led her to her old room where she slid fully clothed into the bed she slept in as a child and Anne cried herself to sleep.

Chapter 32

The next slide appearing on the screen was of the Moloch of Totalitarianism statue by sculptors Nina Galitskaia and Vitali Gambarov at the Levashovo Memorial Cemetery. It was an enormous metal sculpture which made Kate think of a towering Transformer with a flaccid human body sliding out of its midriff. She was listening to the lecturer droning on about its merits when she felt her phone vibrate in her pocket. She was thankful that she had remembered to put it on silent for the lecture. She surreptitiously retrieved it and, covering the screen so as not to distract the speaker, she glanced down and saw that it was Robert calling. She slid silently out of her seat and quickly tip-toed to the nearest exit. Once outside the lecture theatre she just managed to answer before the voicemail kicked in.

'Robert?'

'Hi. Hope you don't mind me calling? Can you talk?'

'Yes, it's fine. I'm glad you rang. I was just in a dull lecture about Russian memorial art. I'm sure they'll cope without me. How are things with you?'

'Pretty hectic actually. I'm just parked up in a side street and am fifteen minutes late for a sale in West Norwood, so I can't talk for long. I just wanted to say hello.'

'Hello to you too.'

'And to see if you wanted to meet up again sometime.'

'Yes. I'd like that. Are you thinking of coming to Bristol? Or do you want me to come to London?'

'I'd like to come to Bristol. If that's okay with you?'

'It's fine. When can you make it?'

'Well, actually I was wondering if next weekend was convenient.'

Kate told him it was perfect and she agreed to text her address to him. She put the phone in her pocket and returned to the lecture with a smile and a bounce in her step.

Sylvia received a text from Kate later that day.

'Rbt coming 2 c me nxt wkd. K8. X'

She replied, *'Cool. Let me know how it goes. Sylv X'*

Sylvia dropped the phone back into her bag and smiled to herself. So Kate and Robert might become an item. She really did want to know how it went. Thinking of Robert and Kate together led her to think about Kevin. How did she really feel about him? He certainly wasn't moving forwards too fast. If anything he seemed to be holding back. In a way, she liked that. But maybe it was time to move things on and see where it went. Perhaps the weekend in Oxford would lead to something.

Kevin checked the balance again. There was over sixty thousand pounds in the payout account. He mentally totted up the items bought but not paid for yet. It came to around nineteen thousand pounds. They needed to work faster to move the money as the money was arriving quicker than they were spending it. In the post, that morning were more catalogues. He browsed through them, looking for items with higher guide prices.

One of the catalogues had a number of music memorabilia lots including a letter written by John Lennon to a friend from Hamburg in the early days of the Beatles. Anyone interested in music knew about the Beatles early days playing the Hamburg clubs including the Indra, Kaiserkeller and Star Club. The guide price was thirty thousand pounds. He had come across memorabilia before but had not considered it as it was outside his normal area of knowledge in antiques. That letter was written just as a part of music history was being made. He shook his head and went back to the other catalogues, but somehow he couldn't get it out of his mind.

Robert arrived at the auction just after it started but still managed to successfully bid on the lots Kevin had circled in the catalogue. He was pleased that Kate wanted to meet up at the weekend, as he had decided it was best to be out of the way when Kevin's soon-to-be-ex-wife Anne arrived. He was intrigued to meet her but didn't want to add to what was likely to be an awkward time for them both.

He had received the text with Kate's address and when he got back to the flat he informed Kevin that he was going to be in Bristol for the weekend.

'Ah. Doesn't Kate live in Bristol?' said Kevin, waiting for the inevitable eyebrow arch and was not disappointed.

'I thought you might need a bit of space when Anne came round.'

'It wasn't necessary, but thanks anyway. I'm not expecting her to stay long.'

Later that evening Kevin received two texts. One was from Anne.

'Still on for meeting at wknd? Hope so. Meet at Euston? 1pm Sat?

Kevin studied the text for a moment thinking about how he should respond. As he started typing, he received the second one. It was from Sylvia.

'Gather Rbt will be in Brl with K8. Fancy a meal or

something?'

Chapter 33

Kevin was waiting at the top of the escalators in Euston station when Anne arrived. As she approached him, he could see that she had lost some weight and her face looked determined as she scanned the crowd. She smiled and waved when she spotted him, then made her way over to join him. They didn't embrace.

'Hi. Good journey?'

'It was easy. Train was on time and managed to get a seat for once.'

They turned and walked out onto the bustling street.

'Are you hungry? Shall we get some lunch?'

Kevin led Anne towards a group of restaurants and they went into one of the quieter ones. After being shown to their table and ordering drinks Anne said,

'So how have you been?'

Kevin told her that he was enjoying life. He told her that he'd managed to get the job at the saleroom and then was lucky enough to find a flat nearby even if the rent was ridiculously high compared to Birmingham. She asked if he enjoyed his job. He told her he did, that it was infinitely more interesting than the job at the insurance company had been, and that he seemed to be quite good at it. He explained how he was also in the process of setting up an antiques business of his own with a couple of people he had met in London.

She said she was pleased for him. He enquired about her job. She told him it was going well. She told him briefly about winning the new account and her new role. He asked how things were going with Tom. He saw her composure alter as soon as he mentioned Tom's name.

'It's over.'

'I'm sorry. ' Surprisingly, Kevin did feel marginally sorry for her and although he didn't really want to hear the details he felt obliged to ask her if she wanted to talk about it.

'Not really.' But then she looked down at her drink as she succinctly explained about the problems that he had caused at work, resulting in his dismissal. Then she told him how she had gone home one day to find her bags all packed and Tom telling her to leave.

In the back of Kevin's mind was a feeling that she had it coming and perhaps now she might feel a little bit how he felt when she moved out and left him on his own, but his face didn't give anything away.

'I'm sorry to hear that. So where are you living now?'

'Back with my parents. Temporarily I hope. And in case you are wondering, all this happened after I rang you about coming down to see you.'

'I see.' And then after a short period of silence 'And what are your plans now?'

'Not sure really.'

'What about your job? Is that secure? I remember you saying that there was talk of laying people off.'

She told him that she thought it was more secure now, as long as the agency could retain the new client by not fouling anything else up.

'I'm enjoying my job; especially now I've been given extra responsibility. So I'll probably just find somewhere to live and get used to the single life again.'

The food arrived and they ate in silence each mulling things over until Anne said, 'And have you met anyone else since you arrived in London?'

'I've made some new friends. The ones I'm in business with.'

'I meant in a romantic sense. Anyone special in your life now?'

'No, not really'

'Not really? That sounds to me like you have met someone.'

'Well, there may be someone but I'm not sure if it's going anywhere.'

'So, are you saying there might be a chance for us again? '

Kevin almost choked on his mouthful of spaghetti.

'What?'

'We're not divorced yet.'

'You are joking I take it?'

Anne put her knife and fork down and stared at him. 'No, Kevin I'm not joking. God knows, I did a terrible thing to you. But I've come to realise that I made a dreadful mistake. Is there any chance at all that you could forgive me and we could try again?'

Kevin was shocked. Of all the reasons he thought she might have wanted to meet up again, this would have been the last on his list. Money, possessions, curiosity would all have come higher up than this.

'Um…I don't know what to say'

'Please, just think about it. Don't say anything now. I don't think I could take another rejection right now. Tell me you'll consider it at least. Technically we're still married. I know you're in London and I'm in

Birmingham but I'm sure we could work things out.'

Kevin was thinking of the text reply he had sent to Sylvia saying that he couldn't meet her this weekend as an old friend from Birmingham was coming down to see him. He wondered what she would be thinking if she could listen in on this conversation.

They finished the meal. Kevin paid. Then Anne asked if he'd mind showing her his flat.

'Just so that I can picture where you live when I think about you,' she explained.

Kevin hesitated about taking her there but she was insistent so they walked there. While they walked, she told him more about her life with Tom and about how things had taken a turn for the worse after the trip to Cyprus and Kevin was left feeling that Anne had wrecked their marriage for a fling with a complete idiot.

At the flat, Anne looked round observing how sparse and basic it was compared to Tom's luxury apartment. Then she spotted the spare room with Robert's things in it.

'Someone else lives here?'

'Yes,' said Kevin. 'My business partner has the spare room.'

Anne looked him questioningly. Then said, 'Thanks for showing me round. I think I'd better go now.' They made their way outside and Kevin hailed a cab. As the taxi left she said, 'Think about what I said. I'll call you'. Then she was gone and Kevin was left standing on the side of the road. His head was spinning.

Chapter 34

'You have reached your destination,' said the female voice of the satnav fixed to the windscreen. Robert slowed down and looked for number seventy-six. As he pulled up out outside a small terraced house he saw the curtains twitch. A moment later Kate was standing on the front doorstep. She was wearing a stripy apron over the top of what appeared to be a short black dress.

Robert reached for the flowers and bottle of wine from the van's passenger seat and walked up the short garden path. Kate took the flowers and kissed him on the lips as he entered the house.

'My housemates have gone out for the evening so it's just us. Hope that's okay?'

'It's great,' said Robert as he took in the table laid out for two and the candles.

'You've been busy,' he said as Kate retreated to the kitchen at the rear of the house.

'Oh, it's nothing special.' She yelled, 'Just a curry. Hope you like curry.'

'My favourite.'

Kate reappeared carrying a tray with several dishes, some naan and poppadoms on it.

'This one is Bhuna, this is Rogan Josh and that one is chicken tikka marsala.'

'Wow. Excellent. A feast.'

They ate, drank wine and talked. Kate asked if Robert had seen Sylvia recently and if the antiques business was going well. Robert asked her to tell him about the course she was doing, and then asked how she came to know Sylvia.

'We were at school together. She was the good one and I was always getting into trouble. Once when we were about fourteen we went out to the shops at lunchtime and I nicked some sweets for a laugh. The shopkeeper caught us red-handed and threatened to tell our parents. Sylvia was completely distraught. So I volunteered to work in the shop on Saturdays for a month without being paid. He relented and actually gave me a paid part time job after that. I think Sylvia was both cross with me and also grateful. My parents were too busy with each other to really notice me, but Sylvia's parents were far more interested in her so they would have been terribly disappointed if she was caught stealing.'

'And did you get into any more scrapes?' said Robert

'Countless. I was expelled from the school eventually, but it was only the last term I missed. I was still allowed to take the exams and just about managed to get into university.' What about you? Have you ever been in trouble?'

'A bit.' Robert told her some of his history including a brief summary of his time in Scotland, including a watered-down version of some of the less savoury activities he had been involved with and how relocating to London was his way of shaking off the past and starting afresh.

'And that's when you met Kevin and Sylvia. Right?'

'Uh-huh. We all met in the hotel we were staying in. I worked there for a while and then went into the antiques business with Kevin.'

'It seems to have gone well for you, and quite quickly too, considering it was only a few months ago when you first moved to London.'

'I suppose that's true.' He then changed he subject

and they talked about the merits of Bristol compared to London. After the meal, Robert helped Kate clear the table and they went into the kitchen to wash up. Robert washed and Kate dried.

As she put the clean plates into the wall cupboard Kate asked, 'Do you think Kevin really fancies Sylvia?'

'Definitely. You can tell by the way he talks about her that he's mad about her. Has she told you whether she's keen on him?'

'Oh yes. I haven't seen her this way for years. She's fallen for him. I hope he doesn't mess her about, though. I'd hate to see her heartbroken again.'

'I haven't known Kevin long but from what I know of him, he seems like a really decent guy. I don't think he'll mess her about.' As he said this he remembered that Kevin was seeing Anne this weekend and wondered what the outcome of that meeting might be. Whenever Kevin referred to Anne it was usually in negative terms but if she really came on to him, perhaps his defences might weaken, especially as they were actually still married.

As if she was reading his mind Kate asked, 'What's happened to his ex-wife? Has she met someone else?'

'Yes, I think so. As far as I know she left Kevin so she could move in with one of her work colleagues. I think it was the combination of that, plus being made redundant, that made him decide to move to London. And actually they are still married although I think the divorce is nearly completed.'

'She must be an idiot. Kevin seems like such a nice guy. If she can dick around with him like that, she doesn't deserve him.'

'No. You're probably right.' Robert replied hoping

that Anne had not got her claws back into Kevin. That could upset everything.

'Thanks for helping out with the clearing up. Want to watch a film? I've got The Godfather 2 on DVD.'

'Excellent.'

They sat next to each other on the sofa and watched the film. After a while, Kate leaned into Robert and he put his arm around her. Before long they were kissing and sliding their hands inside each other's clothes. By the halfway point in the film, they were half-naked and lying on top of each other before Kate suddenly stood up, her pert breasts, freed from their support, jiggling slightly as she reached out for him and led him willingly upstairs to the bedroom.

In the morning, Robert showered and made his way downstairs. There was evidence of the other housemates late night arrival with discarded Chinese takeaway containers stacked up on the table and empty bottles lying around. He started to clear up when Kate appeared wearing a short bathrobe.

'Leave all that Robert. Let them clear it up when they get up. Why don't we go for a walk and get some breakfast while we are out?'

Kate quickly showered and dressed. She put her arm through his as they set off down the road. They found a Starbucks and ordered coffee and muffins. Robert turned his phone on and checked his messages. There was one from Kevin.

'How's it going? Anne's gone. Hope your trip has been more fun. C U later. Kev.'

As Kate fought her way through the crowded café with the tray, Robert quickly replied.

'Sos about Anne. All good here. Back later. R'

'I was just texting Kevin to say that I've had a great time this weekend.'

Kate smiled and touched his hand. 'I'm glad. So have I. I hope we can do it again soon.'

'Yes. So do I. Maybe you could come to London when Kevin and Sylvia go up to Oxford for that sale?'

'It's a date,' said Kate and she gripped his hand tightly.

Part 2

*Justice is a human invention
and it only exists in our minds.*

Mark Stretch

Chapter 35

After thirty-two years of marriage, George and Alexandra Newman were divorcing. George had met someone else from his past and now that the children had left home and were secure he had decided that this was the best time to make the break. They had both engaged solicitors and were currently dealing with the financial settlement. So far, they were still being civil to each other.

George had spent his entire career to date working for a large publishing company based in Norwich. Alexandra had taken time out to have their children and then, when they had gone off to college, she had returned to her job as a primary school teacher. As part of the settlement, both of them had to complete the Form E financial disclosure document.

George had moved in with Jacob and was sitting at the dining room table poring over the form. He was surrounded by several dusty box files and piles of paperwork. Every now and then he would put the pen down and rifle through the paperwork. Sometimes he would rush into the bedroom and then reappear with a building society book or a letter.

Jacob brought him a cup of tea and placed it gently on the table. He ruffled George's hair and said,

'Take a break George, it's only going to get you all rattled and upset.'

'Thanks. I wish I could, but I need to get this finished. I understand why I've got to get it done. I just can't believe how much information they want from me. As you know, I've told Alex she can have the house but the solicitors say I have to fill this in. I have to provide details of every bank account, every building society account, my pension, my assets, liabilities, everything. They want to know where every last penny is. It's bloody exasperating.'

'I know. But it's just a question of going through it listing everything. We've got nothing to hide and you are being perfectly generous to Alex. It'll be fine.'

'It's just that I've got some old accounts that I haven't touched in ages. I don't even know if there's any money in them. I can't find statements for them but if I miss them off the solicitors are sure to find out.'

'Leave it for now. We'll go to the banks tomorrow. I'm sure they'll be able to provide statements and so on. Drink your tea before it gets cold.'

The next day they drove into town in Jacob's Morris Traveller. They had to visit two banks. In the first bank, George was pleased to learn that he had one hundred and nine pounds and thirty-seven pence. He collected a statement and then closed the account and withdrew the cash. In the second bank, after waiting in a queue for fifteen minutes and watching a mini-drama as someone fainted, George arrived at the counter. He told the cashier that he was sure he had an account with them but couldn't remember the number or anything about the account. He explained that he had set it up while he worked away from home many years ago and had just forgotten to do anything with it since.

After a series of security questions and then further discussions about former addresses, the cashier eventually established that there was an account in George's name that had not been touched for thirteen years. She asked to see some identification. George was prepared for this and had brought along his passport and driving licence. He had also brought along some utility bills and other documents that would establish his identity. The cashier amended the address on the account and then printed off a statement and handed it to George.

'Eight hundred and eighty-six pounds! Look!'

He showed the print out to Jacob who smiled. 'Does that mean we can afford a coffee now?'

They thanked the cashier then walked hand in hand to the coffee shop and ordered.

'I had no idea there was so much money in there. Maybe the company paid me a bonus or something after I left the area all those years ago. I wish I'd known.'

'Perhaps it was a tax rebate? What does it say on the statement?'

They looked at the details on the statement. It did appear to be an extra payment by the company.

'I can't remember why they paid again, but it's good news.'

'That's odd George, look at this.'

George looked back down at the statement.

'See how the interest payments were applied regularly every year on the same date but there wasn't one this year'.

'Maybe you don't continue getting interest if you don't use the account?'

'I don't believe that for a minute. I'm sure you are still entitled to interest even if you don't use the account. We ought to check and see.'

'It's hardly worth the effort. It will only amount to a fiver or even less if we are lucky.'

'How much were these coffees?'

'Four pounds sixty.'

'Well, there you are. It might be enough for another coffee, another day. And it's the principle of it too. When we've finished these we're going back to the bank to sort this out.'

Chapter 36

In Oxford, Kevin was examining a set of six chairs by Emile Gallé. The catalogue described them as,

'1889, made of cherry, the backs inlaid with various woods, each with a different design: daffodils, pine cones, fruiting holly, cornflowers, flowering plant with butterflies and flowering branch with butterflies37½ in. (95 cm.) high daffodil and pine cones with horizontal inlaid mark GALLÉ; fruiting holly and cornflowers with vertical inlaid mark GALLÉ; flowering plant and flowering branch with branded mark Emile Gallé.

'Look at these! I thought these would be nice. They are even better than I hoped. Think we'll bid on these.'

Sylvia held his hand. Although she knew very little about antiques, she knew when something was beautiful and she found Kevin's enthusiasm incredibly infectious.

'What about that? It looks lovely too.' She gestured towards a chair by Carlo Bugatti.

'Wow. You do have good taste after all,' said Kevin. 'This was one of the other items I wanted to look at. It is totally stunning isn't it?' He walked around the chair admiring it.

'Carlo Bugatti, who designed this chair, was the father of Ettore Bugatti who designed the cars that were so successful in races in the nineteen twenties and thirties. He also had a son, Rembrandt, who was a sculptor.'

'Sculptors, furniture and car designers all in the same family, they must have been a creative lot, the

Bugatti's'

Kevin nodded and continued to examine the chair. 'They were. But they had their fair share of tragedy too. Rembrandt committed suicide. And Ettore's son was killed testing a newly designed car.'

'Oh dear, that's horrible. How do you know all this?'

'I don't really know. I suppose I just absorbed it while I was working for my Dad in the summer holidays. They had plenty of books lying around about Art Nouveau, Art Deco and so on. I read them all. Some of it must have stuck.'

Sylvia looked at him. 'I like hearing you talk antiques.'

'You must be tired. It's been a long day. I've seen enough now. Shall we go and check in at the hotel?'

At the reception desk, Kevin signed in for both of them. He had booked two rooms, a double room for Sylvia and a single for himself.

They met up an hour later and had a drink at the bar.

'I'm so glad you asked me to come with you. It's been fascinating. And this is a gorgeous hotel. The grounds are magnificent.'

'Seriously, I'm the lucky one to have you here with me. It can get a bit lonely doing this on your own. It's really nice to have some company. Want another drink?'

'Yes please.'

Kevin ordered more drinks. They sipped their drinks and chatted. Kevin asked Sylvia if she had heard from Kate recently. She confirmed that she had. Kate seemed very keen on Robert and she gathered that she was visiting Robert that weekend while they were in Oxford. Kevin told her that Robert was showing similar signs and that he'd never seen Robert look quite so well-groomed or the flat so tidy as when he left it to meet up with Sylvia. They agreed that they made a fitting couple.

There was a moment or two of awkward silence. Then Sylvia said,

'Kevin, I was wondering if ..'

'Another drink? I'll get them.'

When he returned with more drinks, Sylvia tilted her head, smiled and said 'Kevin Walker, are you trying to get me drunk?'

'Not you. Me.'

'Why?'

'So I can pluck up the courage to ...'

'Maybe we should get Room Service?'

With that, she picked her drink and walked towards the lift. Kevin swiftly followed. They took the lift up to their rooms. Kevin stopped outside his room and Sylvia walked a little further on up the corridor to hers. As Kevin started to insert the key Sylvia said,

'Hey, you. Come here. I don't think you'll be needing that room tonight.'

As daylight began to filter into the room around the edges of the heavy hotel room curtains they lay sprawled across the bed. Items of clothing were strewn around the room. Kevin's trousers were by the bathroom door. A bra was lying by the window. Hanging from the lampshade was a tiny pair of black knickers.

'That. Was. Amazing,' mumbled Kevin as he rolled over and put his arms around Sylvia.

'Mmm, yes it was. In fact, I'd like a bit more, please.'

At around ten o'clock Kevin woke from his dozing suddenly remembering the auction. He roused Sylvia.

'Come on. Quick. We'd better go or we'll miss the sale.'

'You go Kevin. I'll stay here and enjoy the hotel. Buy the stuff and hurry back. I'll be waiting for you.'

Kevin quickly showered and dressed while Sylvia ordered breakfast for one from room service.

'I'll get back as quickly as I can.' He kissed her on the lips. She reached up and pulled him to her and held him for a while. The sheet dropped down revealing her small but perfectly formed breasts with erect nipples.

'Remember, I'll be waiting,' Sylvia whispered as Kevin stumbled out of the room and looking back one last time to ensure the image of her naked in bed remained etched in his mind.

The auction went well and Kevin succeeded in his bids for all of the pieces he came for, paying just over a hundred thousand pounds for the lot. He asked the auctioneers to retain the items and put them into their next auction, which was to be held back in London a month later where he felt they might gain a higher price. He sometimes wished that they weren't doing this just to launder money as some of the pieces he would just love to own himself. Maybe one day, he thought.

He hurried back to the hotel. As promised, Sylvia was waiting for him. She had spent the day reading, swimming in the hotel pool, relaxing in the sauna and hot tub followed by a soothing massage. When Kevin returned to the hotel room, Sylvia was stretched out on the bed reading a magazine. She was wearing just her underwear and a broad smile.

The Laundrymen

'How did it go?'

'Well. Very well. In fact.' Kevin was hopping around the room trying to get his shoes and socks off. Sylvia said 'Sit down. Let me do that. You've been working. I've had a lovely relaxing day. Now it's your turn.'

She undressed him slowly, stroking his skin and kissing him all the while. They made love again, this time slowly and sensuously.

Later Sylvia cuddled up to him and said, 'I've been wondering. How come it took you so long to get me into bed?'

'I didn't know if you were interested or not.'

'You crazy man. I fell for you the night we went to the restaurant. You could have had me any time. But I'm glad you waited. It was worth waiting for. I was just curious, though.'

'I suppose it's because I am technically still married. There hasn't been anyone since Anne. I guess I'm a bit out of practice.'

'Well, you'll be divorced soon and then you won't have to have anything more to do with her.'

Kevin felt a pang of guilt as he thought of Anne and her parting words. He hadn't really given her much thought since she had left in the taxi, but now he knew he definitely didn't want to try and re-kindle a relationship with her. He just needed to find the right way to tell her.

That evening Kevin and Sylvia ate in the hotel restaurant before retiring to their room with a bottle of champagne.

They made love again and just before they both collapsed into a deep exhausted sleep Sylvia nuzzled Kevin's hair and whispered, 'I think I'm falling in love with you, Kevin Walker.'

Mark Stretch

Chapter 37

As Kevin and Sylvia were travelling back from Oxford, Robert and Kate were busy tidying up the flat after a busy weekend of sightseeing, takeaways and sex.

Robert took Kate back to the station. On the way there she suggested that they book a holiday, somewhere warm. He told her he thought it was an excellent idea and that maybe she should see what she could find. He watched her board the train. Then he waved until he could see her no longer and made his way back to the flat. He arrived there just as Kevin returned and was unlocking the front door.

'Aha. Here he is. How was your weekend? Did you get the lots you were after? Bet you didn't get that Bugatti chair.'

'I did. As a matter of fact, I got them all' And I got the girl too, he thought to himself, as he lugged his bag inside and Robert followed him in.

'Well done. That's good news. Hopefully, I'll see them go through the London auction at a profit.'

'I think you almost certainly will. I got them at a good price. How was it here?'

'Very nice indeed, thank you. Did the tourist thing, showing Kate round. Went to Buckingham Palace again. Bit more fun than on our last visit there. I also had a call from Chloe. She's really pleased with the phone I sent her and it's great that she can call me direct rather than having to go through Janice. Kate and I had a curry last night. We did tidy up, but I'm afraid that there's still be a bit of an aroma ..'

Once Kevin had unpacked they settled down to

their usual glass of wine and chat.

'So? Are you going to tell me?' asked Robert

'Tell you what?'

'You know. You and Sylvia. In Oxford. In a hotel. For a whole weekend. Something must have happened.'

'I see', he hesitated. 'Actually something did happen.'

Before Kevin could tell him anything, his phone vibrated and than rang. He answered. It was Anne. He mouthed 'Anne' to Robert. Robert raised his eyebrows, picked up his wine and tip-toed out of the room.

'Hi, Anne.'

Anne started to tell him about her week, how her parents were driving her mad and about work. Kevin interrupted.

'Sorry Anne, but I'm quite busy right now with some paperwork so I can't talk for long. But I've been thinking about what you said as you were leaving. I don't think it's a good idea. You're in Birmingham. I'm down here. We've both got new lives. It's probably best if we don't complicate things further. What do you think?'

There was no response. Kevin began to wonder if she had ended the call. He asked if she was still there. Eventually, she spoke up and, in a colder tone of voice, told him that she thought he was making a mistake. They were destined to be together. Her leaving him had just been a stupid mistake, but it was over now. She told him that it wasn't often in life that people get a second chance and that if he was wise he should take it. When he didn't respond, she called him a bastard and that he hadn't heard the last of this. Then she hung up.

Kevin put the phone down on the table and stared at it. Anne had just spoilt what, up until that moment, had been a fantastic weekend.

Robert came back in. He knew straight away that the call had been unpleasant.

'Come on Kevin. Forget her. Let's go to the pub and have a drink. You can tell me all about your weekend, and I'll tell you about mine.'

Kevin allowed himself to be led out of the flat and up the road to their local.

In the pub, and after Kevin had drunk enough beer to take the edge off the phone call, they talked about their respective weekends. Kevin admitted that he and Sylvia had shared a room.

'I knew it!' said Robert. 'From the moment you two met I knew you'd end up getting off with her.'

Kevin reminded him that he'd also suggested she might be 'high maintenance'.

'Well, I bet she is. You'll see I was right about that too.'

Then Kevin said 'I'm guessing you moved things along a bit while you were in Bristol' He looked up to see Robert trying to look innocent.

'It's really great that you and Kate are, um, an item to use Sylvia's terminology. And I know she's pleased too. For both of you. But whatever you do, you mustn't tell Kate anything about the venture. Not a word. Yes. I can see by the look on your face that you had no intention of mentioning it, but I just wanted to say it for the record. Okay?'

Robert told Kevin quite forcefully that he was fully aware of the rules.

'And while we are on the subject of the rules, do you think you and Sylvia can still operate as individuals in this now that you are .. an item, or will it be me and the two of you working together as a team?'

'No, I don't think anything will change as far as that goes. We'll all have to continue to be just as careful as before.' Then he added 'By the way, I don't know if I mentioned it before but I've been thinking we might branch out into music memorabilia too. Some of it fetches good prices. Plus it might be fun. Imagine owning a guitar once owned by Pete Townshend? Actually maybe that's not such a good example as it might be smashed to pieces, but you know the sort of thing I mean. What do you think?'

'Sounds interesting. We both know a bit about music so at least we should know a bit about the people who owned this stuff, but how can you tell if it is genuine?'

'It needs to have all of the provenance to authenticate it. Often it's a certificate but it can be other documents too, like photos or signed statements. I saw that there was a letter from John Lennon when he was in Hamburg up for sale the other day. The guide price was about twenty-five thousand pounds.'

Robert whistled. 'Twenty-five grand for a letter! Well, maybe we can research it all a bit more first. We need to make sure there are genuine buyers out there for this stuff.'

'Okay. Perhaps we'll go to the next big memorabilia sale together and see if we can spot who's buying and who's selling.'

'Fine. By the way, it's your round.'

Chapter 38

The office was buzzing with the news as Sylvia arrived for work on Monday. There was a very strong rumour that the bank was being taken over by an American bank. The word was that the final details had been negotiated over the previous weeks and the deal had been struck over the weekend. The rumours had sent the share price soaring.

Nobody knew exactly what this meant for the bank employees. It might mean redundancies. It might mean promotions. There was very little concrete information and a lot of speculation.

Sylvia had half-expected something like this to happen. She knew that nothing is certain in this life, especially one's job.

She knocked on Brian's door. He motioned her to come in.

'If you've come to ask me about this takeover, don't bother. I'm as much in the dark as you are. We'll just have to wait for the announcement and see what the implications are for us all. In the meantime, we should just carry on as normal. If we are all doing a great job it doesn't give anyone an excuse to say that they don't need the department.'

Sylvia got up to leave.

'Before you go Sylvia. Can you have a quick look at this for me?'

He was looking at his screen and holding out a print of an email.

'It's probably nothing but the IT department have received a few calls from branches about interest not being paid on some previously dormant accounts. As

I said, and I told them too, I doubt if it's anything that we can help with, but as you look after dormant accounts can you have a quick check and see if you can spot anything?'

He still didn't look up as he handed her the email, which was probably fortuitous, as he didn't see the look of fear that momentarily flashed across her face.

Sylvia sat down at her desk. She didn't want to read the message but knew that she must. It had been sent by the IT manager to Brian asking him to see if he knew of any reason why the interest had not been paid on the accounts listed below. The IT manager had then listed five account numbers underneath.

It was quite simple for Sylvia to amend the records in the system so that the missing interest was paid into those accounts. But she knew that very soon it was likely that the same query would be raised again.

The next day Brian called the whole department together.

'As you may have heard it was been announced late last night our time yesterday that we are being taken over by American Municipal Bank. I have a letter here from our CEO Julian McDonald. I'm going to read out the contents.'

He cleared his throat and then began,

'*To all staff of the National Standard Bank,*

We are delighted to confirm yesterday's announcement about the merger between this bank and one of the world's greatest banking institutions, the American Municipal Bank.

The joining of these two banks will allow them both to grow and prosper in tomorrow's uncertain financial world. I am sure all of you have concerns about your future. However, I have been assured by our new partners that they have been impressed by the staff and results here at National Standard and will not be making any wholesale changes in the near future. Whilst some rationalisation is inevitable, any changes will be made with full consultation.

I do hope that this reassures you and that continue to show the level of dedication and support to the new alliance in the future as you have done in the past.

I will be stepping down as CEO and the new leader of both banks will be Eric Rodriguez and he will be based in Washington D.C.

I would like to take this opportunity to thank you for all your effort and support during my time at the bank and wish you all every success for the future.

Yours sincerely

Julian McDonald'

The staff listened in total silence.

Brian said, 'I can't really add much to this as I have yet to hear from or meet with any of our new American allies, but I suggest we carry on as normal. As soon as I hear more, I'll keep you updated.'

Brian then went round the more senior managers and called them into his office. When they had all sat down, including Sylvia, he said, 'Right that's the nice bit done. Now I can speak more plainly but this stays within these four walls. Is that alright with everyone?'

He looked around to make sure that everyone had acknowledged this. 'The fact that Julian has gone means that we are likely to get swallowed up by the Americans. My advice is to start looking for new jobs right now. I am, and you should too. The Yanks can do exactly what we do from their head office and there will be no further need for us. So, the sooner you all get looking the better. Obviously I'll be writing the highest quality references for anyone that needs them but don't wait until it's too late. Move now. Any questions?'

Still reeling from the shock, the managers filed out of the office and resumed their duties. There was a sombre atmosphere in the office for the rest of the day. In the afternoon, Sylvia popped her head around Brian's door and said, 'I've sorted that problem with the dormant accounts. It was just an IT glitch. If the IT guy has any other queries just forward them on to me or if you like I'll contact him and tell him to email them directly to me.'

'Fine. Thanks, Sylvia.' Said Brian in an absent-minded, monotone voice. Again, he didn't even look up from his screen.

* * *

Kevin and Robert were looking around the art, music and writing memorabilia pre-sale display. Some of the items were considered to be so valuable that they were kept in glass cases or were guarded by bored-looking security guards. Robert was examining a cream-coloured guitar signed by the Sex Pistols.

'What's the guide price for this?'

Kevin flicked through the catalogue, 'four hundred pounds' he replied.

'That seems quite cheap really compared to some of this stuff.'

'I think there's a big difference in the value of items actually owned and used by these people and the stuff that's just been signed by them. Did you ever see any of them actually play a guitar like that? It looks like a cheap Fender copy to me.'

Robert looked closely at the guitar again and said, 'Yes, I think you're probably right. Are you sure you know what you are doing with this?' He gestured around. 'The antiques we've been buying look like they are actually worth the money. This memorabilia is only worth something because of its' association. And that feels a bit dodgy to me.'

'Correct. So we have to be even more careful to make sure we don't buy anything that we then regret. So, if we buy anything, it's going to be from a mainstream artist and will be fully documented and authenticated. If there's nothing here that fits the bill, we'll leave it.'

They continued walking up and down the rows of auction lots. Many of the objects were obscure and so were the names of the people who had owned, used or signed them.

'If Kate was here, she would probably know who some of these people are, or were,' said Robert as he circled a glass case contained a palette and brushes which were still covered in paint. He read the card. It said that these had belonged to Frank Bramley, 1857-1915.

They moved to where the literary-related lots were on display. Kevin ignored the lower valued items and sought-out the lots with the highest guide price. He motioned to Robert.

'What do you think of this?'

Robert joined him and peered inside the glass cabinet where Kevin was pointing. As the book inside revolved around and revealed its cover, he could see it was a copy of Ian Fleming's Goldfinger. According to the card, it was a first edition signed by the author. It was fully authenticated with certificates and a photo of the author signing the book at his Goldeneye estate in Jamaica in 1958. The guide price was twenty thousand pounds.

Kevin made some notes in his catalogue.

'Fantastic book. Right, I've seen enough. Have you? If so, let's get something to eat.'

The auctioneer opened the bidding on the book at ten thousand. There was an initial reluctance to bid so he took a starting bid off the wall and it quickly escalated to eighteen thousand. It slowed again. Still Kevin had not placed a bid.

'What are you waiting for? Want me to do it?' whispered Robert.

'No, it's okay. I'm just biding my time.'

'Well if you wait much longer you'll miss it.'

The bidding moved on the nineteen thousand and five hundred. The auctioneer said he would accept a bid of two-fifty more. He glanced over to the phone bidders who were stood to his left. One of them mouthed a figure to him. Then he announced that there was a telephone bid of twenty-two thousand. He asked if there were any more bids, advised that it was going once, twice then Kevin put his hand up and signalled.

'The auctioneer acknowledged his bid by pointing in his direction, 'New blood at the back. Twenty-five thousand I'm bid. Any advance on twenty-five?' The phone bidder nodded. Kevin responded. Robert tugged his arm.

'Steady on.'

It was with Kevin at twenty-seven thousand. The person on the phone was frantically talking to the unknown bidder at the other end of the line and then motioned a bid of thirty thousand. Kevin bid thirty-two. He was out-bid at thirty-five. He bid forty thousand. There was a gasp. Everyone turned and looked at him. Robert just smiled back at them. The phone bidder was talking quietly now on the phone. Kevin willed the auctioneer to end the auction. The phone bidder shook her head. 'Going once, fair warning, going twice. Sold to the man at the back for forty thousand pounds. Well done sir.' There was even a ripple of appreciative applause before the auctioneer carried on with the next lot.

Travelling back to the flat Kevin was thinking about how he could re-auction the book and still make a profit. There was a film memorabilia sale coming up shortly. He would research collectors and have a look at the American market. He felt sure it would sell. It was just a question of finding the right buyer.

Robert was contemplating whether to congratulate Kevin or call him reckless. Forty thousand pounds for a book! Twice the guide price. And it's not even as if this was a really old book. He'd had a copy of this book himself when he was younger, although it obviously wasn't a signed first edition. He couldn't decide, so he turned the radio on to listen to the news. After detailing the days events including more flooding in Devon and the resignation of a senior Labour MP 'to spend more time with his family' after some allegations concerning his sexual proclivities emerged, the news presenter announced that the National Standard Bank had been taken over by the American Municipal.

'Isn't that the bank where Sylvia works?' Asked Robert. Kevin clamped his jaws together and didn't reply.

Chapter 39

The huge pile of ironing was eating away at Anne. She knew if she left it, her mother would do it but somehow she felt that it was her way of contributing to her parents for her keep as they had continually refused her offers of money. They were out for the day at a craft fair in Harrogate so Anne had the house to herself. She carried the ironing board into the kitchen and erected it carefully so should reach the ironing pile on the side and still see the television in the corner.

She started with her father's shirts. She ironed the back first, and then the front. She took extra care with the sleeves, just as her mother did, to get neat creases in them just the way her father liked them. When she had finished the shirts she started on the next pile, which was mostly made up of her own clothes. She glanced up at the clock on the wall. She'd been ironing for nearly an hour. She decided to stop for a break and to watch the news, with a cup of tea.

She dropped a teabag into a mug which said 'Keep Calm and Drink Tea' on the side and was just pouring the water in when she jerked her head up as she heard Kevin's name mentioned on the television. She put the kettle down before she spilt any more water and looked across at the television. She saw a throng of people with Kevin in the centre. He was turning away from the camera. Another man was holding his hand up to shield his face. It was something to do with a record price for a modern book at auction. The news then switched to another topic.

Anne got out her phone and went online looking for a reference to the news item. She found it. In the last few days, there had been a controversial announcement about the re-making of the Bond film, Goldfinger. This had caused huge interest in everything to do with the new film and at a film memorabilia auction in London, a first edition of the original novel signed by Ian Fleming, the author, had just sold at auction for a record amount, fifty-seven thousand pounds. The buyer was a collector from Cheshire who wished to remain anonymous, although the report suggested that it might be a well-known footballer. The seller was Kevin Walker of Enterprise Antiques of London.

Anne sent him a text. *'Hi. Just seen U on TV. Call me. A x'*

Kevin's phone had not stopped ringing all morning. The calls were from other dealers to congratulate him. Everyone loves a winner. He even had a text from Anne, which he ignored. Peter, his boss had been giving him strange looks ever since he got in. Obviously he'd seen or heard the news too. Eventually, when he heard Kevin's phone sound again, he called him into the office.

'Is this true?' he asked, 'That you've just sold a book for a record amount.'

Kevin was really beginning to wish that he had stuck to antiques.

'Yes. It was a bit of an accident really. I bought a book at auction, with my own money and then when I sold it again at the next auction, it seems to have sold for rather more than I expected. Maybe the auctioneer knew that it was going to do well and alerted the press.'

'Fifty-seven thousand pounds, I heard?'

Kevin stretched his neck and ran his finger round the inside of his collar. 'I didn't expect it to fetch that much. Really. It's just all the publicity about the new film they are making just pushed the price right up. I had no idea it was going to happen. I'm sorry if it's caused any embarrassment.'

'It's not embarrassment, Kevin. It's just that I've noticed that you've been spending quite a lot of time away from the showroom recently. I don't really feel that your mind is on your job any more.'

'I'm sorry you feel that way, Peter. I really am.'

'Enterprise Antiques? What's that?

Kevin's heart sank. He knew what was coming next.

'I have been doing a bit of buying and selling in my spare time. It's the name I've been using.'

'So, you've been using your position here to further your own private business.'

'No. Not exactly. Look. Do you want me to resign?'

'I didn't yesterday, or last week. But yes, I do today. I'm sorry Kevin. I've been pleased with your work here but I feel there may be a conflict of interest and I'm not sure that I can fully trust you any more. I don't know if you are working for me, or for yourself.'

'In that case, I'd better leave. I'm sorry I let you down.'

Kevin packed up his few possessions and left. As he walked back to the flat he felt flat. Peter had given him a chance and he had thrown it back in his face. He was not proud of himself, despite the profit. He knew that he was not going to be working for Peter forever, but he was sad that it ended so abruptly. He had always tried to maintain a sense of pride in his work and loyalty to his employer. To be leaving under such circumstances didn't feel right. It wasn't all that long since he had walked away from the insurance company and now, a few months later, it was happening again. His phone rang. It was Sylvia.

'We need to talk.'

'Yes, we do. Shall I come to your place?'

'Okay. See you later.'

Kevin ended the call and looked up at the sky. He felt that there should be gathering storm clouds but actually the sky was clear and blue.

Chapter 40

'Villa nr Nice 1 week just £299 each in 2 weeks time. Last minute deal. Fancy it? Let me know. K8 x'

Robert texted Kate back without hesitation. He could do with a bit of sunshine.

'Yes. Book it. R x'

The reply came back twenty minutes later *'Brill. Done it. Can't Wait x'*

He sent a text to Kevin. *'Have booked 1 wk holiday in 2 weeks time 4 me & Kate, ok?'*

Kevin read the text and checked the diary. It was clear. There were no sales taking place that week that they had planned to attend. He texted back that it was fine. Holidays. The last time he had been on holiday was with Anne. Then he remembered her text. He scrolled through the texts and there it was. 'Call me' it said. He didn't really feel up to calling her so decided to leave it until later.

He spent the morning phoning round the auction houses updating the postal address to his flat for future catalogues. Without the job, Kevin was aware that he would now have more time to devote to the business of laundering the twenty-five thousand pounds that was arriving in the payout account every day, but somehow the buzz that he felt while juggling the job and the bank venture had diminished now the job was gone. Something illogical in his mind told him it wasn't entirely illegal while he was regularly employed at the same time. Now he had to accept that he was a full-time crook and it did not make him feel good.

Kevin moped around the flat for a while, checking

the eBay sales and the spreadsheets. Eventually, he texted Robert,

Where are u?

Robert texted back, '*Bonhams, Knightsbridge. Will be back about 6 pm*'

'*Mind if I join you?*'

'*Absolutely fine - But let me do the bidding this time okay?*'

Kevin smiled and texted back, '*Sure. Be with you shortly.*'

Just before he left he decided to call Anne after all. After three rings she answered.

'Hi, Anne. It's me, Kevin. You asked me to call you.'

'Ah, hello Mr Big Shot. Nice of you to spare the time to call me at last. I suppose it must be nice to be on the TV just because you've made a huge profit.'

He was shocked by her change in tone.

'Anne, that's not exactly how it was ..'

Anne interrupted 'Hopefully, you are aware that, as we haven't had the decree absolute yet, that profit will be forming part of your total assets. And any other money that you've hidden away recently. In case you had forgotten, I'm still your wife so legally I believe I am entitled to at least half of everything you have. And I'll be wanting half of your future income too.'

'Now hang on, I thought we had agreed on the finances already.'

'But that was before you started raking it in and making a name for yourself on television. Perhaps you should have thought of that when I suggested that we might try again. You'll be hearing from my solicitor. Bye.'

Then she was gone and Kevin was still holding the phone to his head. He swore through gritted teeth, clicked it off and thrust it into his pocket. Grabbing his jacket from the hook on the back of the door he left the flat and took a taxi to Bonham's.

Robert glanced to his left and saw Kevin making his way towards him with two coffees held out in front of him. Robert took one.

'So, why the interest in this sale?'

'It's not so much the sale. Just wanted to get out of the flat. Had an uncomfortable talk with Anne. She saw us on TV. And now she wants more money. Half of everything I have, and half of whatever I may have in the future. Which could be awkward.' Kevin looked worried.

'Can she do that? What are you going to do?'

'Don't know yet. I'll call her again when she has calmed down a bit and see if I can reason with her. I don't mind giving her what's left of the house profits, but I really do resent giving her any more.'

'It's unlikely that my ex, Janice, would have seen me on the TV. It was on the news. If it's not a soap or reality programme it wouldn't interest her. Watch out, this is the lot we're after. Better concentrate.'

Kevin watched while Robert handled the bidding. He got the item of jewellery at two hundred and seventy-five pounds less than the guide price figure.

'Well done,' said Kevin. His mood seemed to have lifted somewhat. He told Robert that there was an Art Nouveau collector in Brussels who would almost certainly be interested in the bracelet and that he would contact her when they got back.

They settled the payment, collected the bracelet and made their way out of the auction house. On the way back to the flat Robert suggested they stop at The Crown & Garter for a pint. The call from Anne had obviously unsettled Kevin who was normally so calm and composed. He wanted to make sure that Kevin was okay before he went away with Kate.

As Kevin handed Robert his pint of bitter he said, 'So you're off on holiday?'

'Yes. Kate got a last minute deal. It's a villa near Nice apparently. She booked it so I don't know any more than that really.'

'Sounds lovely. Wish I could get away. Since I left the saleroom, it's just not the same. And that call from Anne didn't help.'

Robert saw a way to lift Kevin's mood. 'Why don't you come too? Bring Sylvia. It would be great!'

'Oh, I don't know. Can we afford to be away at the same time?'

'Bring the laptops and we're as good as being here.'

'Actually, it's very tempting. I haven't had a holiday for ages. Need to speak to Sylvia though. I'm seeing her tonight. I'll ask her then. Are you really sure that you want us there too? Won't it cramp your style?'

'It'll be much better if we all go. I'm certain. I'll get Kate to check with the travel agent.'

They returned to the flat. Kevin got changed and went off to see Sylvia. Robert rang Kate.

'Hi, Kate.'

'Hiya Robert. I'm so excited! I'm so glad you said yes to the holiday. I'm really looking forward to it already. I've been sorting through my clothes.' And then a little less enthusiastically ' Got to earn some money though, to pay for it.'

'Don't worry about the money. I'll cover it. We've had a good week in the antiques business. Out of interest, how would you feel if Kevin and Sylvia came too?'

'Brilliant. The more the merrier. Sylvia will never take the time off, though. I don't think she's had a holiday for years. She takes her work much too seriously in my view.'

'We'll see. Can you check with the agent if they can add two more in case she can make it? We can confirm tomorrow as Kevin is seeing Sylvia right now. And when am I going to be seeing more of you?'

'I think you've seen pretty much all of me already,' said Kate mischievously.

Chapter 41

Up in Stranraer, Kevin had also been seen on the news. The novelty of the Ducati motorbike bought with the money he had brought back from London was beginning to wear off and Mitch was down to his last few hundred pounds.

The gang had assembled in the small wood-panelled snug bar at the Ferryboat Inn. Monkey was decked out in his new mod-style clobber and brandishing a recently purchased smartphone. Jimmy was looking forward to the fortnight's holiday he had booked in Tenerife. Ralph's car had been fitted with a fancy new set of chrome Wolfrace cup wheels and new tyres. Charlie had repaid his Mum the money he borrowed to buy an eternity ring for his girlfriend who had ditched him days later but kept the ring. They were now looking to Mitch to provide their next earning opportunity.

'So when's the next job Mitch?' said Ralph

'Quiet. I'm thinking' replied Mitch. He was running his hand over his shaved scalp, backwards and forwards. The gang all glanced at each other and then looked down into their drinks. No-one wanted to break Mitch's concentration and incur his wrath.

After enough time had elapsed for Charlie to silently finish his pint and stare at the frothy dregs at the bottom of his glass for a minute, Mitch stood up and took his place by the window. He looked out at the wet street for a few moments and then said, 'I think we need to re-visit our friends in the South. They promised us another job and it's about time they delivered. From what we all saw on the news, it seems to me that they've just come into some more cash and I think it's up to us to help them distribute it. So pack your bags lads, we're off to London again.'

A week later they met up in the pub car park and loaded their bags into Ralph's car.

'Cool wheels, Ralph,' said Jimmy and he kicked the tyre before getting in the car and sliding across the back seat. Ralph was pleased that someone had noticed. Charlie and Monkey joined Jimmy in the back. Mitch positioned himself in the front passenger seat.

'Let's go.'

The long drive to London was uneventful. Ralph drove steadily. Monkey spent most of the journey fiddling with his phone while the other two either watched him, or slept. Mitch kept his eyes firmly fixed on the road ahead, planning what he was going to say to Kevin and Robert when he located them. They stopped twice along the route for petrol, sandwiches and to use the toilets. As they reached the outskirts of London, Mitch texted Robert.

It's been a while, old friend. Thought it's about time we visited.

Chapter 42

Sylvia browsed her music collection. She pulled out her current favourite which was the new album by Adele. She wanted to choose the right music for the mood and something that Kevin would appreciate. So she pushed the Adele cd back and slid out a Van Morrison instead. Then she changed her mind again and chose UB40. No, that was too Kevin. She settled on Jack Johnson. Whilst all her friends had their music as mp3's stored on various devices, she preferred her music on cd. She realised that it was old-fashioned, but she didn't care. The cd started playing 'Better Together'. She turned the volume up and after pouring herself a glass of wine, she went into the bedroom to get changed.

By the time Kevin arrived Sylvia had tried on four different dresses. Too formal. Too dinner party. Too sleazy. Too long. She had also tried on her smock top and faded jeans. Too scruffy. Just as he was ringing on the door entry system, she pulled on her new black designer jeans and a short cream cashmere top.

Sylvia knew she's made the right choice as soon as he entered, as she felt his hand slide down onto her bottom as they hugged in the hallway. She wriggled out of his clutches for long enough to put the flowers he had brought into a vase and to put the wine into the fridge. Then she went back to him as he was standing looking at her cd collection and put her arms around him and kissed him on the back of the neck.

'I'm so glad you are here. It's been a difficult week.'

He turned round to face her and brushed her hair

back off her face.

'Same here', he said 'We could both do with getting away for a while.'

'That would be nice.' Said Sylvia as she sat down on the sofa, tapping the space beside her for him to join her.

'Robert and Kate have booked something in a weeks time actually. I was wondering if you'd like to join them.'

Thinking of the current chaos at work Sylvia said, 'I doubt I'd be able to get time off at such short notice.' Then she thought of Brian's words about getting another job fast. And the fact that she had four weeks holiday owing to her. She added 'But who cares any more. You know we're being taken over at work?'

'Yes. I heard about that on the radio. What are the implications of that? Do you know?'

Sylvia went over to the kitchen area and poured them both a glass of wine. She placed them on the table between the two sofas.

'It's shit. The Yanks will take over everything we are doing so it's likely the whole department will go. Everybody is looking for new jobs. Even Brian, my boss.'

'How does that leave our venture?'

'I've been thinking about that. How much have we accrued now?'

'Last time I checked which was a couple of days ago there was about three hundred and twenty thousand in each of our accounts. There is still about a hundred and eighty thousand in stock waiting to be sold so when that's gone we are looking at about three hundred and eighty thousand each so far.'

'Right'. Sylvia went quiet.

'What are you thinking about?'

'Well, we're not even halfway to our target figure yet. The speed with which events are unfolding at the bank means we may not be able to get there if we don't change something.'

'Why don't we just stop now? It's not a bad amount.'

Sylvia twisted round and faced him. 'It's not enough Kevin. And it's in the rules. We said we'd stop at a million each.'

Kevin was mildly surprised at her determined expression. 'Yes, but that was before all this stuff at the bank, and the TV stuff too.'

'I was going to ask you about that. What happened?'

'It was a mistake really. To speed things up, we tried to branch out from the usual type of antiques into memorabilia and bought the Bond book. It's just a coincidence that the new film is going to be Goldfinger. I never expected there to be TV cameras at the sale. It cost me my job too. My boss Peter didn't like the fact that I was 'moonlighting'. I am sorry about all that. But we did make a healthy profit.'

Kevin wanted to tell her about Anne too. But he felt he didn't want to impart too much bad news in one go. Similarly, Sylvia had failed to mention the accounts where the missing interest had been queried.

Sylvia thought for a moment and then replied, 'It's too late for being sorry now. We need to limit the damage by moving quicker.'

'I'm not sure we can shift stock any quicker than we already are doing. Robert and I are on it full-time now. The money is still coming in faster than we can spend it.'

'I was thinking of amending the system so it diverts some or all of the money to some offshore bank accounts. Then it reduces the need to launder it here'.

Kevin took a moment to let that sink in. He didn't fully understand the implications of it. Before he had chance to respond Sylvia said, 'And to accumulate the million each quicker I thinking we'll need to take more out of the accounts than we are at the moment. In some cases that will mean cleaning them out completely, particularly the older ones. The Government is currently taking the money if the account has been dormant for fifteen years or so. I think we can justify removing it first to stop the Government getting its' hands on it. Remember, an account is only dormant while nothing happens to it. As soon as any kind of activity goes on it ceases to be dormant.'

Kevin's first reaction was to point out that it was still theft. But he reminded himself that stealing just the interest, or the interest plus part of the lump sum, or all of the money in the account, was pretty much the same crime. He supposed the end result was the same and doubted if any prosecution lawyer would appreciate the subtle difference that Kevin Walker felt.

'I'm not sure,' was all he could say.

'Here's an idea then. Let's go away on holiday with Kate and Robert. While we are away I'll reset all the systems so the interest is restored and nothing is being moved into our accounts. It will give us a chance to reflect and agree what to do next. Naturally, we mustn't let Kate get wind of any of this.'

Kevin was relieved. He needed a while to get his head around all of this. He didn't like it when events moved faster than he could keep up. He needed to feel in control.

'I like the sound of that. Let me text Robert now.'

'We're on for the holiday if Kate can book us in. Kev.'

Chapter 43

Robert read the text from Mitch once more. '*Thought it's about time we visited*'. This was just what he needed right now. He tried to think if he or Kevin had given any indication of where they lived or how they could be found. As far as he knew they hadn't. Could Mitch and his gang find them any other way? He racked his brain, trying to think of other ways they could track them down but he was as sure as he could be that they didn't know the address and so wouldn't be able to locate them. But he couldn't be certain.

Obviously the brief appearance on TV hadn't helped but he decided it was unlikely that they would have seen it. He tried to relax, but his mind kept being drawn back to the text. He was trying to decide if was sent with menace. Was it a threat? He couldn't tell. On the other hand, why would they come all the way from Scotland without knowing where they were going? Robert thought it through. Then it struck him that it had been several weeks since Kevin handed over the money and that it was probably running low now, so the gang would be after more.

The '*old friend*' bit puzzled him. He had never considered Mitch or any of the others in the gang as friends. Acquaintances yes, but not friends. Robert felt that there was something distinctly sinister in the use of that phrase.

He remembered how Kevin had told him that they might need the gang one day. Maybe Kevin had called them. Unlikely. He was sure that Kevin would have told him if he was thinking of getting Mitch and

Co. involved in anything.

It was a good job they had planned the holiday, as it was possible they all might be out of the country when they arrived. But even if they were, he'd seen how persistent and systematic Mitch could be.

He wondered whether to mention it to Kevin or not. He'd seen how Kevin behaved after the call from Anne and after the TV incident. It had obviously unnerved him. Another visit from the Scottish thugs would only add to his worries. They were leaving for the holiday in two days so they wouldn't be here when the gang arrived. But the problem wouldn't go away. It needed to be dealt with. Robert decided that he would handle this and spare Kevin any more grief. The gang had been paid off so they didn't really have a lever other than the vague promise of a job in the future. Robert reckoned that they had decided to pre-empt the request. Well, Robert would be ready for them.

He texted Mitch back.

'Looking forward to it. Meet in the usual place. Usual time. xx'

Two kisses. Love, hate, like, adore.

The next morning, Kevin went out to purchase a new camera to take on holiday. He had bought several camera magazines. After studying them all and reading the reviews, he had carefully weighed up the pros and cons and finally had selected a Nikon DSLR with HD video capability. He asked if Robert wanted to come with him to buy it from the camera store, but he declined, citing an errand he needed to do that morning. Robert waited until he heard Kevin leave then he went out to meet Mitch and his gang.

From his place buried within the gathering crowd, he watched them approach. As they got nearer, he emerged. Mitch spotted him straightaway.

'Come without your boyfriend this time have you?' said Mitch. They were all standing in exactly the same spot outside the Palace as before.

Robert ignored him. 'What do you want this time?'

'Me and your lover-boy had an agreement. Where is he anyway?'

'He's busy. What sort of an agreement? I can't imagine that you and he would agree on anything.'

'Well, that's where you're wrong. He told us he had a job for us.'

'Oh yes? Has he called you then? And told you all about it?'

'No. Not yet. We got tired of waiting. So here we are. You tell him we're here and he had better have a job for us.'

'As it happens we may have a job for you. If you'd like to step into my office we can discuss it.'

Robert was thinking on his feet now. He guided Mitch away from the rest of the gang and said, 'There may be a little matter that maybe you can help us with.'

'Go on.'

'It's worth two grand. Interested?'

'Mebbee. What is it?'

'It's quite simple really. I just want you to pay a visit to someone, have a quick chat and then be on your way. It's even on your way home. What do you say?'

'Two grand? Just for chatting to someone? Mitch was already splitting the money. Two-fifty each to the others and a grand for him.

'What's the catch?'

'No catch. And with your charming personality, it shouldn't be too difficult, should it?'

'You're a cheeky bastard, you know that, don't you?'

'That's why I'm so popular. Especially with the ladies,' said Robert. 'Now do we have a deal?'

'Add on the cost of the petrol, which I reckon is about another two fifty and you're on. Half now and half when it's done. And you better pay up or we'll be back down here in half a sparrow's fart. Who's the bloke we need to talk to? And what do you want us to tell him.'

'Actually, it's not a bloke. It's a woman. And I'll tell you exactly what I want to say when you are on your way there.'

Chapter 44

It wasn't quite like a blast from an oven, but the air was definitely pleasantly warm and dry as they descended the steps of the plane into the glaring sunshine at Nice airport.

Sylvia and Kate both put on their sunglasses as they walked from the plane to the airport terminal. Kevin had folded his linen jacket over his arm and Robert was wearing a baseball cap back to front.

At the car hire desk, Robert showed his driving licence to the girl in the Avis uniform. She studied it and wrote down some details before handing it back. She beckoned to Kevin but he just shook his head. She looked at Kate and Sylvia, but only Sylvia stepped forward with her licence. After completing the forms, the clerk gave them the keys and the paperwork.

As they walked towards the airport doors Robert nodded at the desk two up from the Avis one. It was for executive helicopter rides to Monaco directly from the airport.

'Maybe we'll take one of those next time.'

Kevin just smiled thinly. They made their way back out into the sunshine and walked to the parking bays.

'This is amazing!' exclaimed Kate. 'The sun. The heat. I can't wait to see the villa. It looked gorgeous on the website. With a pool, a maid and everything! I know it was more expensive than the one I originally booked but it looks stunning.'

The others smiled to see Kate so excited. It was infectious. Even Kevin began to relax. They all felt a bit like teenagers on their first trip away without their parents. The original villa, in the last-minute offer, would struggle to accommodate four so Robert had suggested to Kate that she ask the agent for something more suitable. She had come up trumps.

They found the car, a red Peugeot people carrier, and deposited their luggage in the back.

It took them about an hour to negotiate the winding hillside roads that surround the town of Nice. Eventually Kevin, who was navigating, announced, 'I think this is it.'

They drove down a long tree-lined driveway, which opened out into a spacious parking area with a tall palm tree in the centre, offering some shade to the parked car. The villa itself was hidden amongst more large palms and behind a series of arches covered with vivid red and violet climbing bougainvillea.

The key was hidden behind the flower-box as advised. They entered the villa through the heavy, solid wood front door covered in iron trim. They wandered through the interior, visiting all the rooms. There were two larger en-suite bedrooms, both with roof patios leading off them, two smaller bedrooms, a lounge area, kitchen, al fresco dining area, gardens with orange trees and an invitingly beautiful pool. Beyond the pool was the view. At the end of the view was the sea.

Sylvia walked to the far edge of the patio surrounding the pool. She stared out across the panorama looking towards the sea in the distance. Kevin joined her and put his arm around her waist.

'It's so beautiful, Kevin. Thank you so much for persuading me to come. I didn't realise just how much I needed a break. And now I'm here it's easy to imagine living here all the time. Look out there. It's a whole other world. If there was any doubt before surely you can now see why we are doing this. This is what it's all about. When it's all over I'm going to buy a villa like this, somewhere that's as beautiful as it is here.'

Kevin looked. And yes, he could see what she meant.

Before he could respond, there was a loud splash behind them. They turned to look. Robert had thrown off his clothes and launched himself into the pool. The next minute, Kate, dressed only in a tiny bikini came rushing down the steps from the bedroom they had chosen and started to step gingerly down the steps into the pool. Robert swam over and abruptly pulled her in. She squealed and fell into the water. She splashed him. He splashed her back.

'Come on Sylvia. It looks fun in there. Let's join them.'

* * *

That evening, they drove down to the town again, found a busy restaurant and spent the evening eating, drinking, talking and laughing.

The next day, while Kevin was out taking photographs with his new camera, Robert drove Sylvia to the supermarket so they could stock up on food, drink and other items. On their leisurely journey there, they passed old men with crates of fruit and vegetables strapped to ancient motorbikes and several roaming dogs. Sylvia opened the window of the car and let her arm drape outside feeling the air rushing through her fingers. She took in the smells and the sights and smiled dreamily. After a while, she said, 'How do you think it's all going,

Robert? I mean the money and the antiques and so on.'

Robert thought for a moment and then replied, 'It's all going fine at our end, apart from the TV thing and that was just an annoying coincidence. We're buying as much stuff as we can and we're moving it on quite quickly. We're even making a profit quite often. If the money stopped now I reckon we could just about make it as real antique dealers.'

Sylvia laughed 'And without the fake tans and bow ties too!'

'What about at the bank? How is it for you? And how is this takeover affecting things?'

Sylvia's face dropped a little as she thought about the situation back in London. 'It's not much fun at the moment. There's a lot of spin and confusion. Nobody knows what's going on. People are looking for other jobs. Some people in my department have already left. The Americans are being effusive about us but we know they're bloody ruthless, so things are bound to change. As far as our venture goes, it's not affecting it yet. If anything, it is making life easier in the short term as everyone is looking over their shoulder instead of at the systems.'

'So we're going to keep going, are we?'

Sylvia looked sharply across at Robert as he drove 'Yes, of course. Why on earth would you think otherwise?'

'Oh I just thought that maybe all the changes going on might have made you think about pulling out early, that's all.'

She laughed. 'No way. We're going to get our million each. Don't worry about that.' Then in a slightly more serious tone 'You haven't said anything to Kate, have you?'

'Of course not.'

'Good. Please keep it that way. I don't want her to think badly of me.'

They stopped at the supermarket and Sylvia's sense of humour returned as Robert chased her round the store with the trolley. She kept finding things in the trolley that she hadn't put in. As fast as she was putting the supplies in, she was having to remove the packets of figs, baby milk powder, light bulbs and even a tent that Robert had added.

'You are an idiot Robert.'

He just arched his eyebrows and picked up a large box containing a vacuum cleaner.

As they pushed the trolley to the hire car, Sylvia said, 'Do you think Kevin is okay? He's been quieter than usual recently.'

Robert contemplated whether to tell her about Anne and her threats about the divorce but decided that if Kevin hadn't told her then it wasn't his place to fill her in and anyway, the problem might have gone away as hopefully by now Anne will have decided to curtail her requests anyway. He also thought about Mitch and his visit. He had called him from the airport and given him the instructions.

In the end Robert said, 'I think Kevin was just a bit embarrassed about the TV thing and, of course, it cost him his job. From what I know of him Kevin is a really straight guy and having to resign just knocked his equilibrium a bit. To tell you the truth I suggested that you two come away with us as a way of cheering him up a bit.'

'I'm glad you did. I think we both needed a bit of a lift. And tell me, how's it going with Kate?'

The Laundrymen

Robert told her that Kate was the best thing that had happened to him in ages. 'She's so feisty, and I can be too, so it's inevitable that we are going to have some bust-ups but if you want to tell her I'm very keen, you can.'

'I think the feeling is mutual. I've known her a long time and I've not seen her like this in ages.'

In the afternoon, they went down to the beach. With much splashing, shouting and swearing, Robert and Kevin attempted to windsurf while Sylvia and Kate lay on the sun-loungers and read the novels they had bought at the airport. Later, a leisurely walk along the Promenades des Anglais, was followed by a few drinks in a street corner bar, before returning to the villa where Sylvia and Kate cooked up a delicious coq au vin. Kevin and Robert laid the table and poured the wine. They all dined outside in the warm evening listening to gentle music overlaid with the sound of cicadas. Underwater lighting lit up the pool, while strategically placed wall-lights cast shadows across the arches surrounding the villa.

'This is completely idyllic,' said Sylvia as she sat back with her wine. Kate murmured her agreement.

'What's the plan for tomorrow?' said Kevin.

'Chill out will you, Kevin? For once, let's not have a plan. We're on holiday. We're here to relax, so why don't we just see what the day brings?' said Kate.

Chapter 45

It was nine-thirty in the morning and the team from the client company was running a bit late but it allowed Anne and her colleagues more time to prepare the meeting room. The agency had been working on the first leg of the promotion that was planned for the summer. Today was the presentation of their proposals.

The mood in the agency was positive and up-beat, if a little frantic, as people rushed around with artwork and bits of technology. The tablet was connected to the projector. The projector was pointed at the screen. The images were blurry initially and then the focus and positioning were adjusted until a clear, sharp image appeared on the screen, of a ballet dancer dancing on the top of a mountain. Then it was all turned off again.

Anne made sure there were pens and notepads placed at every seat around the table. As she made her way round the table she nearly bumped into Lydia who was moving in the opposite direction placing glasses and bottles of water in groups at intervals along the table's length.

Lydia's phone rang. The visitors had arrived.

The presentation was a success. The marketing director of the feminine hygiene company was impressed by the ideas and wanted them finessed and progressed. The TV advert concept was also discussed. There were some questions about the budget that needed to be addressed. Could savings be made? But in principle it looked like it was all going ahead.

After the client left, Andy went round each department congratulating them on a job well done.

Anne was glowing with pride as she left the office that day. Even the thought of going back to her parent's house couldn't dampen her mood. She had recently found a flat to move into but the landlord had agreed to decorate it before she moved in. It would be ready in two weeks.

As Anne pulled turned into the drive she noticed the old car with ludicrously fancy chrome wheels parked in the road but she had no reason to be suspicious of it. She parked up and opened the back door to retrieve her bag and laptop when she spotted a large man with a shaved head and wearing a leather motorbike jacket, walking up the drive. He seemed out of place in this middle-class suburban road. She shut the car door and straightened up.

'Hello, can I help you?'

'I think it's us that can help you actually.' He gestured to Jimmy, Charlie, Ralph and Monkey who had assembled on the pavement at the end of the drive.

Anne looked at them briefly enough to decide that they constituted trouble and then addressed Mitch.

'Who are you? What do you want?'

'We just wanted to give you a bit of advice love. But not out here. Can we go inside?'

'No, you bloody can't. My parents are in there and I don't have a clue who you are or why you are here. I think you should leave now.'

Mitch said, 'I don't think you understand. I've got a message for you so if we can't go inside, you'll have to come with us.'

'I'm not going anywhere with you. Okay? And if you

don't leave right now I'm calling the police'. She started to root through her bag trying to find her phone without taking her eyes off Mitch. He stepped forward to take her arm. At that moment, there was a squeal of tyres and the gang all leapt out of the way of a blue Audi that sped up the drive. The door opened. The driver jumped out and stood between Anne and Mitch.

'Tom! Thank God you're here.' Anne moved closer to Tom.

'What's going on?' Tom shouted at Mitch.

'Who the fuck, are you?'

'It doesn't matter who I am. Who are you? And why are you bothering her?' nodding in Anne's direction. You should probably leave now.'

He turned to Anne and said, 'Are you alright? I was just coming over to see you. I've got some more of your things in the car. Are these people bothering you?'

Mitch interrupted. 'We've got a message to deliver and we're going to deliver it. She's coming with us, so I suggest you get lost. Understand?' Mitch reached out again to take Anne's wrist. The rest of the gang had gathered behind Mitch. The curtains twitched as Anne's parents had heard the shouting and were now watching the confrontation through the bay window.

Tom stepped forward and adopted a karate pose. The gang all looked at each other and sniggered. Mitch laughed and gestured for Charlie to come forward. Charlie didn't hesitate. He lurched forward and hit out at Tom who ducked. In return, Charlie received a vicious chop with Tom's foot to the neck. He staggered off across the garden and, tripping on the drive edging stones, fell into one of the bushes. In the window Anne's mother had her hand over her mouth, which was wide open with horror. Then it was Jimmy's turn. He managed to get a punch in before Tom bounced back off Anne's car and hit him solidly in the solar plexus. Jimmy doubled over and collapsed on the drive wheezing and coughing.

Ralph ran off to the car and started the engine. He knew that they would all need to leave in a hurry. He expected Mitch and the others to follow. Monkey was holding back. Mitch nodded to him. Monkey raised his fists and approached Tom. They circled around each other for a few seconds before Tom ran forwards, tucked his leg behind Monkey's tripping him up. With a cry, Monkey fell backwards onto the drive hitting his head on the ground with a loud crunch. He didn't move. Mitch and Tom stared at each other, each waiting for the other to make the first move. Then they looked back at Monkey. He moaned. Suddenly there was a glint of steel. Mitch held a knife out in front of him.

'I don't know who you are mate, but why don't you just get back in your car and piss off. We've got a bit of business to attend to with this woman and you are just getting in the way.'

Tom stood his ground. Then he started walking towards Mitch with his hands held ready. Mitch said, 'I'm warning you. Just leave. Now.'

Tom kept moving towards Mitch. Then he rushed at him. Mitch dodged sideways. As he did so the knife went into Tom's neck. Blood sprayed out. Anne screamed. Tom fell to his knees staring at Mitch. Mitch looked at his own hands now minus the knife. Anne's mother fainted. Anne's dad was already phoning the police. Mitch gathered himself quickly and retrieved the knife. He dragged Monkey, who had been slowly getting to his feet, to the car, looking back once. The others were already climbing in. Ralph floored the accelerator and they were gone.

Anne ran over to where Tom had now fallen on the drive. Blood was pouring out of the wound. She kneeled in the pool and cradled his head. She was crying and wailing at the same time. Tom's eyes were open. He looked shocked and surprised. Then his eyes shut and his head flopped off her lap, crunching onto the sodden gravel.

Chapter 46

Kate was casually caressing Robert's thigh as they lay on the sun-loungers by the pool. Her hand was gently moving up and down stroking his skin. They had all begun to relax now that they were a few days into their holiday. Instead of getting up early and rushing around to pack in as much as possible, Kate and Robert had stayed in bed until mid morning before getting up, moving outside and sunning themselves by the pool. Kevin and Sylvia were not around. Robert's phoned bleeped and vibrated. He ignored it.

'Sounds like a text, aren't you going to read it?'

'No. I'm on holiday.'

Robert continued to lie there with his eyes shut.

'Maybe it's important?'

Robert groaned and reached out for the phone. He sat up and put on his sunglasses to read the screen. Then he stiffened.

'What's wrong? Is it bad news?'

'No, it's okay. I'll be back in a sec.' Robert got up and went inside.

He re-read the text. It was from Mitch.

'Trouble with job. Call me.'

Robert replied,

'What sort of trouble?'

The reply came back thirty seconds later.

'Call Me.'

Robert shook his head and went back out to re-join Kate. She absent-mindedly reached out for him as he sat down.

'Everything alright?'

'There's a bit of a problem with one of the auction lots. I just need to make a phone call. The signal is better down the road so I'm just popping out for five minutes.' He kissed on her forehead as he left.

Robert walked out of the villa and along the drive. He turned right and walked for a while. All the time his imagination was on overdrive. What sort of trouble? Did they mess up the message? It was supposed to be just a gentle warning off, that pressure on Kevin could cause him to do something stupid to himself. That sort of thing. How could they have messed it up? He hoped that Mitch didn't threaten Anne. He had stressed that there was to be no come back for either of them.

He came to a clearing with a concrete bollard. He sat on it and rang Mitch.

'It's me. You said trouble. What went wrong?'

'You never told us she had protection?'

'What do you mean protection? She shouldn't need protection? You didn't threaten her did you? I told you it was to be just a gentle chat.'

'That's what it was going to be then some bloke turned up and it got a bit ugly.'

'Ugly? Jesus. What happened?'

'He got stabbed.'

'What? Who got stabbed? What are you talking about?' As he spoke Robert's heart was sinking.

'I'm not sure but I think he may be dead. We had to get out of there in a bit of a hurry, so I'm not really sure what happened to him.'

Robert's mind was whirling. Dead? He couldn't take it in.

'Who was it? What was he doing there?'

'She knew him. Called him Tom. He just appeared in his car and went for me. Had to defend myself.'

'With a knife?'

'Yeah. Well, he was pretty handy with the karate. I had to stop him. It was self-defence,' he said lamely.

'Jesus Christ, Mitch! What a complete fuck-up. Was this after you delivered the message?'

'I tried, but he just kept shouting.'

'So what did you manage to say to her?'

'Nothing. As soon as we got there he appeared. After he, erm .. Well after it happened, we just drove off quick.'

'Did they get the car registration?'

'Don't think so. But I've told Ralph to remove the plates and dump the car anyway. He's a bit pissed off as he's just bought new wheels for it.'

'Fuck the bleeding wheels, Mitch! You screwed this up. I knew I should have talked to her myself. I can't believe you killed him. Are you sure he's dead?'

'Looked pretty sick to me. Blood everywhere.'

'Where are you now?'

'Back home. Look, when Ralph has dumped the car, there's nothing to connect us. But I still want the money, and Ralph needs another motor.'

'You've got a fucking nerve, Mitch.'

'You wouldn't want her to find out who ordered us to go there would you? And your boyfriend wouldn't want his name in the frame either would he? Just send the rest of the money, plus another grand to replace the car, and we'll keep quiet.'

'There's no proof that I was anything to do with this or Kevin for that matter.'

'Well, you can tell your lover-boy, Kevin, his secret is safe with us. As long as we get our money.'

'You'll get your money. But then I don't want to hear from you ever again. You open your mouth to anyone about this and I won't rest until I've tracked you down and made sure you never walk again. I mean it. Do you hear me?'

'Just send the fucking money.'

Robert sat with his head in his hands. A car pulled up. He looked up. It was Kevin and Sylvia back from the boulangerie. Sylvia was at the wheel. He gathered himself.

'Warm croissants!' Want some?' said Sylvia.

Robert forced a smile and climbed into the back of the car as they drove up the road and into the drive. All the time his thoughts were racing.

After dinner that evening, Kevin and Robert retired to the table by the pool for a beer. After half an hour, Sylvia joined them.

'Kate is spark out.' She looked at Robert with a smile. 'Don't know what you two have been up, to but she looks totally exhausted.'

Robert just raised the eyebrows.

'I thought we might just update each other while Kate's not around. Is that okay?'

'Sure,' said Kevin.

Sylvia kept her voice down then outlined her plan to Robert to move some of the money into offshore bank accounts. She also told him about the idea of taking more of the money in the dormant accounts as well as the interest.

Robert looked dubious.

'Isn't there a chance that people will notice the money is missing?'

'Remember these accounts are dormant Robert. No-one has used them in years. We were only touching the really old accounts. Now we're looking at younger ones but we're still only looking at accounts that have had no activity for seven years or more. And once we've reached our target we'll stop. So it's only for a matter of weeks now. Plus I've covered our tracks with a whole series of interlinked accounts. It would take someone with a lot of skill

The Laundrymen

and several weeks to follow the path. I think the risks are acceptable.'

'What do you think Kevin? Presumably you've already discussed this with Sylvia?'

'We did talk about it but we wanted to run it past you before we did anything. I'm not sure but I think I'm moving towards it just so we can finish it quicker. I worry about Sylvia being in the middle of it, especially with the takeover going on.'

'Actually, that's another reason for needing to speed it up. I'm not sure how long my job there is going to last.'

Kevin gave Sylvia a sideways glance. That was news to him.

'Okay,' said Robert 'Let's do it.'

'Let's do what?' said Kate who had emerged, bleary eyed from the villa. She was pulling on a hoodie as she walked. 'What are we going to do?'

'We're going to have another drink', said Robert, getting up and collecting the empty glasses and bottles. 'What would you like?'

The next day Robert went with Kevin down to the beach. Kevin wanted to take some photos. Kevin was taking typical tourist pictures so Robert acted as art director, pointing out looking around for interesting angles and moving things around to create a better image. Having captured a few images of rocks, waves and scenery, they sat down on a wall by the beach.

Kevin took a picture of the sweeping beach and then put the camera down.

'There's something you need to know Kevin.'

'What?' He had just seen an old dusty car parking up amongst the much newer ones on the side of the road. He picked up the camera, peered through the viewfinder and followed the car, finger hovering over the button.

'Listen, Kevin. Put the camera down. I'll just tell you straight, then you can go mad at me.'

Now he had Kevin's interest. He lowered the camera and paid attention.

'You know how Anne was giving you a hard time about the money?'

'Yes? What about it?'

'Well I thought it was having a negative effect on you so I had a word with Mitch about it and - '

Kevin interrupted 'Mitch? Why would you want to talk to him? I thought we'd sorted it all out with him?'

'So did I. But he came back wanting more. He said you'd offered to get him to do a job in the future. He just turned up to collect. So I thought I could pay him off and get Anne off your back too. Sort of two birds with one stone ..'

'I've got a very bad feeling about this, Robert.'

'Unfortunately you haven't heard the worst of it yet. I asked him to talk to Anne to tell her to back off.'

Kevin stood up and started waving his arms around. 'What? You idiot! He's the last person you should have asked. And it's my business anyway. It's nothing to do with you, or Mitch.'

'Look just calm down and let me tell you first. Then go mad okay? Sit back down, please.'

Kevin sat down again, but his knee was jumping up and down like a jackhammer while he waited to hear what could be worse than Mitch talking to Anne.

'They went to Anne's. Mitch and his crew. Before they could tell her anything, they said that some bloke called Tom arrived. I'm guessing he's the guy you told us about. The guy that Anne went off with. Anyway, there was a fight and Tom got stabbed.' Robert took a deep breath. 'He may be dead.'

Kevin looked incredulous. After a few seconds, it began to sink in.

'What? Dead? I don't believe I'm hearing this.'

'Listen, Kevin, I never meant any of this to happen. I was just trying to help. I had no idea they would mess it up like this.'

'Jesus, Robert. What were you thinking? I can't believe you did this. I've got no reason to like the little shit. But dead? Oh God. Fuck. Fuck. Fuck! That's screwed everything up. We might as well give ourselves up now.'

'You've got every right to be angry. I'm a complete and utter twat. I just didn't think it through. But it's happened and now we've got to deal with it.

'Are you absolutely sure he's dead?'

'No, but Mitch is pretty sure he was. He said he stabbed him and there was blood everywhere. If it's any consolation he doesn't think they got the car registration and the car has been destroyed anyway. Christ, I'm really sorry Kevin.'

They sat in silence for a while. Then Kevin picked up the camera and stood up.

'Come on. The holiday's over. We're going back. We've got stuff to do.'

Chapter 47

Amidst a cacophony of wailing sirens, two paramedics arrived rapidly on motorbikes at the same time as several police cars. Within minutes, the whole area was awash with flashing blue lights, and fluorescent jackets. Anne's father had stayed on the line after calling the police. When Tom fell forward he shouted that they had better bring an ambulance too.

The medical team moved fast and worked on Tom. A policewoman led Anne back into the house. As she looked back she saw them pumping his chest. The ambulance arrived moments later and pulled onto the drive. Neighbours came out of their houses and watched intently from their drives.

Machines were rushed out of the ambulance and hitched up to Tom's body. Lines were inserted, an oxygen mask attached. Eventually, he was placed on a stretcher and the ambulance pulled away hastily with a police escort and more sirens.

Tape incident barriers were placed around the area, blocking off part of the road and several policemen efficiently erected a police tent over the dark stain on the drive where Tom's body had fallen. Police photographers and forensic experts carried out their work well into the evening.

Police officers took initial statements from Anne and her parents and radioed back any relevant information. They asked about the gang and the car. She told them the car had fancy wheels and was grey or was it silver? Maybe, dark green. She couldn't be sure. She didn't know what model it was. It was dusk and she wasn't paying much attention. She described Mitch as about six foot with a shaved head, and he wore a motorcycle jacket. She couldn't remember much more. She told the police there were four others with him but when asked what they looked like she drew a blank. Just men, she said. Her parents couldn't add much either, as they had been further away inside the house and their view was obscured by Anne's car.

After a few hours the police withdrew, leaving a lone policeman on guard outside the house overnight. Anne's parents enveloped her in their arms and they all cried together.

The police were back early in the morning. Anne had woken up thinking it had all been a bad dream only to find three police, two men in suits and one woman in uniform with her hat neatly placed by her side, sitting in the lounge drinking tea.

After introducing themselves, one of the men said, 'Sorry about the early start, Anne. We just wanted to go through the information you gave us last night again, please. We know it's an ordeal for you but we need to get a clear picture of the events while it's still fresh in your mind.'

They asked her the same questions as they asked her the previous night and some extra ones. Did she have any idea why these men might have come round? Did they attempt to steal anything? Did she have any enemies? Did Tom have any enemies? What was her relationship with Tom? Had they had a row or fallen out? Why was he there?

Anne answered as best she could. She was still in shock so her answers were monosyllabic. The police were used to this. The needed a picture fast so they could act quickly before the trail went cold.

After two hours, there was a break in the questioning so Anne asked how Tom was doing. They agreed to take her to the hospital. On the way there Anne stared out of the window. Her father was sitting next to her holding her hand. It's odd, she thought, how when it all turns to shit, it's always your family who is there for you. She pitied people who had no family. Who did they turn to? She kept thinking about Tom. She was trying to remember what he had said. Something about things in the car. Then it dawned on her. He had come over to bring the rest of her stuff. He was sealing off the end of their relationship. And yet he had defended her. And it may have cost him his life. Was it bravery? Or gallantry? Or just machismo? Maybe he did care about her after all. She may never know.

She squeezed her dad's hand. At least there was one man in her life who had never let her down. Yes, they'd had all the rows that fathers and daughters have but at the end of the day she knew he loved her. It was a love that had real meaning and consistency, unlike the other men in her life. She thought of Kevin. She could see his easy-going, smiling face. Had he ever really loved her? He obviously didn't now. He'd probably be pleased that Tom was in hospital. She stopped that thought. No, he wouldn't. Whilst he might have every right to loath Tom, he wasn't the sort of person to wish ill on another.

At the hospital, before she was allowed to see Tom, and after the police had briefly explained who she was and that she was present at the incident, she was taken to meet the doctor who had treated him.

He explained that Tom had lost a lot of blood. His heart had stopped more than once on the way to the hospital. He had been revived each time. Now he was in a medically-induced coma. She could stay for five minutes with him as the intensive care staff needed to monitor him closely. As Anne turned to leave the doctor said.

'He's stable at the moment but in a severely critical condition. He may not pull through. You had better prepare yourself.'

Anne edged into the room and peered at the bed in the centre. In amongst the tubes and machines Tom's body was lying still. As she approached him one of the police guards in the room stepped forward to stop her getting any closer.

The police woman whispered in her ear that, until further notice, everyone at the incident had to be treated as a potential suspect as well as a witness and that they were just doing their job.

Anne stared at Tom for a minute or two. She spoke his name, softly at first and then louder. There was no response. Then she asked if she could leave. She was driven to the police station where she and her father had to make formal statements. They were asked if they wanted legal representation but both declined.

Eventually, they were allowed to return home. As they arrived at the house there was a huddle of press photographers and journalists waiting. Flashguns flashed and questions were shouted out as they drove up the drive and hurried into the house where Anne's mother had drawn all the curtains.

Chapter 48

Kate and Sylvia noticed the change in mood. They assumed that Kevin and Robert had had a disagreement. They didn't pry and went shopping instead with Sylvia footing the bill for most of it.

Bags were packed and the car was loaded up quickly and efficiently. It was as if Kevin and Robert couldn't wait to get back. When they collected their cases at the baggage reclaim area Sylvia and Kate didn't need telling that the holiday was over. Kevin was already calling people on his mobile and checking the results of sales while they had been away.

Kate was waved off at the station. Sylvia drove back from the airport and dropped Kevin and Robert off. Kevin apologised for being a bit quiet towards the end of the holiday explaining that he had got a lot on his mind. Although she was a bit cross with him for being so moody, Sylvia said it was fine and that she would call him in a couple of days. She drove off.

As soon as they got into the flat Kevin said, 'We need to find out whether Tom is dead.'

'What do you suggest?'

'I'm going to call Anne. She'll be expecting me to call to try and iron out the money situation.'

'But what if she thinks what happened to Tom had something to do with you?'

'Best to find out now.'

Robert wasn't so sure. He bitterly regretted involving Mitch, but it was too late for regrets. They needed to take action to limit the damage.

'Is there anything I can do?' offered Robert.

'You can get some food in. There's nothing in the fridge or cupboards.'

Robert shrugged and went out to the shops. Kevin rang Anne's mobile. She answered, 'Hello'

'Hi, it's Kevin.'

'Oh, Kevin. It's good to hear from you.'

'Why's that? Last time we spoke you sounded like you wished me dead.'

'Don't mention death. Tom has been stabbed. He might die.'

'What? Really? What happened?'

Anne told him. It was clear from the way she described the events that she had not connected it with him or Robert. Just to be absolutely sure he asked her if she knew why the gang had arrived at her house. She said the police kept asking her the same question. She told him, as she had repeatedly told the police, she had no idea why they came. She said that one of them had said something about a message but Tom had launched into them before she found out what the message was. Kevin said maybe it was something to do with work. Anne thought for a moment and told him it was possible but she thought it was unlikely.

'And how is Tom?'

'He's in a coma. The doctors don't know if he'll make it. I really hope he does. I didn't think I loved him any more, but he was trying to help me.'

'Is there anything I can do?'

'No, nothing Kevin. But thanks for phoning. By the way, why did you phone?'

'It seems a bit irrelevant now. It's just that last time we spoke you were talking about changing what we'd agreed about the settlement. I've been on holiday abroad and it's been on my mind and I wanted to talk to you about it.'

'Don't worry about all that Kevin. I was angry. I was lashing out. After what has happened to Tom it all seems a bit trivial, arguing about money. I'll tell the solicitors to leave it as it is, and I'm sorry I made a big deal of it. If you are making a success of your life now, you are entitled to the money.'

'Thanks, Anne. And I hope Tom pulls through. You will let me know, won't you?'

'Yes, of course. Thanks for phoning, Kevin. It's good to hear a friendly voice. It's been horrible here. Call me again soon?'

'I will. Bye.'

When Robert returned with the groceries Kevin looked a bit happier. He told him about the phone call.

'So now we are hoping that your ex-love-rival pulls through.'

'Bizarre, isn't it?'

Chapter 49

Jo Morgan had only been working for the bank for seven months. This was her first proper job since leaving university after successfully finishing her degree in economics. Her previous paid employment had included being a sales assistant in Thornton's which she enjoyed apart from having to work with a rather bossy shop manager, six weeks as a waitress in Pizza Express which she loved until the offer of being a runner on a feature film starring Ewan McGregor tempted her away from it. But these were just a means to an end while she was an undergraduate.

When she was offered the job at Standard Chartered with a starting salary which was the same as her father's was when he reached forty, Jo was so excited she rang her parents and they rushed all the way down to London from Reading to take her out for dinner. Jo was ambitious but knew that she would have to start at the bottom and work her way up. She watched how some of the other women who worked there looked so confident, with an air of authority about them and dressed so stylishly. The woman she most admired was Sylvia McEvoy.

Jo was relieved when she saw Sylvia arrive back at her desk looking tanned, healthy and relaxed. Jo waited until Sylvia had taken a few sips of her coffee and turned her computer on before wheeling her chair across the office and perching on the edge of it opposite her.

'Hi, Sylvia. How was your holiday?'

'Great thanks, Jo. I mean, *really* great. We had a lovely time. How has it been here while I've been away? I see a few more people have gone.' As she glanced around she took in the empty desks.

'That's what I wanted to talk to you about actually. While you were away I've been covering for some of the others who have left and Brian asked me to have a look at your stuff too. Most of it I couldn't make head nor tail of, so I concentrated on the simpler stuff. I had a look at the dormant accounts reports. I couldn't help noticing one or two anomalies. I'm glad you are back so you can tell me that it's just normal.'

'Oh,' said Sylvia, attempting to look nonchalant, 'What sort of anomalies?'

'I'm sure we can figure out what they are and I expect there's a perfectly rational explanation for it, but there seems to have been rather more activity than one would expect amongst the dormant accounts and they've been dropping off the dormant accounts list.'

'Okay. So you've been looking at the reports produced before I went on holiday?'

'Yes, Brian said I might as well make myself useful while you were away so I started familiarising myself with the various reports. I was comparing the current reports with some of the earlier ones. I noticed that recently the numbers of accounts that are dormant seem to be dropping whereas a few weeks prior to that numbers seemed fairly constant as the accounts that were joining the list roughly equalled the ones coming off the list. It's probably nothing and maybe I've missed something but do you have any idea why that might be?'

Sylvia was trying to remain calm. 'It may be something to do with the Governments dormant account initiative where money from dormant accounts is transferred to the Government after a period of time. Don't worry about it though; I'll look into it. As you say, there's almost certainly a perfectly logical reason for it.'

'Cool. By the way, you are looking great. The suntan really suits you.'

'Thanks, Jo.'

Jo moved her chair back to her desk and carried on with her work. Sylvia looked at her hands. She expected them to be shaking but they appeared quite steady. She gathered herself, told herself to calm down and then started checking her emails and reports as normal. All the time she was processing the information. Jo had become aware of what she thought was an anomaly. Jo had passed it on to her. Now she must investigate it. It was her job.

Her phone rang. It was Brian calling her from his office just yards away. He asked her to pop in. She got up and walked over to the office. He asked her to shut the door and motioned that she should sit down.

'So how was Nice?'

'It was lovely, thank you. Has everything been okay while I've been away?'

'No. Not really. In fact, it's all going tits-up. People are leaving like rats deserting a sinking ship. The workload is as high as normal. We can't recruit any new people until the implications of the merger are spelt out to us. Between you and me, it's complete and utter shit right now. So no more short-notice holidays, okay?'

'Sure. Sorry, if it caused a problem. It's just that I hadn't had a real holiday in ages,' then changing the subject, 'Have you heard any more news about the merger? Were there any announcements while I was away?'

'No, there are rumours, of course, but nothing definite. I had Jo look after the urgent stuff on your desk while you were away.'

'Yes, I know.'

Brian looked up at her, 'Did you have a problem with that?'

'No, it's just that I was right up to date when I went and I didn't think that there was anything of mine that would need to be handled. It was only a week.'

'I know, but she's a good kid and I wanted to see if she has got the instincts to be on the inspection team.'

'And has she?'

'I don't know yet. I haven't really spoken to her much during the week but now you are back I can schedule a meeting with her to see what she's learnt.'

Chapter 50

The emails had accumulated while they had been away and so both Kevin and Robert had to get busy again quickly to deal with them. There were sales to attend, paperwork to be done, antiques to be collected, deliveries to be made, buyers to be called, money to be banked and catalogues to be perused and annotated.

Robert would leave early in the morning in the van and arrive exhausted back at the flat in the evening. Kevin was on the phone for most of the day negotiating and moving money around. Sylvia had reinstated the computer systems so money was pouring into the account again. Kevin tried to keep the amount waiting to be spent less than a hundred thousand but they had to work hard to get it spent before the account filled up again.

Robert's day would occasionally be interrupted by a phone call from Chloe. She seemed to be calling him more often now. He asked her if everything was alright. She assured him it was, but the calls kept coming. Sometimes she would call twice in one day. Despite her assurances he felt something was wrong. He decided to arrange to see her at the weekend. Although it was a very long way round, he went via Bristol and collected Kate on the way.

'It's about time you met Chloe,' he explained as they drove up the M5 before joining the M42 to Tamworth. 'And I'm worried that she's not telling me everything. She's ten now and is more aware of things around her.'

'I'm looking forward to meeting her. Presumably you've arranged it with Janice?'

Robert admitted he hadn't but he felt sure it would be alright as long as he could get to see Chloe even if it was only briefly. Kate was a bit dubious about this but said nothing.

They arrived outside Janice's house.

'So this is where you used to live?' Kate indicated the house.

'No. We rented that one there.' He pointed to a similar house a few doors up. 'But she moved in with the guy here. They'd been seeing each other during the day while I was at work and Chloe was at school. It all came to a head one day when she invited him round for dinner and they told me what had been going on. I left the same day and moved in with a mate in Glascote, which is just down the road. To be honest, Janice and I were just too young when we got together. All we had in common really was Chloe.'

'Weren't you angry?'

'Oddly enough I wasn't. I wasn't even surprised. I guess we had grown apart and wanted different things. Apart from having to leave Chloe, which was difficult, it wasn't hard to leave Janice. I always imagined that I'd still be able to see Chloe just as much as I only lived down the road but it just got too difficult and confusing for her so I backed off. Eventually, the job I had at the time went as well so I decided to leave the area and start again.'

'That's when you went to Stranraer, right?'

'That's it. Right, let's give Chloe a call and see if she's there.' He dialled her number and she answered.

'Chloe, it's Daddy. How are you darling?'

He listened patiently while she told him about everything in her life right now.

'Listen, Chloe, I've come to see you. We're outside the house. Can you ask your mother if you can see me?'

Chloe's face appeared briefly at the upstairs window. Then she went out of view again. He turned to Kate. 'She's asking her mother.'

Kate nodded. The front door opened and Janice looked out. Robert jumped out of the van and crossed the road. Then Chloe appeared beside Janice. Kate watched the three of them. There was a short conversation between them. Kate eyed Janice up. Bleached blonde hair, quite petite and pretty but her face was hard like someone who has had a difficult life and not always been able to eat healthy food. Chloe disappeared for a moment and then reappeared wearing a denim jacket. Robert and Chloe walked hand in hand across the road towards the van. Janice gave Kate a stare. Kate waved but Janice didn't wave back. She just retreated inside and closed the door.

Robert opened the passenger door and Kate moved along the seat to allow Chloe to climb in next to her. Robert went round to the driver's side.

'We've got an hour. I vote we go to KFC. Seatbelts on, girls. Kate this is Chloe. Chloe, meet Kate, my girlfriend.'

Kate smiled at being referred to as Robert's girlfriend. She held out her hand to Chloe who shook it solemnly. They drove round to the fast food restaurant and ordered. They sat down in one of the booths and Robert said, 'So Chloe, tell me and Kate all about your week.'

Chloe looked up them both and then, between bites and noisy sucking on the milkshake straw, she launched into an account of her last few days detailing all of the goings-on at school with her friends and the teachers. She told them about the new anti-bullying policy at school, and how a fire engine came to the playground, and how they were allowed to look inside it. She told them about her friend Sally who broke her arm on the climbing frame and how excited she was when her mum had said they would soon be going to live in America.

Kate stared at Robert. Robert stared at Chloe. 'America?'

Chloe munched on her chicken. 'Yes, Stephen's got a job there. We're going in four weeks and two days. Mum said I wasn't allowed to tell you but today she said I could.'

Robert looked at Kate. Kate looked sympathetic. 'How do you feel about going to America Chloe?'

'Can't wait. I'll miss you though Daddy.' She put a handful of fries into her mouth and talked with her mouth full. But Mum says I can go to Disneyland. And we're getting a puppy when we get there.'

Robert had to suppress the rage building up inside him. How could Janice do this? Just as he was getting his life organised, and building a relationship with Chloe she was going to be snatched away to live on the other side of the world. He hoped that his face was not showing his true feelings.

'A puppy. That's fantastic. And have you thought of a name for the puppy yet?'

'Yes. Bone if it's a boy and Jordan if it's a girl dog. And Mum is going to have a baby too. I nearly forgot to tell you. Thinking of names reminded me as Mum and Stephen have been talking about lots of different names.'

Kate reached out and squeezed Robert's knee under the table. She asked Chloe 'Super. Are you hoping for a brother or sister?'

'A sister of course. Boys are horrible and they smell. Can I have an ice cream, please? The oreo one?'

Robert went to the counter to organise the ice cream.

'Your Dad loves you a lot, you know. He's going to miss you when you go to America.'

'I know. I'll miss him too but you will be able to come out and see me won't you, when you two get married. You could live there too. Then I could have two families.'

Robert placed the tray of ice creams on the table.

'Chloe was just telling me that when we get married we could live in America and see Chloe all the time.'

'I see, young lady. You've got it all figured out, haven't you?'

'No Dad. It was just an idea. Silly.'

The Laundrymen

Part 3

*The extinction of desire
is the prerequisite to Salvation*

Mark Stretch

Chapter 51

'Kevin. I need to talk to you. It's urgent. Call me'. He listened to the message twice before calling just to be sure. Her voice was breathy and sounded far away. Was it fear, anxiety or just excitement? He couldn't tell.

Kevin pocketed the bundle of notes just released from the cash machine and was walking along the road with the phone in his hand about to make the call when a lad on a silver bike that seemed far too small for him swept up behind him, grabbed the phone out of his hand and then pedalled off wildly down the street and around the corner. Kevin took a moment to recover from the shock and then quickly ran after him but the thief was out of sight.

His first reaction was to go to the police to report the theft but somehow he felt that he couldn't. Not now. Now that he had crossed the line. He went back to the flat to ask Robert if he could use his phone. Robert wasn't in. So he looked up the details of his service provider online and then walked to the nearest phone box to call the mobile phone provider. After waiting for ages and answering interminable security questions, he was eventually put through to the department that deals with stolen phones and arranged for the phone number to be immobilised. Then he went off down the high street to purchase a new phone. As soon as he got one he would call her.

Sylvia needed to talk to Kevin. She wanted to see him. She had become accustomed to spending time with him during the holiday. Now she was missing his company. She also felt she should let him know that she was having to tread very carefully around the office as one of her colleagues had spotted something while she was away.

Just as she was thinking about him her phoned bleeped. It was a text. From Kevin.

'Hey bitch, send me a pic with your tits out.'

She didn't understand. Why was he saying that? She called him. It rang and was answered. 'Sylvia. Hey, babe. What can I do for you today? Bitch!' said a voice that definitely wasn't Kevin's. And then there was a cackling laugh.

'Who is this?' she asked. 'Where's Kevin?'

'Last time I saw him he was leaving the country, Sylvia. So now you've just got me. When are we going to meet up?' The voice sounded like a teenage boy.

'What are you talking about? Who are you? Why have you got Kevin's phone?'

The voice just laughed again and said 'Bored now. See ya' Sylvia.'

The call was ended. Sylvia was confused and worried. She needed to be reassured that Kevin was alright. She called Robert.

'Robert, it's Sylvia. Have you seen Kevin?'

'Not since this morning. Why?'

'I'm worried about him. I've just called his phone and someone else answered. Sounded like a crazy teenager.'

'How odd. I'll try him calling him, shall I?'

'Okay, let me know, please.'

'Will do. Don't worry, I'm sure everything is fine, though.'

Robert called Kevin's phone. It didn't ring. It was a single tone, as if it was disconnected. He called Sylvia back.

'The phone's been disconnected. I'll try and find him and I'll call you back when I have. Okay?'

'Be careful. I hope he's alright'

'I'm sure he will be. Sit tight. I'll call you as soon as I know anything'.

'Thanks, Robert'.

Robert turned the van round and headed back to flat. There was no sign of Kevin. As Robert was coming back out Kevin appeared in front of him.

'Where have you been? Sylvia is worried sick about you. She said some kid was on your phone.'

'The phone was stolen. I've just been out to get a new one.' He held up a bag.

'Well, ring Sylvia will you and let her know you are okay. She sounded pretty frantic.'

Robert held out his phone. Kevin took it and dialled Sylvia's number.

'Robert. Any news!'

'It's me. It's Kevin.'

'Thank God, are you okay? I've been so worried about you. I got this text.'

'I'm fine. My phone was stolen. In broad daylight. I just went out to get another one.'

'That's a relief. I thought that gang was back and they'd kidnapped you or something.'

Kevin smiled 'Nothing quite so dramatic, I'm afraid. There was a message on it. From you I think, saying you wanted to talk to me.'

'No, that wasn't me. I did try and call you but I got the git that stole your phone I suppose. Why did you think I left you a message?'

Immediately it dawned on Kevin that it must have been Anne. He now realised why he thought there was something different about her voice.

'Forget it, Sylvia. I'm getting confused. Must be the shock of the phone being nicked, I guess.'

'Okay. Sounds strange, though. Anyway, I'd like to see you. Can you come over?'

Kevin agreed to see her later on that day, ended the call and handed the phone back to Robert. 'Thanks'.

'Anne?'

'Yes, I suppose it must have been. I'd better call her and see what she wants.'

'You can take it or leave it, but my advice is to be careful. Or tell Sylvia that you are still in communication with Anne. If Sylvia finds out …'

'I know. You're right. It's just a question of finding the right time.'

'Well, you're seeing her tonight, yes? So maybe that's the right time.'

With that Robert shrugged his shoulders, went back out to the van and drove off.

Chapter 52

Tom opened his eyes. And blinked several times. The light was bright. It hurt his brain. Or was the pain there anyway? He couldn't tell. His vision was blurred. But he wasn't dead. He tried to move and winced as pain shot through his body. He could hear noises. A face swam into his view then went away. Then another face, with glasses.

'Tom, can you hear me? I'm Doctor Wardle. You're in the Queen Elizabeth Hospital in Birmingham. You had an accident. But you are safe now.'

Tom blinked and tried to speak. Only a faint noise emerged.

'Don't try to talk. We'll get some of these tubes removed first. But you are awake again. That's a great sign.'

Tom lapsed back into a troubled sleep. The dreams were vivid. The next time he woke up it was because he heard his name being spoken over and over again. He opened his eyes and tried to focus. The face was familiar. Someone from work, maybe. Then he remembered. It was Anne. As her name registered in his consciousness so did the events that led to him being there.

'Tom, you're awake. You've been out for ages. How are you feeling?'

Tom croaked 'Terrible'

'That's really good' said Anne. 'You must be on the mend.'

The doctor came into the room and smiled at Anne. 'I think that's enough for now. We don't want to tire him. Perhaps tomorrow?'

Anne got up and left the room, taking a last look at Tom as she did so. He was going to be okay. What a relief. She called Kevin but just got a continuous tone. Kevin called her later that day.

'I got your message. I'm calling you on my new phone. The other one got stolen.'

'Oh. That probably explains why I couldn't get through to you when I tried earlier.

'I'm sorry about that. I hope you didn't get any horrible calls or texts. I guess the kid who stole the phone was just having fun pissing off everyone on my contact list. Hopefully, the phone has been immobilised now.'

'Anyway, it's Tom. He's conscious. And he's talking. I think he's going to be okay. I thought you should know.'

'That's great news, really great.' said Kevin, with a huge sense of relief. He was certain that his conscience couldn't cope with the addition of a corpse.

'Apparently though, the police have drawn a blank on the people who did this. They're still investigating, but it doesn't look like they're going to find them. They said they might call you, as we're still married. They told me it's just routine. I explained to them that you were abroad at the time, though. I expect they'll have a way of verifying that, somehow.'

Kevin felt cold at the thought of the police contacting him, but at least being out of the country meant he couldn't have done it. 'Well, I suppose the main thing is that Tom is going to be okay.'

'Yes, but what I want to know is why they were on my drive in the first place. The one that seemed to be in charge, sounded Scottish but that's all I can remember about him. It really seemed as if they were there for a reason. I just can't work out what it might be, though.'

'Unless the police can find them, you may never find out. Thanks for letting me know about Tom and everything. I've got to go now. I'm late for a meeting.'

They ended the call. Kevin went straight out to see Sylvia. As soon as he got inside the apartment she hugged him and held him tightly.

'Whoa, steady on. You are cracking my ribs.'

Sylvia slackened her grip on him.

'What's up?'

'Sit down. Please. There are some things I need to tell you.'

Kevin sat down. Sylvia told him earnestly about the earlier incident with the account where the missing interest had been queried, and then about Jo and what she had uncovered while they were away, and how she was now going to have to go through the motions of investigating the anomalies. She explained that she could deal with it, but if there any more alerts and she wasn't around to intervene, other people might pick them up. Even if they did, it would still take them a while to trace them to the source, and the source could still be anyone in the bank.

Kevin let it sink in for a while. Then he took a deep breath and told Sylvia that, while they were on the subject of things going wrong, he'd better tell her about Anne, her threats, how Robert had involved Mitch and his gang, and that they'd been to see Anne, and how Tom had intervened, and got stabbed and that, for a while it seemed that Tom might die.

Sylvia sat in silence while Kevin told her all this, her eyes growing rounder with each revelation.

'I can hardly believe all this. Why didn't you tell me all this before? You should have told me.'

'I didn't know how to tell you. I'm sorry. If I'd told you in France, it would have spoilt the holiday for you. The main thing is that so far, it can't be traced to us. It seems that the police are getting nowhere in finding out who the gang were and it looks like Tom is going to recover. Plus, Anne has retracted her demands for money. But I suppose you should have also told me about what was going on at the bank.'

'How much does Robert know about all of this?'

'Obviously he knows about Anne and Tom. What about the bank? Does he know about what's been happening there?' said Kevin, suddenly worried that Sylvia may have divulged information to Robert that she had kept from him.

'No. I haven't told anyone, until you, tonight.'

They both sat in silence for a while collecting their thoughts, neither wishing to say something they would later regret. Eventually, Sylvia spoke first. 'Look Kevin, we're all in this together. Keeping secrets from each other is no way for partners to behave. Is there anything else you haven't told me?'

'Yes, there is, actually. I'm worried. This whole thing is getting out of hand. I think we should stop.'

'But we can't stop now. We haven't reached our target.'

'We've got to stop this before someone else gets hurt, or someone catches us. We've been lucky so far and I think we should quit now while we're ahead.'

'What does Robert say? Does he share your view?'

'I don't know. I haven't said anything to him.'

'Do you think he'll want to stop?'

'Frankly, no I don't, but we've got to be sensible. It's getting dangerous.'

'Look. I don't want to stop. I know it's getting a bit difficult right now but we always knew it wasn't going to be easy. I think we should stick to the plan.'

'But we agreed we'd stop if any one of us wanted to. That was one of the rules too.'

The Laundrymen

'What if Robert doesn't want to stop?'

'We agreed that if one of us wants to then we all would'.

Sylvia sighed. This wasn't how she wanted the evening to go. She had hoped that Kevin would reassure her and tell her everything was going to be fine. Instead, he seemed to be tearing everything down and dashing her hopes and dreams. She weighed up the risks of being caught, and the fear of discovery against a lifetime of being a wage slave. In her mind, there was no contest. Better to be a prisoner for attempting to be free, than a prisoner for not even trying.

'Kevin. I understand how you feel, and I know a lot of how you are feeling now is because you are worried for me. You're right. I'm closer to the danger than you. But I went into this with my eyes open. I knew the risks. And I think they are acceptable. The potential gain is greater than the risk. And you must know that if anything happened at the bank and if by some miracle they managed to eventually trace it back to me that I would never, repeat never, mention your name. Or Robert's. It would be my crime and mine alone. You do understand that, don't you?'

Her chin was quivering and her eyes were filling up, 'This is so very important to me, Kevin. I've dreamt about this for years, and we are so very close to pulling it off. Please don't end it now. If you really love me, say you'll see it through.' She leant her head on his chest. 'Please. For me.'

She was now in tears. Kevin was in turmoil. He had been so determined on his way over. Now his resolve was melting fast. His feelings for Sylvia were taking over from his logic and it was unnerving, like a fog descending over him, blurring his vision and numbing his other senses. He put his arms around her and pulled her close to him. He could feel her sobbing against his body and it make his heart ache for her. She pressed against him. His resolve softened, as another part of him hardened.

'Okay, okay. But this is totally against my better judgement. Let's see it through, if that's what you really want.'

Sylvia relaxed into him. They stood like that for a while until her sobs subsided, then Sylvia pulled out of the embrace and stood in front of him at arms length holding his hands and looking into his eyes with her red eyes surrounded by black smudges she said. 'Thank you, Kevin, I can't tell you how much this means to me.'

Then she found a tissue and dabbed away the tears. She peered into the mirror and tried to clean off the mascara that had run. She said, 'I know you are nervous about this Kevin, so let's move more of the money direct to the offshore accounts, then you won't be under so much pressure to move it around. That way we can get to the target figure quicker with a bit less stress. What do you think?'

'Anything that reduces the risk of getting caught is fine by me.'

Sylvia turned back to him and tilted her head to one side. 'I really enjoyed the holiday, you know. Especially being able to spend so much time with you. When this is over, I hope we can do more of it.'

Kevin nodded. He hoped so too.

'Those warm nights, and that big bed ..'

He didn't need a second invitation.

Chapter 53

Janice remained firm. No amount of cajoling or persuasion was going to change her mind. They were going to America. It was all organised. A new start for them all, and Chloe was guaranteed to get a better future. It was hard for Robert to argue with that, although naturally he gave it his best shot. He had to resign himself to the fact that Chloe was going and so he had better make the most of the time left to them.

He persuaded Janice that, as time was now limited, Chloe should be allowed to come over to stay with him for the weekend. She relented. Chloe arrived on the train, with a rucksack containing a change of clothes, washbag, teddy-bear and her pyjamas. Robert took her out for lunch and then returned to the flat. Kevin was staying at Sylvia's so they had the place to themselves. Chloe was fascinated by the antiques that were stacked in the corner awaiting shipment to other sales or to buyers. Robert enjoyed being able to tell her as much as he knew about each item, and was sometimes surprised at how much knowledge he had accumulated. He described what it had been like while he was bidding for them, how tense it was and he victorious he felt when he had won the bids. Chloe listened without interrupting. Her dad had never spoken to her like this before and she liked it.

When it came to bedtime, he tucked her up in his bed. He made up a bedtime story about a duckling that was scared of the water and despite lots of encouragement from the daddy duck and the mummy duck, the little duckling refused to leave the safety of the shore. Until one day when a fox came.

The ducks quacked warnings until the duckling finally saw the fox and jumped into the water to escape it, and then realised just how much fun it was, to be paddling around on the water. Chloe smiled with pleasure and told him how much she enjoyed the story. Tomorrow she would draw a picture of the duckling and the fox. She told him she hoped that, when he moved to America too, he could tell her more stories, when it was her turn to stay at his house.

As Chloe shut her eyes and began to doze, Robert silently crept out of the room. He could already feel the pain of losing her, even though she was just feet away. She would be going home tomorrow. He wasn't sure when he would be seeing her again. He poured a glass of wine, put on some music and sat in the armchair listening to a Lou Reed on a low volume before phoning Kate. She answered on the third ring.
'Hi, Robert.'

'Hi. I was thinking about you, so I called. What are you up to this weekend?'

She told him she had a big project to hand in, so she was going to be busy all weekend, and she would probably have to work through the night to finish it. Robert could sense that her mind was on other things so he kept it brief.

'Chloe's here. She was asking after you.'

'Tell her I said hello and give her a big kiss from me.'

Kate was obviously distracted with her college work, so Robert wished her luck with it and left her to it. He moved over to the where the laptop was sat on the table and searched on Google to see whether it was possible for him to move to America. Depressingly, the visa requirements for actually emigrating there looked prohibitively daunting and the cost of healthcare, which we take for granted in the UK, just saddened him further so he turned the laptop off and shut the lid.

Robert sat back down in the armchair, shut his eyes and thought about the recent twists and turns in his life. In the past, he had allowed events to dictate his life. Now he had access to money, and soon he would he would have plenty of it, he hoped it would enable him to take some control and allow him to shape his own future. He needed to decide what was important to him. He took a sip of the wine and thought of Chloe lying asleep in the next room. He wanted to be part of her life, but it was just that, her life. One day she would have grown up and left home to create her own future. It would be wrong to try and influence her life too, especially considering the way his had turned out. Perhaps just being there when she needed him would be enough. As long as she knew that he loved her, the physical distance that was going to come between them could be overcome with holiday visits, email, Skype and whatever other communication developments were made in the future.

Robert's thoughts turned to Kate. He wondered whether they would perhaps live together when she finished her course and maybe try to forge out a life as a team. It seemed a little far-fetched and probably too much to hope for as it was such early days but when he was with her it felt the way he had hoped it would. Was it love? He didn't know. Love was such a complicated emotion. He knew he felt something. It wasn't the same as the way he felt about Chloe, and it was different to how he had felt about Janice and all the other women in his life, so maybe it was love. Was it a weakness to feel that way? By falling in love are you handing power in your relationship to the object of your love? If so, is that a price worth paying? So many unknowns. Such uncertainty. He could understand why people sometimes walked away. The power of the feeling was so strong and it would be easy to feel intimidated by it. The hurt that could be caused by that power being misused was immense. But he was pretty sure he wouldn't be the one to walk away.

His mind switched to his friendship with Kevin. That one had come out of the blue. Obviously he'd had friends before, and band mates but he'd lost touch with nearly all of them over the years. And they had not made contact with him. So were they really friends? Kevin had become a friend. On the face of it, it was an unlikely pairing but it seemed to work. Kevin had helped him when he needed it, and given him money, and a place to live. Robert felt he could be himself around Kevin. He didn't have to big himself up, or play the hard guy. It was a relaxed friendship, as Kevin was an easy-going guy. In their business, they seemed to be playing to their strengths. And although the money they were using wasn't theirs, the profit they were making, by buying and selling, was genuine. They were doing it successfully and that was exhilarating. But maybe it's a bit gay to be thinking about friendships with another guy, so he decided to think about something else.

The money. He had deliberately tried not to dwell on it. He didn't see it as his yet. Like the pot of gold at the end of the rainbow, it might prove to be elusive. So he hadn't made any plans for it. But it was accumulating and he would need to think about it soon. After living so precariously, he felt he wanted a home, something stable in his life, so a property would probably be near the top of his wish list. But where? Any decision about that would almost certainly depend on several other people and their circumstances at the time. Kate, Chloe and maybe even Kevin. Having briefly looked into the entry requirements, it really didn't look like America was going to be an option. And he knew he didn't really want to leave the country anyway. However, if it looked like their crime was coming to light, it might be necessary. And if so, would it have to be somewhere without an extradition agreement? Presumably, that meant somewhere outside of Europe. His head was buzzing with so many unanswered questions. And he had so few answers.

The next day was spent wandering around the local park, buying ice creams, bowling and eventually returning to the station. Robert hugged Chloe for a moment too long before helping her onto the train and making sure she was settled, comfortable, had money for a drink and that she knew where to get off. As the train pulled away, she waved and he waved back until the train was just a dot in the distance. He felt the saltiness stinging his eyes as left the station and quickened his pace.

***

Kevin returned to the flat in a good mood. His weekend with Sylvia had been mixed but had ended harmoniously. Now he was looking forward to getting back to work. Robert was slumped in the armchair when he entered the living room. As Kevin hung up his jacket, Robert straightened up and asked, 'Good weekend?'

'Great thanks, how was yours? Did Chloe enjoy London?'

'I think so. It's hard sometimes to see what they like or don't like. We got on okay though and that's the main thing. I'm really going to miss her when she goes to live in America.'

Kevin wasn't sure what to say so after a few moments he decided to change the subject. 'I tried to persuade Sylvia that we should halt things at the bank. Someone who works with her spotted an anomaly while we were in France.'

Robert looked up.

'Don't worry. She's smoothed it over, but she wants to move more money to the offshore accounts. I told her maybe we should stop now but she's determined to see it through. How do you feel about that?'

'If she's confident that no-one is onto her, then I'm alright with it. Presumably we're not too far from the three million?'

'If she increases the movement, I think we'll be there in another three or four weeks. We'll be getting less come through for laundering which should enable us to move the outstanding stock and start winding things down a bit.'

'Then we'll have to decide what to do next. I was just thinking about it earlier.'

'And did you come to any conclusions?'

'No, not really. A lot depends on other people I suppose.'

'Like who?'

'Well, Chloe for one. And Kate and even you, mate.'

'Me?'

'Well. I've quite enjoyed the last few months and we seem to make quite a good team with the antiques and everything. I wasn't sure if maybe that could continue?'

'I'd assumed you would want to move on as soon as we had met the target.'

'A while ago, I would.'

'And now?'

'I don't know. It's just that I quite enjoy the antiques business and I feel like I've learnt quite a lot. Pity to waste it.'

'I had no idea you felt like that. It's odd really, because I haven't spent any time thinking about what I'd do with the money. The truth is, the money wasn't really the big attraction for me. The challenge of whether we could do it was probably the main driving force.'

'And the possibility of seeing more of Sylvia, perhaps?'

Kevin smiled and raised his hands palms outwards. 'Guilty as charged. '

Chapter 54

Over the next few weeks, Kevin and Robert were hard at work buying and selling antiques. After the unwelcome publicity brought about by the selling of the book, they steered clear of similar items and stuck to the Art Nouveau and Deco period, which they had previously specialised in.

Chloe and her family departed for America. Robert went out and got very drunk the same night. When Kevin returned from seeing a film with Sylvia, he found Robert comatose in the armchair, a half empty bottle of Jack Daniels at his feet. Kevin found a blanket and gently placed it over him.

Sylvia made sure she was at her desk for as much time as possible. While she was there she felt in control. She tried to stay later in the evening than the rest of her department. It wasn't hard. Morale was so low that many people who previously had worked diligently for long hours were now leaving on the dot of five o'clock. The work still needed to be done and Sylvia was only too willing to do it. Brian had spotted it and was impressed by her dedication. When the new owners of the bank finally made an appearance he would ensure that they were made aware of how hard she had worked during the difficult transitionary period, assuming she hadn't left before they arrived.

Kate was pleased to discover that, now her university project was out of the way, she had more time to come over to London to spend time with Robert. She tried hard to fill the gaping hole left in his life since Chloe had left and Robert was grateful for the distraction.

As time went on, the amount of money arriving at the payout account began to slow down. Kevin checked with Sylvia and she explained that she had changed the ratio so that more was now being moved directly to the offshore accounts. Kevin knew that this meant the end was in sight and re-doubled his efforts to get all of the money moved swiftly through the antiques business. He was choosing some higher-value items but also selecting a number of lower ticket pieces too as sometimes there just weren't enough good quality high-value items available to buy.

Robert was busy rushing from sale to sale. The van was nearly always full of pieces of furniture, jewellery, figurines, lamps, paintings and various types of crockery and vases. He kept large rolls of bubble-wrap in the van which he used to carefully envelope the purchases to protect them as he transported them around. Whilst he enjoyed the antiques trade, he would be glad when they had reached their target figure, as he wasn't sure he'd be able to maintain this pace for very much longer.

The pressure finally got too much for Robert when he found the road to a sale was closed and, while he was trying to turn in the road to go back the other way, the van was hit broadside by a taxi. The side of the van was badly dented, but luckily the antiques inside were undamaged. When Robert got home that night he showed Kevin the damage to the van.

'It's lucky you weren't hurt.'

'Yes, but this only happened because I was rushing, and didn't look properly.'

'Don't worry about it, we can either fix it or get another van.'

'That's not really the point Kevin. It's the fact that I messed up. I was rushing. I didn't look properly. I think it's all getting a bit too much.'

Kevin realised that he had not noticed that Robert was beginning to feel the strain. He tried to reassure him.

'I know it has been really hectic, but we must be nearly there now.'

'How much longer do you think?'

'I'm not sure. I need to check with Sylvia to see how much she has moved to the offshore accounts. It's probably just another couple of weeks or so I expect.'

'Can you find out? I suppose we really need to decide what happens next. We've all been concentrating on getting to the end, but not really looking beyond that.'

'I'll check with her and we can start planning. I think I'll start by getting somewhere a bit bigger to live in,' laughed Kevin as he lugged a pair of large anonymous bubble-wrapped items out of the van and into the flat.

Later that evening, Kevin checked the accounts again. He called out to Robert. 'We've got just under six hundred thousand in each of the three accounts now plus about a hundred and twenty thousand in stock ready to be sold. If we add on whatever Sylvia has sent offshore we must be really close now.'

Robert was in his room reading a book. 'Good.' He called back 'Let's see if we can find out just how close we are, then we'll know pretty much when we will be finished.'

'Will do.'

The next day, Kevin went out for a walk. Recently, he found that a brisk walk every morning helped to clear his head. Any doubts or confusion in his mind could be analysed and solutions developed as he made his way around the streets of London. He liked to keep moving. He had tried finding a bench and sitting for a while, but that's when any negative thoughts would come rolling back into his mind. It was almost as if the pumping of his heart, while he was walking, was pushing away the problems and replacing them with answers. He strode away from Islington and found himself walking past the elegant townhouses bordering Highbury Fields. He stopped and admired the Boer War memorial at the south of the park before passing the play areas joyful with the sound of children playing whilst watchful mothers sat nearby. He crossed the grass and thought of home in the Midlands and how the fields that surrounded the areas where he used to live were just taken for granted by the residents.

Sometimes he missed the gentle mocking of his fellow Brummies. Many people found their accent annoying, but he had always found it to be friendly and calming, compared to the staccato London-speak, which had always seemed to him to be so hurried, anxious and impatient. He made his way north and could hear the sound of tennis balls being knocked across the nets. He was tempted to stop and watch, but kept going instead.

He left the park and started to make his way back towards the flat. He stopped at the cashpoint to withdraw that day's five hundred pounds. After tapping in the pin and selecting the amount Kevin turned and looked around, as was his custom while waiting for the money to be counted. He didn't hear the normal sound of the money coming out of the slot so he squinted at the screen. It said 'Insufficient Funds'. He cancelled the request and retrieved the card. He tried it again, carefully tapping the pin into the machine, then re-entering the amount. The same message appeared. He tried a third time, this time entering one hundred pounds in case the message meant that it was the machine that was low on funds. Same result.

Kevin retrieved the card and walked off towards his flat. He spotted another cash machine on the other side of the road. He crossed over and tried the transaction again. The result was the same.

Gritting his teeth, he hurried back to the flat. When he got inside he thumped on Robert's door. 'Get up! Get up Robert. We've got a problem.'

Robert opened the bedroom door and looked out. He was wearing a t-shirt and boxers. His receding hair was sticking out at all angles and he was rubbing sleep from his eyes. He saw Kevin flitting between the two laptops.

'What's up?'

'I don't know. I couldn't withdraw any cash this morning. It said there wasn't enough money in the account. I tried two machines.'

'Maybe there's a glitch at the bank. It's happened before.'

'That's what I'm hoping. I want to check the other accounts. Just waiting to see which laptop fires up first.'

Robert joined him and watched while he entered the login details of the accounts. They were all rejected.

'If it's a glitch, it's a big one. All the accounts are affected,' said Robert. 'I'll put the kettle on, shall I?' He started to make his way into the kitchen, but Kevin stopped him.

'No. Wait. Something's very wrong here. We need to find out what's going on. You'd better get dressed.'

Fifteen minutes later they were on their way to Sylvia's. Robert was driving. Kevin was busy texting

The Laundrymen

Sylvia to see if she knew what was happening. He had tried phoning her, but her phone wasn't responding.

'You'd better get a move on, Robert. She's not answering her phone. Hope she's alright.'

Robert accelerated but even with him going as fast as he could the build up of traffic meant that the journey to Sylvia's apartment was painfully slow. Finally, they arrived. Kevin leapt from the car and bounded up to the entry phone. He pressed Sylvia's number. There was no reply. At that moment, a woman in a raincoat, with a small dog on a lead came out and Kevin grabbed the door. Robert joined him and they raced upstairs to Sylvia's apartment. Kevin thumped on the door. There was no answer. He thumped and shouted. Eventually, the door opposite opened to the limit of its security chain. An unshaven guy in a dressing gown peered through the crack.

'Hey, there's no point in making all that racket, waking everybody up. She's moved out. They put all her stuff in a big yellow removals truck. Yesterday.'

Chapter 55

At a dark industrial estate near Brentford, there was just one lit window in the unit furthest from the main road. Parked outside were four large yellow removals trucks. As the last box was placed in the warehouse, Jack breathed a sigh of relief and patted Steve on the back.

'Fancy a pint before you head off?'

'Yeah, why not? Let me just get out of these bloody overalls.'

While Steve got ready Joe pondered the day's work. This had been a bit unusual. Tasty bird. Classy. And no bloke around, which was a bit odd, he thought. Then she'd wanted everything done so fast. Quite often house moves had to be completed quickly as sometimes another removals firm would be waiting to move in as they finished up. But this stuff was just going into storage and there didn't seem to be anyone moving in. It was almost as if she was doing a flit. But that was unlikely because she was clearly worth a few quid. He could tell that from the quality of all the gear in her place. Nice furniture and paintings and so on. Plus the size of her tip. It was almost a week's wages to split between them. So they could have a few pints and hand over a nice little bonus to the wife. She'd be pleased. Might even show her appreciation.

Steve reappeared. They turned out the light, set the alarm, locked up the warehouse and walked down the road to the pub. On the way there Jack handed Steve his half of the cash neatly rolled up.

'Wow! There must be three hundred quid there! Nice lady! Actually I thought she was quite fit. Didn't you? And so was that other one that turned up. I thought our luck was definitely in.'

'In your dreams!'

Jack got the first round in and bought peanuts for them both and tipped the buxom barmaid. She had smiled sweetly back at him. Actually she was more his type than the woman they'd moved today but he can always wonder.

'What did you think of that move today Steve?' as he placed the pints and nuts on the table. 'She seemed in an awful hurry.'

'Yeah, I thought that. See how she jumped when that entry phone thing buzzed. It was like she was scared of something. And it was just her friend turning up. Wonder if she was doing a runner or something. Maybe she hasn't paid her rent for months. She said something about moving to a warmer climate or something.'

'Well, she paid us a nice big tip, so she's alright in my book.'

'Yeah, cheers to her. And her friend. And when they get settled wherever they've gone we might be the ones to deliver the furniture to them and who knows what else they'd like us to hump, eh?'

They laughed, then clinked their pint glasses and peered upwards to watch the football on the big screen on the wall.

* * *

One hundred and thirty-five miles away Dean and Grace were entering the terraced house in Bristol. Dean went straight through to the kitchen to put the milk away. Grace went into the lounge to open the curtains and, amongst the piles of post, magazines and DVD boxes on the coffee table, she spotted a large brown envelope. It was addressed to her, Dean and Cass. She recognised it as Kate's handwriting.

She called to Dean, 'There's an envelope from Kate here.'

'Oh yeah? What's in it?' Dean replied from the kitchen.

Grace slid her finger under the flap and opened the envelope. Inside was a wad of twenty-pound notes and a letter. 'There's money in it.' She said to Dean, waving it at him as he came into the room.

'Fuck me! There's loads of dosh there. He took the money and fanned the notes. 'I bet there's over a thousand pounds here. What does the letter say?'

Sandra opened the letter up. Dean peered over her shoulder. They read the letter at the same time. When they'd finished reading, they looked at each other.

'So she's gone then. Didn't see that coming.'

Dean ran upstairs and checked Kate's room before coming back down into the lounge.

'Her room's empty. All her stuff has gone. Didn't realise how big her room was without all her art stuff in there. Bet it's something to do with that Robert bloke she's been seeing. She's probably moved in with him.' said Dean.

'Just seems odd that she didn't tell us first or give us any notice.'

'Does seem strange, but she's more than covered her rent. In fact if we can get someone in to take over her room quick, we'll be quids in.'

Dean went back upstairs. Grace read the letter again, looking for any indication why Kate had left so suddenly. Then her phone went. It was her mother. The letter was dropped on the sideboard and Kate was hardly mentioned again in the house.

* * *

The Laundrymen

Kate and Sylvia were sitting in the departure lounge at Heathrow. Sylvia kept glancing down at her phone.

'Kevin again?' asked Kate.

'Yes.'

'Maybe you should talk to him. Explain.'

'No, I can't. Not yet. I need some distance first.'

'They are going to be pretty cross. In fact, they'll be livid. Do you think they'll try and find us?'

'I doubt if they'll just sit there and take it. So yes, they'll try and find us. But they won't succeed. I'm pretty sure of that. We're changing planes a few times.'

'What's this place like that we're going to?'

'It's gorgeous. I went there on holiday once with Neil. I just fell in love with it. It's even better than the South of France.'

'Surely you can tell me now. I'm obviously not going to get the chance now to accidentally tell Robert.'

'When we're up in the air, then I'll explain the plan.'

Chapter 56

As they drove rapidly back to the flat, Kevin kept on trying to call Sylvia. Sometimes the phone rang out. Sometimes it just cut off. His mind was rapidly sifting through various different scenarios. The one scenario that he did not even want to contemplate was that Sylvia had disappeared taking their money with her. He looked over at Robert.

'Have you heard from Kate? Maybe she knows where Sylvia is?'

Robert braked the van sharply, pulled up onto the pavement and tried calling Kate. The phone just rang out and then stopped. 'No answer,' he said.

'Jesus! I hate this. What the hell are they doing? Why aren't they answering?'

'I've got a really bad feeling about this,' said Robert.

'Don't.' Said Kevin holding his hand up. 'Not yet. I refuse to believe that she's stitched us up.'

'Oh God, I've just had a terrible thought. Maybe it's not just Sylvia? Maybe it's both of them together.'

Kevin thought about that for a few moments. 'Fuck. It's possible I suppose. I just can't get my head around them doing that to us. There must be another explanation.'

'I haven't got a number for the house in Bristol where Kate lives. I always called her on her mobile. The only way to check to see if she is there is to go there and see.'

'It's a hell of a long way to go just to see if she's in.'

'I don't care. I've got to see for myself.'

'Okay, drop me at the flat then. I'll see what I can find out while you are away.'

Robert pulled up outside the flat. Kevin jumped out. 'Let me know as soon as you're there. I'll keep trying Sylvia. If I find out anything I'll call you.'

Robert drove off. It was going to be a long drive getting out of London and crossing the country to Bristol.

Kevin went back into the flat and sat down. He needed some calmness to get his head straight. He thought back to their very first meeting back at the hotel. Who approached who? He forced his brain to replay the moment they had met. He remembered. She had spoken to them about her phone and then they had got chatting. Could it have been anything else other than coincidence? He thought about how she'd suddenly tossed the idea of syphoning off the money into the conversation and how surprised both he and Robert had been. He had assumed that it must on her mind and she was just itching to tell somebody whom she trusted. Even now he still couldn't believe that they had been set up. It just seemed too elaborate. Too well planned. Surely he or Robert should have suspected something? And becoming lovers? Was that set up too? Was Robert in on it? He began to feel sick. If any of this was true, he, and possibly Robert too, had both been played like complete and utter fools.

Kevin turned on his laptop and tried the accounts again. He still couldn't access them. Then he almost cried out with pain. Every last fibre in his body was hoping that there was a rational explanation, but deep down he knew then that it was all going to be true. He was going to have to believe it and then deal with it.

He took a few deep breaths. Then he went through everything in his mind again. It was like watching a video of the last few months. This time, though, instead of being the hero of the story, he was the poor victim.

For a moment, there was a tiny part of him that almost felt relief. If it wasn't so sad, it would be funny. The money had been stolen off them by the very person who had stolen it in the first place. Robbed by the robber. Did that mean he was now removed from the crime and, therefore, innocent? He doubted it. The relief was short-lived. Somehow, if Sylvia was caught, it would become apparent that she must have had accomplices. Then, he and Robert would certainly end up paying the price, without even getting the reward.

* * *

Robert drove fast. He stayed in the fast lane all the way along the M4, powering the van past all the other commuters, but keeping an eye out for police too. He was desperately hoping that he was wrong. He really didn't want to find that Kate had been part of this. If she had, it meant that she had known about what they had been doing but not once did she even hint that she knew. He grimaced. All credit to her, she must be a superb actress to carry it off. Fuck. Fuck. Fuck. How could they not have even suspected them?

Then he calmed himself. No point in getting worked up until he knew for sure.

Forty minutes later it was confirmed. He had rung the doorbell. Dean had answered. They had met briefly once before when Robert had stayed over. When Robert asked if Kate was in, Dean shook his head and invited him in, showed him Kate's letter and asked if he knew where she had gone.

'I was going to ask you the same thing,' he said. He had asked to see Kate's room. He had a quick look round, opening the drawers in the bedside cabinet and looking in the empty wardrobe, but there were no clues as to where Kate had gone.

'She never had much furniture in her room, as you know,' volunteered Dean. 'Just a few bits and pieces of art stuff, clothes and so on. When she left, she cleaned the room out. We found a lot of her stuff in the bins outside, afterwards.'

Robert thanked Dean and left. Once outside, he dialled Kevin. 'Kate's gone too. Just packed up and disappeared. Left a note for her flat-mates and some money to cover the rent. No indication where she's gone.'

'Shit. So they were both in on it. I really hoped I was wrong. You better get back here. We need to decide what we're going to do now.'

'I'm on my way. I reckon I should be back there in about two and a half hours. And Kevin, don't get all worked up over this any more than necessary. They aren't going to get away with this. We'll find them. Even if it takes years. We will find them. We both need answers.'

Chapter 57

Brian now hated Mondays. From the minute his phoned buzzed and vibrated its way into his dozy subconscious at six-thirty in the morning, through the rushed tea and toast breakfast to the stifling tube journey to the office it was all so depressing. It hadn't always been like this. When he had first been appointed to the more senior job at the bank it had seemed so exciting. He had always woken up in advance of the alarm, leapt out of bed, jumped in the shower, often skipping breakfast, running to the tube and arriving at work with bright shiny eyes eagerly looking forward to the day's challenges. The takeover had changed all of that. The staff resignations and subsequent departures had broken his team - and his spirit.

He glanced at the printout that Jo had deposited on his desk. He moved the post-it note sticker that said *'Odd, don't you think? Jo.'* It's all odd, he thought. It's odd how one minute we had a thriving happy, effective department and now we have a disparate group of individuals walking around like zombies, with haunted expressions. It's odd how he used to take such satisfaction in wandering around the department keeping an eye on his 'troops' and now, since the takeover announcement, he only reluctantly left the sanctity of his office. Amongst the remaining staff, there were a couple of notable exceptions, though. One was Sylvia, who had worked tirelessly throughout the changes and the other was young Jo, who didn't seem to have been phased at all by the upheaval going on all around her.

He glanced over to Sylvia's desk expecting to see her in her familiar pose, scanning the screens in front of her. But she hadn't arrived yet. He looked up at the clock, then checked his watch too. That's unusual for her, he thought, and picked up the report again. He looked at it half-heartedly. What's odd Jo? Apart from everything, obviously. He couldn't concentrate. He put the report down and cautiously ventured out into the department. A while ago he would have felt people stiffening to attention when he was in their presence, wanting to make sure he knew they were hard at it, but now the staff just carried on at their usual pace. They didn't even look up from their desks. He didn't blame them. He felt the same way. And he certainly would have felt the same way in their position. He went over to Sylvia's desk. It was neat and tidy as usual..

'Morning, Jo. I assume Sylvia's not in yet. Has she phoned in?'

'No, I don't think so. It's not like her. She's usually in early, especially on a Monday,' said Jo, whose desk was closest to Sylvia's.

'Yeah. I know. Okay, let me know when she's in, will you?'

'Yes, Brian. Did you have chance to look at that report yet?'

'I did. We'll talk about it later,' replied Brian, giving himself more time to familiarise himself with it when he felt a bit more alert.

Jo watched Brian walk off. He seemed so distracted. When she had first started at the bank Brian had a presence about him. He oozed an aura of authority and confidence. She felt that he'd been somewhat reluctant to offer her the job, as if she hadn't quite convinced him at the interviews and so she felt that she needed to continually impress him and overcome any lingering doubts he may have had. Now he looked as if he didn't care any more. She realised that it must be the takeover that had knocked him off balance. His poise and attention to detail seemed to have taken quite a hammering. Jo knew that something was going wrong in the department. The figures on the reports didn't look right. She couldn't put her finger on exactly where the problem was but it was there somewhere and she wanted to root it out. But Brian didn't seem to be interested so she was going to have to do more work on it in her own time and then, when she had located the source of the problem, she could present the whole case to him after it had been solved. That should eradicate any misgivings he may still have. If only Sylvia was in, she could have tried discussing it with her. But she wasn't, so Jo had to check over Sylvia's desk in case where was anything urgent that needed attention.

Jo picked up the latest dormant accounts report and went through it again. Like the one she had placed on Brian's desk earlier, there was a sharp reduction in the number of dormant accounts. Jo wondered why these accounts were suddenly becoming active again. She decided to check on the activity that had taken place. She selected a number of accounts and, using the supervisor access details that she had only recently been allowed to use, she viewed the details on her screen. She noted down dates, times and amounts. Before long she began to notice that, with a few exceptions, the accounts had similar amounts taken out on similar dates. She selected more accounts and widened her search. There was definitely a pattern emerging. She extended her grid of dates and amounts. If Sylvia had been there she might have suggested an explanation. Jo tried to think of what it might be. But it just looked like these accounts were being systematically emptied. The exceptions were where the accounts had been accessed, a balance check done or a few pounds removed or added. The exceptions looked like the normal sort of behaviour that one might have expected. The other accounts looked like something very unusual was happening.

Jo worked on this for another few hours, with occasional breaks while she did some other routine checks. The office had gone quiet. She looked up and found that she was alone. Everyone else had gone. Brian hadn't come back to her about the note on the earlier report. She gathered up her notes and put them in her desk drawer. Then she left. On the way down in the lift she began to wonder if she uncovered something serious, or if there was an obvious explanation that she wasn't aware of. Hopefully, Sylvia would be in tomorrow and would shed some light on it or if there was a problem, then hopefully she would recognise Jo's contribution in discovering it and put in a good word for her with Brian. She looked forward to being able to discuss it with Sylvia.

Chapter 58

'So, you are going to have to explain it all to me again. How come we've flown halfway round Europe and now we are on a freezing fucking car ferry heading back to Dover?'

Sylvia was checking her make-up in her compact mirror. She clicked the lid shut and put it back into her bag. She sighed and then, as if talking to a child, replied, 'We needed it to look as if we've moved out of the country.'

'But we haven't, have we. We're on this bloody stinking tub full of pissed-up chip-eating chavs and it looks like we're going back to where we started' Kate said sulkily.

'Look, Kate, Kevin and Robert aren't stupid, agreed? So, as soon as they realise the money's gone, and that we've gone too, they are going to know it was us and then try and find us. They'll almost certainly figure out that we must have used a removals company to shift all my furniture somewhere. Assuming they do, they'll no doubt track down the one I used. And if they do that, they'll be told that we mentioned something about going somewhere warm. I reckon they'll assume that we've gone back to Nice or another Mediterranean resort.'

'And instead we'll be homeless back in Britain. Great. I liked the South of France idea myself.'

'But I can't run away like that' said Sylvia. 'It would look very suspicious at the bank.'

'Well, it's going to look pretty suspicious anyway isn't it? You haven't been to work for three days.'

'I phoned in sick on Monday. I left it until lunchtime and then phoned Brian and explained that I had been in hospital over the weekend. I told him that I would get back as quickly as I could. With all the uncertainty there at the moment, it's no surprise that people are having time off.'

'So you are going back? Are you crazy? They must know about the missing money by now.'

'Why should they? Nothing has changed. I covered my tracks pretty well you know. And I think it's very unlikely that Kevin or Robert will have said anything as they are just as guilty as we are. Besides, I need to tidy up any loose ends and then I'll resign. Most of the others there are leaving anyway so it'll come as no surprise to Brian.'

'Then what?'

'Then I plan to move abroad, but not for a little while. I want the dust to settle first.'

'And what about me?'

'We'll, it's up to you really. You don't have to do the same as me, although it would be fun if you came too. You are very wealthy now so you might decide to do something completely different.'

'I hadn't really thought about it. I suppose I imagined that we'd be on the run for a while until we found somewhere safe.'

'I don't know about you, but I don't want to spend the rest of my time looking over my shoulder, worrying that someone is going to turn us in at any moment.'

'I suppose you're right. I feel bad about Robert though. And Kevin.'

'Listen, it was always part of the plan, wasn't it? You weren't supposed to actually fall for him, just to play along.'

Kate fixed her gaze on Sylvia 'And were you just playing along? You didn't feel anything for Kevin?'

Sylvia hesitated for a moment and bit her top lip before responding, 'We needed them on board. I did what I had to do.'

'You didn't answer my question.'

The bored sounding voice over the tannoy announced that ship would be docking in ten minutes and that drivers should begin making their way to the car decks.'

'Come on' said Sylvia. 'We'd better get moving.'

Chapter 59

It took thirty-two phone calls before Robert struck lucky. He had concocted a story about owning a car which had its wing-mirror damaged by a removals truck in Chiswick. He explained that he hadn't been in the car, but a witness had said that the truck was yellow. The receptionist of the thirty-second removals company he called admitted that they had yellow trucks and were based near Chiswick. Robert went straight over.

Kevin had gone to the Standard Chartered bank where Sylvia had worked. As he entered the bank, he wasn't sure what approach to take. He worked through the options. He could try and get up to the floors where her department was located and demand to speak to Sylvia if she was there. He discounted that option as she may have fled because the leaked money had come to light, in which case his appearance could be regarded as suspect. Then he thought he might try and talk to her boss but he again he couldn't think of a way that wouldn't arouse suspicion. In the end he couldn't decide what to do, so he stood outside and called her direct dial number from her business card that he still kept in his wallet. When it was answered, he asked to speak to Sylvia.

'I'm afraid Sylvia is not available today, can I help?' came the reply.

'Oh, who's that?'

'My name is Jo. Can I help you?'

Sylvia had mentioned Jo to him, in passing. So he knew that she worked in the same department. 'I hope so, Jo. Would it be possible to speak to Sylvia? It's important.'

'If you let me know what it is in connection with, I should be able to assist.'

'Perhaps you can Jo. Sylvia gave me her card. I've been working to acquire information that she wanted. Can I tell you and will you pass it on to her?'

'Yes – of course.'

'Not over the phone, though. I can meet you. I'm down in the lobby. Perhaps you could come down. I'd rather tell someone face to face. I'm David by the way.' It was the first name that came into his head.

'Okay, I'll be right down.'

Kevin waited for a minute or two and then went inside the building and stood beside the large windows near the entrance. Jo appeared carrying a notepad.

'David?' she asked.

Kevin smiled and nodded. Jo was very attractive, probably in her early twenties, he guessed. She gestured to the plush mulberry leather sofas. 'Shall we sit down?'

They sat and Kevin groped for something to say.

'You say you have some information?' Jo asked.

'Yes. I was dealing with Sylvia and helping her with an investigation she was carrying out. Is she not here? Maybe I should talk to her instead?'

'Unfortunately Sylvia is off sick today. She's in hospital. So I'm standing in for her until she's back.' Jo had decided to assume this position in case this man knew something that was useful. Again, if Jo collected the information it would look good when Sylvia returned. She'd probably be cross to discover that a potential informant had been allowed to walk away.'

'We met before in a coffee shop down the road. I feel a bit uncomfortable being here – in the bank

The Laundrymen

where it's all going on.' Kevin was still not sure where he was going with this.

'Okay, if you'd feel more comfortable, let's go there then shall we?' Jo collected up her pad and pen and he followed her out of the building.'

'How long have you known Sylvia?' she asked as they walked around the outside of the building and along the road.

'Not long,' said Kevin, 'And I don't know her very well.' He was being truthful now.

They arrived at the coffee shop and Kevin ordered coffee while Jo found them some seats.

'So Sylvia is in hospital. I hope it's nothing serious,' said Kevin as he placed the cups on the table and then slid into the booth.

'No, we gather she should be back in a couple of days.'

'Oh really? Then perhaps this conversation can wait until she gets back.' Kevin was desperately trying to think on his feet.

'Are you sure? It sounded urgent on the phone.'

'Look, Jo, the information I have got is dynamite. It could affect the takeover of the bank. I want to make sure it gets into the right hands.'

'David, I can assure you ..'

Kevin interrupted her holding his palm towards her. 'I'm absolutely sure that the details would be perfectly safe with you Jo, but Sylvia knows the wider issues involved, including my rather delicate position so it's probably best if it keeps until she is back. When did you say you were expecting her back?'

'She said that she should be back in a couple of days.'

'It'll keep until then, Jo. Rest assured, I'll be certain to let Sylvia know how impressed I've been with you and your obvious integrity. Perhaps you could let Sylvia know that David wanted to talk to her about the antiques project, that's our little code name for the issue.'

'I certainly will. I'd better be going. Thanks for the coffee.' Jo got up and left, leaving most of her coffee untouched. Kevin waited until she had left the shop and then called Robert. 'How are you getting on?'

'I've found the removals firm she used and I've just paid one of the guys there a hundred pounds. He told me he was one of the guys who moved her stuff. She told them she was going to somewhere warm. And she was with another woman too. Presumably that was Kate. But oddly enough he said all of her stuff was now in storage, which I think may mean she's coming back for it.'

'Or that they never went away. I've just spoken to her colleague at the bank. They think she's in hospital. They are expecting her back in a couple of days.'

'What? That's bizarre. What do you think?'

'There's only one way to find out. We'll have to keep watch at the bank to see if she appears. But I also think we should try and find out if they did fly out too.'

'I'm not sure how we could do that.'

'Nor am I. Maybe your mate Mitch might know a way.'

'Oh God, not him again. I'd rather never see his ugly mug again.'

'You don't have to see him. Just call him up and ask if he knows how you can track someone who may have flown out of the country.'

'Okay. I'll give it a go. I doubt if he'll know, though. I'll meet you back at the flat.'

Kevin pondered what Robert had said. He closed his eyes and tried to imagine Sylvia and how her mind worked. Surely she must have known that he and Robert would be able to trace the removals company. If so, then by telling the removal guys that they were going somewhere warm she was deliberately aiming to let them know. So what did that mean? He then replayed the conversation with Jo. Was it really conceivable that Sylvia would go back to the bank? He hoped it was. He knew that if he ever wanted to see her again he was going to have to stake out the bank for the next few days. And then what?

Chapter 60

The grand reception area of the Dorchester on Park Lane was bustling with activity. It was late afternoon and the new arrivals were checking in. Smartly dressed porters weaved around the guests with trolleys piled high with designer luggage. At the main desk, the immaculate and poker-faced Head Receptionist asked Sylvia and Kate to sign the registration details while he stared at his computer monitor. Sylvia was aware that Kate was feeling a bit let down and dejected after their brief visit to Europe and the subsequent ride back on the choppy car ferry so thought a little bit of luxury might cheer her up.

They needed to kill a bit of time before Sylvia could return to the bank and damp down any problems that had arisen while they were away. They had booked two junior suites.

'This is very pleasant. Very pleasant indeed.' said Kate as she was shown to her room. The porter deftly accepted the ten-pound note tip. As soon as he had left and shut the door behind him, Kate kicked off her shoes and launched herself onto the bed, bouncing on it a few times before walking all round the suite opening the cupboard doors and peering inside. 'This is more like it,' she said to herself. There was a gentle tap at the door. Kate opened it and let Sylvia in.

'What do you think? Nice isn't it? Mine is opposite and pretty much the same as this one.'

'It's simply amazing!' Kate pointed to the little statuette in the corner. 'Look, it's even got antiques. Reminds me of Robert.' With that, her face fell a little.

'Right, get yourself freshened up. We're going out on the town. Meet you downstairs in one hour. Don't be late.'

Kate found Sylvia in one of the plush leather armchairs in Reception. She was on the phone. Sylvia looked up and beckoned Kate to sit opposite her and the placed her finger on her lips in a gesture that told Kate to be quiet. Sylvia was clearly talking to someone at the bank and reassuring the person the other end that she would definitely be back at work the next day. She ended the call and dropped the phone into her bag.

'I managed to catch Brian before he went home. I'm going in tomorrow. So where shall we go tonight? Do you fancy a show, or a meal, or what?'

They took a taxi to Leicester Square and walked across it, people-watching all the time. They found a bar and ordered drinks. Kate took a sip of her cocktail and then asked Sylvia what was on her mind.

Sylvia looked directly at Kate for a second and then scanned the couples and crowds in the bar. Eventually, her eyes rested back with Kate. 'It's just that.' She looked down at her drink.

'What?'

'Well, you asked so I'm going to tell you. It's just that I'm not sure about you, Kate. I don't know how committed you are to this. I know when we first discussed it you were totally behind it. Now we've nearly done it, I'm not so sure.

Kate took her time before answering. 'It's too late to be having doubts now.'

'Yes, I suppose it is.'

'I've done everything you asked so far haven't I?'

'Yes.'

'So you've no real reason to question my commitment.'

They both fell silent, lost in their own thoughts. After a few moments had elapsed, Kate asked if Sylvia was worried about going back into the bank the next day.

'No, not especially. Although it's always a bit nerve-wracking returning to work after a few days away, knowing that there will almost certainly be some stupid problem that's cropped up that needs to be sorted out. It's rare to have a leisurely shoe-in back to work. What always makes it worse, of course, is when you've just had a really enjoyable time away.'

She sipped her drink. 'It's been great spending these last few days with you, Kate. I don't really have many real friends and you and I go back a long way.' As Kate looked up at Sylvia, she saw Sylvia gazing at the middle-distance as if she was remembering something. Kate began to feel slightly uncomfortable and suggested they get something to eat.

The following morning Sylvia went into work. As she arrived she saw bank staff walking in the opposite direction carrying bags and boxes. She walked into the department and immediately knew that something major had happened. She collared Tim, one of the supervisors., 'What's happening?'

'You obviously haven't heard.'

'Heard what?'

'About the closure.'

'The closure? Of the department?'

'Of the bank.'

'The bank?'

Tim walked off while Sylvia stood open-mouthed.

Sylvia darted over to Brian's office and looked inside. It was empty, but his photos and other nick-nacks were still on his desk.

'Where's Brian? Anybody know?'

'Probably upstairs in a meeting,' came the reply.

Sylvia dashed up the stairs and looked in all the meeting rooms. She spotted Brian in one of the smaller rooms sitting opposite a female employee who was clearly upset. Sylvia walked in and demanded to know what was going on. Brian apologised to the girl and led Sylvia out of the office and down the corridor. He found an empty room. They went in and he gestured to the seats. Sylvia ignored him and repeated her question.

'What the hell is going on Brian?' He turned and looked out of the window.

'There's been an announcement this morning. The press knew about it before we did. I bloody heard it on the radio as I was getting up this morning. They are closing the bank, Sylvia. Those American fuckers have shafted us royally. Jesus.'

He sat down and put his head in his hands.

'I expected a few people to go. Well, I expected a lot of people would go actually, but shutting the whole thing down. I really didn't see that one coming.'

Sylvia had so many questions that she could hardly articulate them. Her brain was having trouble taking it all in. In the end she just stared at Brian. He lifted his head and said, 'And before you ask, I have no idea why. Maybe we'll find out in the fullness of time. Our department results have been good. The performance of the bank overall has been exceptional. We thought that's why they were buying us, so they could learn from our expertise. Instead, it just looks like they wanted us out of the way so they could expand their operation. It wasn't a takeover. It was a culling. Don't ask me anything about redundancy or anything. I have no idea. You could try the HR department, but you'll probably have to join the queue.'

He looked up at her. 'Anyway, are you better now? You were in hospital weren't you?'

Sylvia told him she was fine now and was inwardly surprised that, in the midst of all the mayhem, he had asked after her health. Brian was definitely one of the good guys. Her thoughts were racing. She thanked Brian for everything he had done for her and told him she was going to clear her things. All the way back to her desk, she saw people in tears, packing up boxes. Men in overalls were unplugging electrical items and carrying them out. Some young black females in tabards were loading the pots of office plants onto sack trucks and taking them out to the lifts. There would probably have been less pandemonium if the building had been burning down.

In the department, there was a general din of drawers being opened and shut, of items being tossed into waiting boxes, with people talking on mobile phones. At her desk, Sylvia saw Jo packing her things. Jo eyed her and frowned.

'I know,' she said.

'Know what?' said Sylvia, hunting round for a suitable box. She found one and started putting her photos in.

'About you and what you've been up to.'

Sylvia felt her heart start racing. She calmly carried on opening her drawers and selecting any personal effects.

'Sorry. Not sure what you mean.'

'Yes, you do.'

Jo shouldered the huge bag she had been filling and then picked up her box and walked up to Sylvia. Their eyes met.

'I'll be in touch. Soon.' Then she walked off and didn't look back. Everyone else in the department was too busy to notice the conversation. Sylvia took a quick look round and then swept up the rest of her effects into the box and left the building a few minutes later. On the way out she picked up a copy of the evening newspaper. The headline glared *'Bank Goes Under'*. Her eyes drilled down to the detail of the article.

'UK Standard chartered bank closes down as takeover company discovers 'holes' in its' finances amounting to several million pounds.'

Kate stuffed the paper into the box and hurried out.

Kevin had spotted her leaving. He'd been waiting outside since seven. He'd seen her arrive and expected to have to wait all day. He set off in pursuit keeping some distance behind her so she didn't spot him. He followed her as she weaved in and out of the other pedestrians. When she stopped to cross roads and looked around he dodged in and out of doorways and shopfronts and waited till she had moved on. Finally, she arrived at the Dorchester. She went straight to the lifts. Kevin hovered in the reception, tucking himself behind a pillar. When she stepped into the lift alone, he neatly slid through the shutting doors to stand beside her as the lift ascended. She did a double-take.

'Kevin!' He was pleased to see that she looked shocked.

'Hello, Sylvia. Can I help you with that box? It looks heavy.'

'No, no, thank you. It's fine. Look, I'm ..'

Kevin quickly interrupted her, 'No need to say anything now, Sylvia. I assume you've got a room here. Let's go there now and we can have a chat about what you've been up to, shall we?'

Sylvia led the way out of the left and stopped outside her suite. She handed the box to Kevin while she found the key card and inserted it into the door. She stepped inside the room and Kevin followed her. He placed the box down on the luggage rack and looked around the room.

'Impressive. Must have cost a bob or two. But then money's not really a problem for you now, is it?'

Kevin, I can explain ..'

'I'm sure you can. In fact, I'm really quite eager to hear how you thought you could get away with this. How you could use me and Robert and just disappear without any thought for how it might affect us.'

'It wasn't like that ..'

'Wasn't it? But why don't you tell me how it was then?'

Chapter 61

Robert was getting nowhere checking flights out of the UK on the day when Sylvia and Kate had disappeared. There were just so many of them. And even if he knew where they were heading, there was no way of knowing if they were on any given flight. To test the theory he tried ringing one of the airlines and enquired about a flight that had left for Naples on that day. He pretended that he was trying to trace a relative, his sister Sylvia McEvoy, who had flown out of the country that day after a family argument. The airline apologised profusely but advised that they could not confirm or deny that she had been on the plane. They quoted 'Data Protection' as the reason for their refusal to help. He tried some other airlines and asked about other flights but got the same answer. After racking his brain for other ways of finding out, he got his phone out and was reluctantly going to call Mitch when the phone rang. It was Kevin.

When Kevin had told him that he'd located Sylvia, Robert breathed a huge sigh of relief and then asked what Kevin wanted him to do. Five minutes later Robert was on his way to The Dorchester. He joined Kevin, Sylvia and Kate in the restaurant.

'Well, well, well. This is all very cosy,' he said as he pulled out the chair and sat down.

Kate kept her eyes firmly pointing down at her cutlery.

'Sylvia was just about to divulge the rest of her plan. Now that you have arrived, you can hear it too.'

Sylvia looked very uncomfortable and smiled weakly at Robert.

'Listen, Robert, I'm really sorry.'

'Sorry! Sorry. Jesus, is that all you can say?' said Robert rather louder than he intended. The other diners glanced over.

Robert lowered his voice.

He hissed, 'Is that sorry that we found you? Or sorry that you tried to stitch us up? And what about you?' He was looking at Kate, but she still wouldn't meet his eyes.

'How much of this was your idea?'

Kate's mouth opened as if she was going to respond but after quickly glancing up at Sylvia she closed it again and continued to stare at the place setting.

Sylvia spoke instead. 'It was all my idea. Just mine. I'm not even sure that Kate was in full agreement. I persuaded her to go along with it.'

Robert was staring intently at Kate. She was still looking down.

'I brought Kate in as I couldn't do this own my own. She's as much a victim as the two of you. I need to apologise to all of you. I let my own greed and stupidity get the better of me. I got nervous and tried to conclude this quickly. I made a mess of it. I can assure you, Robert, that it wasn't easy to convince Kate as she wasn't at all happy about what I was proposing.'

And with a fleetingly quick glance at Kevin she added, 'Nor was I, for that matter. Although I know that there is not the slightest chance that you'll believe me now.'

There was silence at the table for a few moments. The waiter came and took the order. Kate looked up at Robert briefly and mouthed a 'sorry' at him, then resumed looking down again.

Kevin signaled the waiter again.

'A bottle of Champagne please – not your best one but make it a good one.'

While the waiter was fetching it, Kevin said 'We should celebrate our good fortune. We're all back together. We can forgive and forget, can't we Robert?'

Robert gave him a pained look. The angle his eyebrows adopted indicated that it was probably the very last thing he was prepared to do but said nothing. The champagne cork popped. The frothy liquid was poured and when the waiter had wafted away Kevin proffered a toast.

'To us,' he said ' And to the job we pulled off.'

They all raised their glasses and wondered where Kevin was going with this.

'Look,' he said suddenly leaning forward and taking a quiet and deadly serious tone. 'You two tried to fuck us off and you very nearly succeeded. But in the end you didn't. And now things are going to change. Sylvia, I want all the details of the Swiss bank accounts and any other accounts you opened to stash away the money. We are going to locate and account for every last penny. Then we are going to divide it equally as we agreed. Until that time, ladies, you are not leaving our sight. Do you understand?'

They nodded.

He raised his glass again and smiled grimly.

'Cheers!'

Chapter 62

Jo was doodling in her diary. She was drawing lines and circles around two figures. One said five and other said ten. Next to the numbers she drew a series of zeros. The zeros got bigger and bigger and then encircled the numbers. She picked up her phone and typed a text. She smiled to herself and pressed send.

When the text announced its arrival on Sylvia's phone with a bleep she was sitting on the bed in the hotel suite. Kevin was sat in the chair opposite glaring at her. The scene was almost identical in the suite across the corridor.

'Oh God,' moaned Sylvia.

'What is it?'

'It's Jo. Jo from the bank. She's put two and two together and wants fifty thousand.' She showed him the text on her phone.

Kevin let it sink in for a moment. 'Shit'. He stood up, 'Fifty grand.' He went over to the window. 'Fifty grand' he repeated. 'She's quite a smart kid. I met her recently.'

Sylvia looked up at him. She was about to ask him to explain and then changed her mind.

'We've got enough money but if we pay her, we're admitting what we've done.'

'And if we don't, do you think she'll go to the police?'

'Presumably.'

'What proof does she have?'

'I don't know. She must have something, though. I doubt if it's just a wild guess.'

'How come? I thought you what you were doing was undetectable?'

'I was. I don't know what she's got. I've been racking my brains, but I can't think of anything that would give us away. I'm not sure we can take the risk though. Can we risk calling her bluff?'

'You'll need to meet with her and find out what she knows, or thinks she knows.'

'Yes, I suppose so.'

Sylvia typed a reply and pressed send.

Meanwhile across the corridor Robert and Kate were sitting in silence. Kate was staring at her feet. Robert was pressing the tips of his fingers together, forming shapes with his hands. Eventually, Kate raised her head and looked directly at Robert.

'I know what you're thinking. You think I'm an evil bitch.'

'That's putting it mildly.'

'I would too, if I was in your position.'

They lapsed into silence again. Then Kate leant forward. 'I know you won't believe me, but I had no idea that Sylvia was planning for us to leave so suddenly.'

'That didn't stop you clearing out of your place in Bristol though did it? And your flat-mates had no idea you were going either.'

Kate rubbed the carpet with the ball of her foot and her eyes watched the action. She mumbled 'She told me I had to.'

'You could have refused.'

'I did try, but she said that it was all part of the bigger plan.'

'When exactly did you become part of this plan?'

'Do we really need to do this?'

'It's up to you.'

'Alright then. It was shortly after you and Kevin met Sylvia. I came to London to visit her on a whim really and she told me all about it then. I was to become your girlfriend so that you'd help us. I just went along with it.'

'So when we were in France, you knew all about it.'

'Yes.'

Robert gestured with his hand as if he was swatting an invisible fly and shook his head.

'Well, you're a brilliant actress. I'll give you that. You had me completely fooled.'

'Robert, I wasn't acting. It was real.'

'Yeah right, and I'm supposed to believe that?'

'It was real,' she beseeched him, 'You've got to believe me. I know it must be hard after what's happened, but it's the truth. I got caught in the middle between you and Sylvia. She's my oldest friend. I trusted her. I really didn't want to hurt you.'

'Too bloody late for that.'

'Please, Robert. You must know how I felt - how I feel, about you.'

'I really thought I did.'

'I loved you. And I do still. I've been a complete idiot. All the time on the plane and that horrible, shitty ferry I kept thinking about you, trying to think of a way I could tell you all this. I was terrified that I'd never see you again. I'm so glad I've finally been able to talk to you, even if you don't believe me and even if you never speak to me again. I realised that there's absolutely no point in having pots of money, if you can't share what it could buy with someone.'

Robert was clamping his jaw so tight that the muscles were aching. It sounded heartfelt. He was having a huge internal debate with himself whether to believe her or whether she was just adding to the lies. He desperately wanted to trust her again, but in his experience giving people second chances usually didn't work. They just did the same thing all over again. Before he'd made his mind up, his phone buzzed. It was Kevin. Robert listened briefly and then pressed the end call button and pushed the phone back into his pocket. He stood up, slid the chair back under the desk and said to Kate, 'Better get your jacket. We're going out.'

Chapter 63

The four met in the hotel lobby and then took a black cab across the city.

'Just here is fine, thank you,' said Kevin. He paid the driver. They got out and the taxi pulled off. They were on the corner of a busy main road.

'What now?' asked Robert.

'We're going to watch, while Sylvia meets up with Jo.'

As Sylvia went to walk off, Kevin caught her arm, leaned in towards her and whispered brusquely in her ear.

'Just remember what we said. Don't do anything stupid. We won't be far away. We'll be watching your every move.'

'Don't worry. I won't.'

'Shouldn't we all go?' said Robert.

'No. Presumably, Jo only knows about Sylvia's involvement. And we'd rather keep it that way. We don't want her to think that anyone else is involved.'

'But what if she does a runner?'

'One, I don't think she will. And two, we're going to keep a close eye on her. From a discreet distance, of course,' replied Kevin.

Sylvia crossed the road and walked up a side road. The other three followed a hundred yards behind. She stopped outside a bar with a few tables outside and looked back. Then she slipped inside. A few minutes later, Kate, Robert and Kevin entered the same bar. Kevin tucked up behind Robert so that his face was hidden. He didn't want Jo to spot him. Robert went to the bar and nodded in the direction of Sylvia and Jo so that the others knew where she was sitting. When Robert had bought the drinks they sat at a table where they could observe them. Kevin sat back in the shadows, out of Jo's line of sight. Sylvia had her back to them. Jo was looking intently at Sylvia.

They watched the discussion between Sylvia and Jo. Sylvia shook her head a few times. Jo looked nervous and fidgety. After a few minutes, Jo got up and departed grim-faced. Kevin bent down to re-tie his shoelaces as she passed their table. She didn't appear to have even noticed them. Sylvia stayed for a while, sipping her drink and then made her way out of the bar and down the street. The three immediately followed her out and joined her outside.

'Well?' said Robert.

'She's spotted the changes to the dormant accounts. She's convinced that I'm involved somehow. As the bank has closed and she doesn't have a job right now, she wants money.'

'Will anyone else have spotted this?'

'It's very unlikely, as only our department gets the reports. And it's our job to monitor them. No-one else is interested right now. And within our department it was just me, really. Jo must have looked over them while I was away.'

'Has she told anyone else?' asked Kevin.

'No, I don't think so. In fact, I'm pretty sure she hasn't. Not yet anyway. Obviously I asked her if she had informed anyone else. She said that she had tried to let Brian know that she thought something was odd, but what with the redundancies and so on I doubt he didn't even look at the reports so she got them back. Plus I don't think she'd be trying blackmail me if she had passed the information on.'

'What are we going to do?' asked Kate.

'Clearly, we don't want her going to the police. But paying her off may be a mistake too as there's nothing to stop her coming back to us for more money, later on.' Kevin began pacing and rubbing his chin.

'Surely if she has blackmailed us, that makes her complicit in it?' countered Robert.

'That may be the case but refusing to pay her more at a later date might just tip her into making sure the police find out. Maybe, anonymously. We just can't take that risk.'

'So we can't pay her in case she comes back for more, and we can't not pay her as then she'll go to the authorities. That doesn't leave us many options. Apart from maybe making her disappear?' Said Robert lamely.

The others all looked at him.

'That's not a serious option, by the way,' he said 'I was just thinking out loud.'

Kevin shook his head as he was pacing.

'Hang on! What about making her part of the team and offering an equal share?' offered Kate.

'No,' said Sylvia firmly. 'I don't want her joining us. There's got to be another way. And I think I might have it. I need to get back into the office.'

That night all four spent the night in Sylvia's suite. The women occupied the bed with Robert and Kevin shifting uncomfortably in the armchairs. They took it in turns to keep awake.

'You don't really think they'd try to disappear again, do you?' whispered Robert.

'Actually I don't. But equally I don't want to take any chances.'

At breakfast the following morning Kate asked Sylvia about her plan.

'Jo wasn't part of our team, but she was part of my team at the bank. If I can get into the systems again I should be able to reset things to look as if she was involved. I can use her computer input code and login details to implicate her.'

'And what if you can't get back in?'

'Then we'll have to come up with something else' said Sylvia looking directly at Robert.

Kevin went with Sylvia while Robert stayed behind to keep an eye on Kate.

At the bank, Sylvia showed her badge and persuaded the bored security man to let her pass as she had left some of her personal possessions in the office while Kevin waited in the main reception. In the office, some workmen were already there dismantling furniture. The computers were still working and Sylvia logged in and checked the systems. She pored over the computer for an hour occasionally switching to Jo's terminal. Then she went downstairs to the floor below and using her passkey unlocked the door of an empty office. She logged onto one of the computers in there using Jo's login details and carried on making what changes to the system that Jo's security clearance allowed.

When she had finished she returned to her desk, picked up some pads of paper and then rejoined Kevin on the ground floor.

'Well?'

'All done,' she said and slipped her arm through his. Kevin looked down at her arm and shrugged as they left the building.

As they travelled back to the hotel by taxi, Sylvia sent Jo a text requesting a meeting.

***

Back at the hotel, Kate and Robert were still tip-toeing around each other.

'So, how much longer is the silent treatment going on for then?'

'I don't know what you mean.'

'Yes, you do. I've told you I'm sorry. You can see I'm not going to run away. You don't need to glare at me like that and give me the cold shoulder. I'm sorry. There, I've said it again. You'll have to believe more or not. It's up to you. I was foolish to listen to Sylvia. I knew it was the wrong thing to do. What do I have to do to make you trust me again? I love you, Robert. I love you. Do you hear me? You bloody stupid idiot.'

With that, Kate leapt off the bed and dashed into the bathroom slamming the door on the way. Even though the shower had been turned on, Robert could still hear her sobbing through the noise of the cascading water. Once more he was left with the dilemma. Could he really believe her? Did he dare trust her again? Was this all part of the act? He shook his head as the conflicting emotions whizzed round in his head.

Chapter 64

Alone in her flat, Jo fidgeted with her phone. She wasn't used to this. The bank had closed. She had no job. She was confident that she could secure another job, but the thought of the merry-go-round of job applications, interviews, assessment days and so on, made her heart sink. And even when she was successful, it would be like starting all over again, just as she had been making some headway at Standard Chartered. At least the money from Sylvia would buy her some time. Maybe she should take a break and do some travelling. All her university friends had done this, either before, during or after their degree. A gap-year. It sounded good. She thought about that for a while, imagining herself in Mongolia or Nepal, or maybe the plains of Africa. She could almost feel the African sun on her face as she leant her head back and closed her eyes. The feeling only lasted a moment before she jerked forwards and back to the matter in hand. She wondered if she should have told someone else about this. But she reminded herself that the less people who knew the better the chances of getting this wrapped up quickly. She brought up the previous sequence of messages between herself and Sylvia. The last one from Sylvia was suggesting another meeting. Jo typed *'Okay. Have you got the money?'* and pressed send.

Sylvia received the text and replied straight away *'Too late. No deal.'*

Jo stared at her phone in disbelief. She started to reply and then deleted the message. Instead, she rang Sylvia.

When Sylvia answered with a curt 'Yes,' Jo said 'Just what the hell do you mean, no deal? You do realise you leave me with no choice. I'll have to go to the police.'

'Fine. You do what you have to do. Before you do, though, there are a couple of things you might want to think about. You should be aware that the police will not be very impressed with the fact that you've tried to blackmail me and, more worryingly from your point of view, if the police examine the records at the bank they may find that some of the records were altered from your PC with your login details. I've got enough print outs to throw a lot of doubt onto your innocence. You might find that hard to explain. Do you want to take that chance?'

'You bitch! You fucking bastard scheming bitch,' spat Jo and rang off.

* * *

Sylvia gave Kevin full details of the new access codes. She also furnished him with the account numbers and login details for the Swiss bank accounts. He flipped open his laptop, checked online and was pleased to see that the accounts were intact with the amounts he expected. While Sylvia hovered in the background, he tested that he had full access by successfully moving some money between accounts. He sent a text to Robert to let him know the good news.

As Robert received and registered the text, the bathroom door opened. Kate stepped into the room in a cloud of steam, wearing just a towel. Her eyes were red. Her mascara had run. A wave of pure emotion instantly drilled through Robert. He dropped the phone, crossed the room in two strides and took her in his arms as the towel dropped to the floor.

Kevin and Sylvia went for a walk. To any passers-by, they would have looked like a happy good-looking young couple. No-one could possibly guess that between them they had amassed a small fortune through criminal means and that they were struggling to trust each other. They turned off into a quiet side road and strolled up the tree-lined avenue. Sylvia slipped her arm through Kevin's again. He didn't remove it.

'So. What now?' He said.

'That's rather up to you I think.'

'Why?'

'Well. I'm the one that screwed up. You're in the driving seat now.'

Kevin pondered that for a moment. Then he said, 'Okay. How do you want this to end?'

'Naturally, I would prefer a happy ending.'

'So would I.'

They walked in silence for a while.

'I still don't get how you thought you could just ditch us and then come back here as if nothing had happened. It takes some determination .. and a heart of stone.'

'It wasn't like that, Kevin.'

'Well, tell me how it was then.'

Sylvia stopped and turned to face him. She put her arms on his shoulders and looked right into his eyes.

'I had a plan and I stuck to it. I overruled my own feelings. I made Kate do it too. Now I realise how stupid that was. Unfortunately, I can't undo it. That's why it's your call now. I am at your mercy. You decide. I'll go along with whatever you want.'

Kevin absorbed this and then turned to continue their walk. An elderly man walked past them in the opposite direction with his dog. He didn't look up. They crossed a road, walking in silence. Eventually Kevin asked, 'Do you regret starting this?'

'Starting what? The money? Or do you mean what happened between us?'

'Both, I suppose.'

'The money yes, you no. There are lots of things I'd do differently now. But it's pointless doing this. We are where we are. And we need to decide what to do next and where we go from here.'

'So you do regret taking the money?'

'Yes, I do. At the start, it was a challenge. It was a question in my head. Could it be done? We've shown it can be done. But the cost is not worth it. That's the bit I didn't consider. I was consumed by the technical details. The planning came next and then the implementation of the plan. I never thought about how it would make me feel inside.'

'Do you want to give the money back? And cover your tracks?'

'It's crossed my mind. But I'm not sure I can. It would probably cause more ripples than siphoning it off. Plus I'm not sure I can get back into the bank again now it's closing. And I don't think it will solve anything. What's done is done.'

'You could give the money away.'

'I've thought about that too. And in a way, I will.'

'How?'

'I'm not sure yet but I'll make sure it's spent wisely, so people benefit. What about you? What will you do?'

'I know exactly what I'm going to do.'

Sylvia waited for him to elaborate, but he didn't. They walked on. They were heading back to the hotel now. Eventually, she plucked up the courage to ask the only question she really wanted an answer to. 'And us?'

Chapter 65

Omar Hussain had been attending the Regency English Language College in the evenings for two months. He had expected it to be a large, period institution like the famous British universities he had read about before he arrived in the country. Instead, the college was above a Lithuanian supermarket in a run-down area of Beckton, in London. He had to catch the tube and then two buses to get there every evening. By day he worked in a warehouse, which stored parts for gas fires. Today he had phoned in sick at eight o'clock. By eight-thirty he was dressed and ready to go. He hoisted his weighty black rucksack with the converse logo onto his back. He took a look around his bedsit room to make sure it was tidy and made his way downstairs to the ground floor. He opened the front door and blinked at the bright sunshine. He put on his sunglasses. With a quick glance in both directions and turning his baseball cap round he exited onto the high street. He walked purposefully to his destination keeping his head down.

Sylvia waited until Kevin, who was exhausted, had dozed off in the armchair and then silently slipped out into the corridor. She listened briefly at Kate's door. There were no sounds coming from her room. She hurried to the lifts. As she waited for the lift, she kept glancing back up the corridor, half-expecting to see Kevin rushing out to grab her. But he didn't. The lift arrived and she pressed the button for the ground floor. She left the hotel and walked as fast as she could, in the direction of Park Lane.

Jo was surprised to get the text from Sylvia. And agreed to meet her. Maybe Sylvia had changed her mind after all. She hoped so. She hurried to the rendezvous.

Omar was sweating slightly as he strode along. He had walked for several miles now. He had been told not to take the bus. His mission was critically important. He was fulfilling his destiny. His place in heaven would be assured. His name would be remembered forever. And those virgins were waiting for him. He licked his lips and pressed on determinedly. He entered the entrance to the tube station, bought a ticket with cash, slipped it into the machine and passed through the barrier.

Sylvia alighted on the tube at Hyde Park Corner. Omar joined the central line at Bank and then changed again at Holborn. He got off at Leicester Square. His rucksack was still tucked under the seat on the tube train. Sylvia was just stepping off the next carriage. Omar reached into his pocket and pressed the green button on his phone. His body was instantly slammed into the wall of the tube station, crushing his skull into a thousand fragments as the deafening blast ripped violently through the train and along the platform, sending shards of lethal metal shrapnel in all directions.

Chapter 65

Jo was trying to make her way to Covent Garden, but it was utter chaos. The emergency services were pouring into the area. The air was filled with the smell of burning. Sirens wailed in the distance and people rushed by in all directions. Police vehicles with flashing lights were parked at every junction and traffic was at a standstill. Obviously something major had happened. Jo texted Sylvia had told her that she might be late. Frustratingly, she did not receive a reply.

Kevin woke abruptly from a deep sleep to find that Sylvia had gone. He sprang out of the chair, checked the bathroom and then rushed out into the corridor. He banged on the door of the other suite. Robert came to the door. Kevin quickly explained that Sylvia was missing. Robert and Kate quickly got ready and joined Kevin in the reception. He was asking the reception staff if they had seen Sylvia leave. They told him apologetically that they'd been very busy and hadn't noticed if she had passed by. Kate was frantically trying Sylvia's phone. There was no response. Robert tapped Kevin on the arm and pointed at the large television on the wall. The screen showed a reporter with ambulances and fire engines in the background. The sound was off, but the subtitles running across the bottom of the screen indicated that there had been an explosion at Leicester Square tube station and it was clear that it was a major disaster. Kevin looked for a moment and then said 'That's awful. Let's split up. We need to find her. This is just going to make it a lot more difficult.'

It was several days before Sylvia McEvoy's name was included amongst the thirty-four people who were killed instantly by the explosion. She had been identified by a combination of the charred remnants of her credit cards in conjunction with her dental records. Many more victims were reported as having received horrendous life-changing injuries. Hundreds had received other injuries and had been admitted to hospital suffering with trauma. The reporter went on to advise that it was likely that the eventual death toll would be higher. Around the same time, Jo was staggered to find an extra fifty thousand pounds in her bank account.

When Kevin heard the news about Sylvia, he went into his room at the flat and did not come out again. Kate suggested that Robert try to coax him out. Robert refused. 'He'll re-appear when he's ready.' Kevin did not attend the funeral.

Kate and Robert spent the next few days talking seriously. They ironed out their differences, decided to make a fresh start and began to plan for the future. They took a room at a small hotel close to Kevin's flat. Robert went to the flat every day to see if Kevin was ready to talk. A week after the announcement Kevin came out of his room when he heard Robert arrive. He apologised to Robert for his absence. Robert waved it away.

They walked to the pub and talked about their plans. Robert explained that he and Kate were going to try and make a go of it. Kevin patted him on the back and told him he was pleased. Kevin said he would arrange for their share of the money to be transferred to them. Robert declined it. He and Kate had agreed to re-start their lives and the money would just get be a constant reminder of their duplicity. Despite Kevin's repeated attempts, Robert was firm. Finally, Robert did agree to take on the antiques business with the current stock.

'What about you? What will you do now?' asked Robert.

'I'm going to travel,' said Kevin. 'I'm going to put some of that money to good use. It's what Sylvia would have wanted. I think it's what she was planning to do anyway.'

'In what way?'

'There are lots of things that need to be done to improve peoples' lives and sometimes it's just money that's standing in the way. I thought I'd try and find some of those things and help out where I can.'

'You're one of the good guys, Kevin.'

'Not really. And if there are checks and balances, I've still got a lot of making up to do.'

'If you are in society's debt, where does that leave me?'

'You're a survivor, Robert. I suspect most of what you've done in the past was just to get by, not because it's a life you really enjoyed or admired. Clearly, it's your choice, but if I was you, I'd do what I can to make Kate and Chloe's lives as good as they can be, on the right side of the law where possible.'

'That's pretty much my plan.'

'No more dodgy stuff, then?'

'No. I don't think so. I've learnt a lot over the past few months, thanks to you.'

Robert finished his drink. They shook hands and then hugged. Robert left Kevin and went back to meet Kate at the hotel.

Chapter 66

Several months later, Robert had sold enough of the stock to fund the deposit on a small house in Enfield. Kate had started painting again and was now in the early stages of pregnancy. Robert had set up an anonymous email account and using a computer in the local library had sent Kevin a short message to tell him the new address and about the forthcoming baby. The next time he checked, he had received a reply.

Hi Both,

Brilliant news about the forthcoming offspring! Hope he or she doesn't inherit your looks, Robert. Only kidding! I'm very happy for you both. And I'm sure Chloe will love the idea of a new brother or sister. I'm looking forward to when we can all meet up again and I can meet the little one – and see your new house, of course.

Hope the business is prospering. I'm sure it is, Robert and I can't wait to see your first exhibition, Kate. It'll be a huge success, I'm sure.

I went to Australia for a while. I travelled for a bit and then, when I felt up to it, I visited Sylvia's parents. They were pleased to meet someone who knew her and after I explained that the funeral was just too painful, they understood why we didn't meet them there. I told them about you too. (Obviously not about what we were up to) but I think it made them happier to know that Sylvia had some close friends in the last few months of her life.

Then I went to Africa and ended up in Jinja, which is in the south of Uganda, on the shores of Lake Victoria. It's truly a beautiful place. I found a small village nearby and have got involved in a project to build a school. I'm really enjoying it and everyone here seems to appreciate my small contribution. I finally feel as if I'm doing something worthwhile. So maybe I'll stay for a while before coming over to see you. Hope you don't mind.

Robert smiled. That was so like Kevin. He was sure that his small contribution was probably the entire cost of the building.

One more thing. I came across this on the internet. I thought you might be interested to see it.

Kevin had attached a scanned copy of a page from the Galloway Gazette. In the bottom left-hand corner was a short feature about a fatal motorcycle accident involving local bad boy Peter ' Big Mitch' Mitchell.

Oh, and I had a text from Anne. She and Tom have got married. Apparently Tom has turned over a new leaf since the stabbing and she says they are very happy.

Finally, attached to this message are some login details. I know you said you didn't want anything, but I thought you might need something towards the school fees in a few years, or something else. Anyway, I hope it comes in handy. (Don't worry, it's clean. Well, sort of!)

Look after yourselves. I consider myself very lucky to have you as friends.

Kevin

When Robert checked the account some time later he found there was a quarter of a million pounds in there. After much soul-searching and deliberation, Robert and Kate decided they would keep it, but only use it sparingly. They wanted to live on their earnings where possible. Their first act was to book flights to America to see Chloe.

Chapter 67

The sun was rising above the lake and fishermen in tiny wooden dugout canoes were casting their nets already. Kevin gazed at them for a while, enjoying the quiet repetitive activity which was probably unchanged in hundreds of years. Then, shutting his eyes, he lifted his head towards the sun and soaked up the gentle warmth as it spread across the red earth. After a few moments, he finished his coffee and poured the dregs onto the dusty ground. He walked past a rusting motorbike, which he was using as transport and went back inside the rented bungalow to finish getting ready for the day ahead. As he shaved, he looked in the mirror and seeing his reflected tanned face and long hair he thought back to those grey days at the insurance office in Birmingham and smiled wryly before toweling off and locking up. He kick-started the bike and then rode off to the school building site.

The End

Proof

Made in the USA
Charleston, SC
27 November 2015